TF105286

D0586485

This item is to be returned on or before the last date
stamped below.

ST SP   MILBURN

31 OCT 00	23 APR 01 ST	4 FEB 02 ST
17 NOV 00	28 APR 01 ST	26 FEB 02 ST
28 AUG 03 ST		28 MAR 2002
11 FEB 03 ST	E 3 AUG	
7 JAN 00	01 ST	13 MAR 02
30 JAN 01 ST	E 2 JUN 01 ST	11 APR 02
20 FEB 01 ST	25 JUN 01 ST	2 MAY 02
	16 JUL 01 ST	17 MAY 02 ST
E 2 MAR 01 ST	20 AUG 01 ST	

HEART IN ICE

Recent Titles by Iris Gower from Severn House

DESTINY'S CHILD
EMERALD
FIREBIRD
HEART IN ICE
HEART ON FIRE
A ROYAL AMBITION
THE SEA WITCH

HEART IN ICE

Iris Gower

TF   Dumfries and Galloway
      LIBRARIES

      1 0 5 2 8 6   Class F

This edition first published in Great Britain 2000 by
SEVERN HOUSE PUBLISHERS LTD of
9–15 High Street, Sutton, Surrey SM1 1DF.
Previously published 1984 in paperback only in the USA
by The Berkeley Publishing Group,
under the title *Beloved Captive.*
This title first published in the USA 2001 by
SEVERN HOUSE PUBLISHERS INC of
595 Madison Avenue, New York, N.Y. 10022.

Copyright © 1981 by Iris Davies.
Copyright © 2000 by Iris Gower.

All rights reserved.
The moral right of the author has been asserted.

British Library Cataloguing in Publication Data

Gower, Iris
    Heart in ice
    1.   Russia - Courts and courtiers - Fiction
    2.   Love stories
    I.   Title
    823.9'14 [F]

    ISBN 0-7278-5615-4

All situations in this publication are fictitious and
any resemblance to living persons is purely coincidental.

Printed and bound in Great Britain by
MPG Books Ltd, Bodmin, Cornwall.

Author's Note

When I first began to write for publication, I was unsure
which direction I wished to pursue. So the reader of this
reprinted novel will find it differs greatly from my currently
published historical books.
In the past I wrote historical romps and Victorian thrillers
and tried my hand at modern romance. These are the books
you will have taken from the shelves if you are reading this
author's note. In spite of the differences from my later
novels, I do hope my readers will find these stories a good
read and a glimpse into the past efforts of the author.
Best wishes to all my readers, old and new.

© *Iris Gower 2000*

1

"Hussey blood is bad blood."

The voice of the old housekeeper was harsh and it carried on the soft spring air to where Seranne Hussey was sitting on the terrace. She crouched deeper into her chair and her fingers plucked nervously at the jet beads gleaming against the black folds of her gown.

"I'm that sorry for young Miss Seranne," Mrs. Pegg continued remorselessly. "But, say it I must, there was bad in that father of hers, for didn't he tumble every country wench from here to Plymouth afore he died?"

There was a soft reply from one of the maids that Seranne could not quite hear and she held herself still, realizing with relief that she could not be seen from the drawing room. The plethora of plants set outside in the *jardinière* made a more than adequate screen. She felt she should make some protest and stop the gossiping, but her nerve failed her and she listened on.

"And this one that's coming from London, the master's sister, she's no better than she should be. Ten years it is since she was down here in Devonshire last, and then the tales her maid told me about her would make your hair curl, Ellen."

"You shouldn't take on so, Mrs. Pegg." Ellen's voice was clearer now, with the softness of the Devonshire countryside in its tones. "I suppose Miss Seranne will be glad of the company, poor little duck, she's that weepy lately. She needs cheerin' up."

"Perhaps you're right," Mrs. Pegg said. "I dare say my ideas are a bit old-fashioned, and times change. Still, I'm not looking forward to having Mistress Mildred here, and that's a fact."

Seranne felt trapped. She closed her eyes and orange particles of sunlight pierced her lids. She wished she could make herself invisible. She had no desire to face the housekeeper, for Mrs. Pegg could be more than a little tart on occasions.

"Put that figurine down, Ellen." Mrs. Pegg had apparently finished gossiping. "You're supposed to be dusting it, not kneading dough. Now come on out of 'ere, help me check the linen cupboard, or we'll be caught in a muddle by Miss Mildred and that I'll not have. Move, girl! The coach is due any time now."

Seranne sighed as she heard the double doors of the drawing room bang shut behind the servants. Her stomach was churning and she clenched her fists in her lap. Was her aunt really such a dragon that even Mrs. Pegg feared her?

She opened her eyes and looked over the parapet

down into the rippling waters of the River Dart. Usually, the flowing of the sun-yellowed water brought her a feeling of peace, but not today. Now she felt only unease and apprehension, wondering what effect the visit of her aunt would have on her life.

She scarcely remembered her Aunt Mildred. Seranne had been only seven years of age when her father had quarreled loudly and violently with his sister, practically ordering her out of the house. The scene had printed itself indelibly on her young mind and Seranne could only think of her aunt as some sort of outcast, one who had recklessly flouted William Hussey's authority.

That her father had been the pivot of her own life, Seranne could not deny. His word had been law to her, and she could no more have angered him than she could have stooped to scrubbing the floors alongside the kitchenmaid.

William Hussey on his part had never made any secret of the fact that he would have preferred a son to the delicate, pale child his ailing wife had produced. He treated Seranne with a casual affection, while teaching her to ride and shoot as well as any boy. He allowed her to accompany him on his visits to the tenants, but gave her no quarter. She kept pace with him or she was left behind.

Seranne had been dismayed when her mother, rousing herself from her usual state of languor, had insisted she be taught more ladylike pursuits. It was not fitting, she had insisted, that a young lady of twelve years should ride around the country as disheveled as any peasant girl.

Her mother's wishes had prevailed. Seranne had endured the confinement of the music room with bad grace, knowing that her father had been wearied by his wife's constant nagging, preferring to give in rather than make a battle of the situation.

"She's not very well, my dear," he had explained to Seranne. "And in a way your mother's right. You should be groomed for marriage now, though it's a damn waste, if you ask me." He had laughed good-naturedly. "You'll have no difficulty finding a husband, not with those looks." He had pinched her cheek. "But don't go leaving me just yet, little one."

He had spoken casually enough, but Seranne had taken him seriously. She needed her father's approbation as she needed the air she breathed, and she had no trouble declining the attentions of the few pimply youths who were invited to the Hall for her inspection.

Seranne was fifteen when her mother died, peacefully and unresistingly, in her sleep. She had always seemed a remote being, locked up in her bedroom in semidarkness, untouched and untouchable, and her passing made but a slight impression on Seranne.

But after her father's passing, Seranne still grieved for him deeply, even though it was almost a year since he had died. The Hall had been silent, the huge rooms empty of laughter. That was what she missed more than anything, Seranne thought, laughter and joviality—two attributes her father had possessed in abundance. It was true he had left her a large inheritance but to Seranne that meant very little. She had never lacked anything and so took her great wealth for granted.

And now there was to be more change. Aunt Mildred was about to arrive, suddenly concerned with the plight of her niece, buried in the heart of the country without proper companionship.

A chill breeze had sprung up and the waters of the Dart were swelling into waves. Seranne went into the drawing room, closing the French windows behind her, standing for a moment in the shaft of sunlight that warmed her through the glass. She looked around her, trying to see the room as her aunt would see it.

There was elegance in the high ceiling with the huge, cut-glass chandelier hanging from the center. The multiplicity of the pieces caught the sun, gleaming as though the candles were already lit. Seranne's eyes traveled to the Adam fireplace and, above it, the portrait of her father, looking stern and rocklike, as though he were with her still, scolding yet affectionate.

At the far end of the long room was a screen, veneered and inlaid with woods in a variety of colors from pale rosewood to deep mahogany. This hid the door that led to the kitchen and the passageway outside which was always cold and drafty. As a child, Seranne had imagined all sorts of evil creatures lurking in the darkness of that mysterious corridor.

She sank down into a chair, feeling restless and miserable. She had told herself countless times that she must not be biased against her aunt just because of a family quarrel that had occurred many years ago. But she wondered if the Hall would appear antiquated, even stark, to someone who had spent the past ten years in fashionable London.

It had irritated Seranne greatly to see the way the servants, under the direction of Mrs. Pegg, had worked with a vigor that had been noticeably absent in the past few months, and all for the visit of an unknown aunt who was not even welcome. The housekeeper, of course, would have clear memories

of Mildred and it said volumes that the redoubtable
Mrs. Pegg should make such an effort to have the
Hall looking its best. Aunt Mildred must be a for-
midable person indeed.

There was a sudden bustle of activity outside in the
hallway. Seranne heard doors banging and the
sounds of voices. She rose to her feet with a feeling of
apprehension. It seemed her aunt had arrived.

Footsteps approached the drawing room. Seranne
took a deep breath, trying to calm herself. It was absurd to feel nervous at her age. She was no longer
seven but seventeen and mistress of Hussey Hall,
whatever ideas Aunt Mildred might have of taking
the reins into her own hands.

Mrs. Pegg's lined face registered obvious relief
when she saw Seranne.

"Mistress Hussey has arrived," she said rather
pompously. At any other time, the housekeeper's attitude of reverence might have made Seranne laugh.

"My dear niece, how wonderful to see you again!
And haven't you grown!" Mildred did not simply
walk into the room, she made an entrance. Seranne
suddenly felt frumpish and dowdy in comparison.

Mildred was an imposing woman, tall, well-built
and dressed in the very latest fashion. Her high-
waisted coat was plum-colored, the collar so large
that it was almost a cape. On her glossy hair was
placed a bonnet, the brim dipping over her smooth,
unlined face, and decorated with bobbing feathers
that picked up the plum of her coat.

"Well, my dear, aren't you going to kiss me?"
Mildred bent toward Seranne, brushing her cheek in
a quick gesture. "Are your servants well-trained,
dear?" she said, moving toward the fireplace and

drawing off her gloves. "I shouldn't like my luggage to be damaged."

"Everything will be quite all right, Aunt," Seranne said quickly. "I shall ask for your boxes to be taken directly to your room."

Mildred's eyebrow lifted slightly. "Ask, dear, ask? Why, you must make an order of it, not a request." She removed her hat carefully, smoothing back the strands of hair that had been barely ruffled. "Don't be too familiar with the servants, dear, otherwise they will tend to become confused and uncertain of their place."

Her coat removed, Mildred made herself comfortable in one of the chairs at the side of the fireplace. She leaned back and looked around her, eyes narrowed.

"Nothing, but absolutely nothing has changed since I was here last." Her tone was derisive.

"You must admit that it is very tasteful, Aunt," Seranne protested.

"Tasteful, yes, but so old-fashioned, my dear. These chairs, for instance—they are in the French style, all bright colors and padded upholstery. Don't you know that simple cane chairs are the vogue in London now?"

Seranne was silent but resentment rose within her as she watched her aunt from under her lashes. As though sensing her niece's feelings, Mildred smiled brilliantly, setting out to charm.

"You like riding, of course. Being my brother's daughter you must sit a horse well," Mildred said suddenly and Seranne was caught off guard, confused by the turn the conversation had taken.

"Riding? Well, yes, my father made sure I could

ride almost before I could walk." Seranne could barely hide her satisfaction. She was sure of her ground now, confident that in the saddle, at least, she was more than a match for her aunt.

"That's a relief," Mildred said. "Then I shall have some diversion while I'm here." She stared openly at Seranne. "You are far too pale, my dear." Mildred smiled as though to soften her words. "We must take the air for at least an hour every day, put some color into your cheeks. Yes, I'm sure I shall be able to make something of you."

Seranne felt outraged by her aunt's criticism. She had no wish to be "made something of"; she was quite content to be what she had always been, a country girl with no pretensions of being a society fashion plate.

"Perhaps for today we shall simply walk," Mildred was continuing, oblivious of the effect of her words. "I have traveled enough over the last few days and I ache from the bumping of the coach. But tomorrow, we must ride."

Seranne sat gazing wide-eyed at her aunt. In the face of such determination she felt helpless.

"I think I shall go to my room and rest now, dear." Mildred rose from her chair. "But you must promise to be ready to show me something of the countryside when I have slept a little." She smiled. "We must start straight away with our efforts to banish that unattractive pallor of yours."

Seranne clenched her hands into fists in her lap as the door closed behind her aunt. How was she going to endure the presence of her father's sister in her home without quarreling? Mildred was given to frank, if not tactless, remarks and Seranne fervently hoped that her aunt's visit would be brief. Surely

Devonshire would seem exceedingly quiet after the
colorful life Mildred was used to leading in London?

Strangely enough, Seranne found herself dressing
with more care than usual as she prepared herself for
the proposed walk. She discarded the shapeless black
gown in favor of a soft purple velvet one, that was
pleasantly full in the skirt, with a simple bodice that
accentuated the swell of her breasts. She would show
her aunt that country girls weren't always dowdy and
plain.

The sun had risen higher in a cloudless sky by the
time Seranne and her aunt left the Hall, taking the
path at the edge of the river. Seranne had replaced
her soft pumps with stout high-buttoned boots, but
Mildred had taken no such precaution and she was
forced to pick her way with care over the rough stony
ground. After only a few minutes, she sank onto a
fallen log, her face flushed.

"What a fool I am, my dear," she proclaimed.
"You would never think I was brought up in these
parts, would you? I have quite forgotten what it is
like down here. I must confess that the only walking I
do in London is on smooth pavements or over the
green outside my house."

Seranne was surprised by her aunt's self-criticism;
it seemed she could be equally as hard on herself as
she was on anyone else who appeared foolish. She
suddenly found herself envying Mildred. She was so
strong, so self-assured, never at a loss, not even when
she was laughing at herself. Seranne had little idea
that her aunt was feeling envy of a different kind as
her eyes rested on her niece.

Mildred was almost forty years of age and, though
she had undoubtedly enjoyed her life, she had lately

begun to wonder if she should have settled down to marriage and a steady domesticity.

Looking at her niece now and seeing her natural, youthful beauty, she felt a sudden nostalgia for the innocent young girl she herself had once been. But all that was a very long time ago. Mildred had the same hot blood in her veins as her brother had had, and she had enjoyed her first adventure with one of the employees of the Hussey estate while still a girl. Since then she'd had many lovers, none of them making a lasting impression.

Her latest romance had shown more promise than the rest, however, and so the shock had been doubly hurtful when Phillip Carey, who was fifteen years her junior, had suddenly left London without even a note of explanation. To save face, Mildred had immediately packed her bags and made for Devonshire. The visit was long overdue, of course. She should have returned to the Hall the moment she had heard of her brother's death.

Her niece, though, was another matter. With a twinge of conscience, Mildred reproached herself for not thinking about the girl's future before this.

Seranne had grown into a very lovely young woman. Her hair was pale, spun gold under the sun, her skin almost translucent. She was small of stature —she inherited that from her mother, of course. That she was immature was apparent at once, and as yet she was unawakened by a lover. Mildred would have wagered on it. The girl needed a husband and Mildred felt an almost maternal interest in her welfare, determined that Seranne should not waste her life as she had done, not if Mildred had anything to do with it.

"Would you mind if I asked visitors to the Hall, dear?" she said.

Seranne looked at her, eyes large with uncertainty. She would have to learn to be decisive, or her aunt would soon take over control of her whole life.

"Not too many, of course," Mildred said quickly. "We don't want to make a great party of it all. No, just a few selected friends—that's all it shall be, I promise you."

"If you like, Aunt Mildred," Seranne replied, but it was obvious she was not delighted by the prospect of having strangers in the Hall.

"Another little thing, dear," Mildred said slowly, not wanting to hurt Seranne's feelings. "I'm a little worried about your dress. Outmoded, my dear, definitely. Surely you must have noticed that waists are higher now? It's all because of this silly Frenchman, Napoleon, of course. Some of the more extreme of the London set are even wearing epaulettes on the shoulders of their outdoor coats."

"That wouldn't do for Devonshire, Aunt," Seranne said, and her eyes were downcast as she studied her own carefully chosen gown.

It was a pleasant enough dress, Mildred thought, good quality velvet and well-fashioned, but how much prettier Seranne would look in one of the new gowns that were made of soft, clinging material, meant to flatter not cover a woman's charms.

"Leave it all to me, dear," she said out loud. "I shall see you have new clothes that are suitable, so don't worry your head about it." She smiled at her niece. "Thank goodness you didn't cut your hair, as all the young ladies seem to have done lately, because now the fashion is for a plait pinned up at the back of

the head." She got to her feet. "Let's go back, dear.
I think we've done enough walking for today." She
laughed. "Remind me to wear something more sensible on my feet next time."

As they retraced their steps back along the river's
side toward the Hall, Mildred, preoccupied with her
own thoughts, noticed nothing of the beautiful
scenery. She was making a mental note of the more
promising men of her acquaintance. Lord Cornwallis, now, not only was he a personal friend of the
Regent himself but his two sons were extremely eligible young men. Fenn Cornwallis was a Government
Consul and a very handsome man, but he was a sec-
ond son, so perhaps his brother Dervil was the one
for Seranne. Dervil Cornwallis was quite wealthy in
his own right, so Mildred believed. At any rate she
had witnessed the way the more eager of the London
mothers had sought his company, hoping no doubt
to foist some favorite daughter upon him. He was an
official of high standing in the Foreign Office, a hard
man to impress, and yet Mildred felt that Seranne
might just manage to catch his eye.

As soon as they reached the Hall, Mildred de-
parted to her room. To her delight, a fire had been lit
in the grate, as the sun was fading and the air was
growing chilly. She slipped off her muddied pumps
and wriggled her toes before the bright blaze, sighing
with satisfaction. The journey from London had
tired her more than she thought, and she decided to
relax for a moment on the bed while composing a
carefully worded invitation in her head to the men of
the Cornwallis family. But soon, the warmth and
silence of the room overwhelmed her and she slept.

Mildred was awakened by the appetizing smell of

roast meat, and she sat up quickly. She'd better hurry if she was not to be late for dinner.

She dressed in a soft blue gown that revealed rather too much of her full breasts. She stared at her reflection in the mirror, wondering if perhaps she might be overdressed by country standards. Then she shrugged; most of her gowns were cut on the same lines, and anyway, who was there to disapprove except for her niece and a few servants. All the same, it might be a good idea to have some new clothes made up, just for wearing while she was in the country.

She smiled with inward amusement as Mrs. Pegg the housekeeper passed her in the hallway, the astonished look on her face quickly turning to prim-lipped disapproval as she observed the revealing neckline.

"Silly woman," Mildred said as she entered the dining room and Seranne looked up from her place at the table.

"The housekeeper," Mildred explained. "I don't think she approves of my gown." She took her place at the table. "No matter. She'll have to grow used to my little ways, because I mean to stay a while. So long as you don't mind having me here, dear," she added as an afterthought.

"Of course I don't mind, Aunt."

Seranne spoke politely but Mildred sensed a certain tone of reserve in her niece's voice. She looked carefully at Seranne and, though there was no expression on the girl's face, Mildred realized there could be a great deal going on in her head. Seranne knew the sudden visit had more to it than met the eye, but she would never ask questions, she was just not the type to pry. Mildred found herself drawn to Seranne; they might get on very well together. Yes, there was a great deal of the Hussey spirit in her niece, and Mildred promised herself she would do her best to bring it out.

As the days passed slowly into weeks, Mildred found that the barrier which had initially been present between Seranne and herself was crumbling. They went riding together almost every day, and when the weather prevented their outings they spent long hours gossiping cozily by the fire in the drawing room. And then a consignment of dress material that Mildred had sent for arrived from London. They had been like children, choosing bales of cloth for new gowns and deciding on the patterns they would have made up.

Mildred had been fortunate in finding the perfect seamstress, a little woman from the village who had a bit of style and flair about her and was not hidebound by old customs.

Seranne had demured at first when she had tried on her new gowns, protesting that the necklines were too bold, but Mildred had talked her out of her false modesty, telling her that in London society such gowns were commonplace. The girl looked delightful and all Mildred could hope for now was that Seranne would conduct herself well before the guests who had agreed to visit the Hall.

As yet Mildred had not told Seranne whom she had invited to stay in the Hall, but one morning she decided she could no longer keep the good news to herself. It would surely brighten the dear girl's day to know there were some elegant and extremely eligible young men already on their way to the Hall.

Seranne was on the terrace, her young face dreamy as she looked down into the waters of the River Dart.

Mildred drew a quick breath as she gazed at the slim figure. Her niece was a lovely girl, far too lovely to be wasting away her young days in solitude. It was a fortuitous day for her when she, Mildred, had taken it into her head to come to Devonshire.

"I have something to tell you, my dear," Mildred said and as Seranne turned to look at her there was a smile of welcome on her face. It seemed that in spite of everything a bond had sprung up between the two of them.

"I believe, my dear," Mildred said, speaking slowly so that the full import of her words would strike home, "I do believe I've found you the perfect husband."

2

Seranne found as the weeks slipped past that her initial apprehension at her aunt's outspoken nature was indeed giving way to genuine liking. Mildred remained as bluff and immodest as ever but it soon became apparent that all her gestures were well intentioned and generous.

Under Mildred's hands, the Hall took on a new appearance. The old furniture was swept away in favor of fashionable Regency pieces. Dainty side tables stood beside new sofas covered with delicately striped damask. Even the pale green silk wall hangings were taken down and cast aside, and curtains of rose-colored damask with gold fringing hung in their place.

Mildred had by no means finished her task of refurbishing the Hall but she had been forced to suspend her activities for the moment because of the impending visit of her friends from London.

One morning, Mildred had left the Hall with a flurry of instructions about what should be done in her absence. She had gone to meet the afternoon mail from London, and when she returned, it would be with the man whom she had decided would make an excellent husband for her niece.

In a fever of impatience, Seranne awaited her aunt's return. On impulse, she hurried up the wide, curving staircase to her room. She wanted to look at her reflection once more in the new ornate mirror that hung at her bedside.

The reflection staring back at her was that of a stranger. Her gown, far more revealing than anything she had ever worn before, showed the full white rise of her breasts. Would the visitors think her immodest? she wondered in sudden panic.

Her hair was pulled straight back from her face and braided up behind her head, and her eyes appeared wider, even slightly apprehensive, as they stared back at her in the mirror. She was suddenly aware that this moment could be a turning point in her life. But then she told herself not to be foolish. She was merely meeting some friends of her aunt's and there was no need to overdramatize the situation.

There was a commotion downstairs in the hall. Doors were opening and closing and the sound of male voices was accompanied by a tinkling laugh from Mildred. The visitors had arrived.

Seranne forced herself to walk sedately along the

corridor and down the curving stairs. She prided herself that no one would have guessed from her appearance that she was trembling inside. Her heart was beating so swiftly that she could hear it pounding in her head, but she made herself walk slowly, as though she had all the time in the world.

Then she saw him. He was standing in a shaft of sunlight and he was like a golden god. His hair, paler than her own, framed a square bronzed face. His, eyes met hers and she could not look away.

How she descended the last of the stairs without tripping, Seranne never knew, but she found herself standing in the hallway, still looking up at the towering man who was smiling at her appreciatively. She felt a momentary confusion as his glance lingered on her neckline, but she forced herself to remember that she was merely following current fashion.

"Please listen when I speak to you, my dear," Mildred said chidingly. "This is Dervil Cornwallis, elder son of my dear friend Lord Cornwallis."

Seranne was being drawn away from her golden god and, reluctantly, she forced herself to concentrate on what her aunt was saying.

"Unfortunately, Dervil's father could not make the trip—pressure of work, poor dear."

Seranne was vaguely conscious of the tall dark man looking down at her. He had an almost saturnine appearance and a strength in his jawline that suggested a ruthless streak. There was a trace of disdain in the curve of his mouth and Seranne turned back to his brother with a feeling of relief.

"This is Fenn." Mildred sounded waspish and she brushed over the introduction as quickly as she could but not before Seranne had felt her hand engulfed in strong brown fingers.

"Come along, dears." Mildred's smile managed to include everyone. "Dinner is ready. I'm sure our guests must be famished after their long journey."

When everyone was seated at the long table laid with gleaming silver, Seranne was overjoyed to find Fenn next to her. He leaned closer, the male, spicy scent of him banishing everything from her mind except the excitement of his nearness. He stared into the cleavage between her breasts and she shivered as though he had caressed her.

"I think you will find that we set a good table, even though we are in the country." Mildred was speaking rather loudly and as Seranne looked up she gave a slight shake of her head.

Seranne was puzzled. What was her aunt trying to convey?

"We have mock turtle soup," Mildred continued. "And for entrées some delicious larded fillets of rabbit. I do hope you like rabbit, Dervil."

He inclined his head without speaking and Mildred rested her hand on his shoulder.

"I see from your face you do not. No matter, there is plenty for you to choose from. How about roast pigeon or stewed beef?"

"Excellent." Dervil Cornwallis was a man of few words, Seranne realized, and even when he spoke, she could not be sure he was saying what was really on his mind.

"You have a most charming home." Fenn leaned toward her again and Seranne glanced up at him shyly.

"Aunt Mildred is to thank for the new furnishings," she said. "She's worked so hard since she came down from London."

"I find you charming too." Fenn almost whispered the words, and for a moment Seranne was not quite sure that she had heard them. "I don't want to talk about your aunt, I'm far more interested in her niece."

"Have some meringue, my dear." Mildred's voice was like a sword thrust, effectively separating Seranne from Fenn.

"No thank you, Aunt, I'm not very hungry." Seranne looked down at her hands, twined together in her lap, hoping Mildred would leave her alone. She did, but only until dinner was over, then she took her niece to one side.

"My dear, where's your sense?" she demanded in a throaty whisper. "Why waste your time with Fenn? It was Dervil I wanted you to impress."

"But, Aunt, Fenn is very charming," Seranne said defensively. "And I can't see that it matters which brother I talk to."

"Silly girl!" Her aunt's annoyance was obvious. "Dervil will inherit his father's title some day and along with it all of Lord Cornwallis's assets. Fenn on the other hand is a charming rake. He is a womanizer, he likes fine clothes and good brandy. He is not the one for you."

Seranne bit back a sharp retort as she saw Fenn and Dervil coming toward them. The contrast between the two brothers was striking. Dervil was as dark as his brother was fair and he seldom smiled. No, whatever Aunt Mildred might think, it was Fenn and not Dervil she found attractive.

In the drawing room, Mildred proudly pointed out the changes she had made and Fenn set out to be agreeable, admiring the color scheme of rose and gold. Dervil simply sat in one of the cane-backed chairs, watching the proceedings with a smile on his face that Seranne found supercilious and irritating.

It was late by the time Mildred decided to retire to bed and yet Seranne had never felt so awake in her life. But it was expected that she follow her aunt from the drawing room, and she felt a pang of regret as she gave Fenn a last quick glance. He smiled at her as he held the door open and she fiercely resisted the urge to touch his face with her fingers.

In her room, Seranne paced restlessly across the carpet. Her whole being seemed to tingle with life and, when she stopped before the mirror, she saw that her cheeks were flushed and her eyes held a sparkle she had never seen before.

Gray streaks of dawn light were penetrating the room and still Seranne lay wide-eyed in her bed. With a sigh, she slipped from beneath the sheets and pulled on a robe of cream satin, tying the sash tightly around her waist.

She would go downstairs and make herself a hot toddy; perhaps the whisky in hot water would help her relax. It had been her father's favorite remedy for sleeplessness. At any rate, anything was better than remaining in her room.

She was startled to see the glimmer of candlelight from under the door of the drawing room. She pushed it open and went inside and a tall figure rose from the chair before the fire.

"Fenn!" She breathed his name and then he was beside her, taking her hands, leading her toward the warmth of the blaze. His touch sent shivers coursing through her body.

"You're cold," he said, still holding her hands.

She shook her head, unable to reply, but her eyes rose slowly to meet his.

The strangest sensations were sweeping through her. She was so close to Fenn that she could feel his breath on her cheek.

"Do I frighten you, Seranne?" he asked in concern, and she made as if to withdraw from him a little. He smiled, holding her tightly, his fingers entwined with hers. "I do frighten you. Come along, admit it." His voice was soft, teasing, and Seranne felt the hot color flood into her cheeks.

"You have no effect on me whatsoever." She tried to sound cool but her voice quivered.

"I don't think you mean that." He pulled her slowly, relentlessly closer to him and Seranne had no wish to draw away, not now with his arms closing around her waist.

She felt the long length of his masculine body close to her own soft curves and she melted against him. He bent his head with deliberation and his lips brushed her eyelashes, then her cheeks, finally coming to rest against her mouth.

The contact took her breath away. Her arms crept upward, encircling his shoulders, clinging, holding him close. She felt dizzy as his lips parted hers and his tongue probed sweetly, drawing an immediate response from her.

"So much passion," he said softly, almost as though speaking to himself. "And shall I be the one to awaken you to the delights of love, little one?"

She tried to control the emotions that raced through her. She had met this man only today, he was virtually a stranger and yet she was allowing him unspeakable liberties.

His hands were sliding down her shoulders, pausing for a moment at the hollow of her waist before shaping the outline of her hips, pulling her nearer to him.

"You're so beautiful." He whispered the words against her mouth. "I would like to possess your loveliness. You feel as I do, don't try to deny it."

He led her to the sofa and drew her down beside him, pushing her back against the scrolled cushions. His mouth took hers once more and then his hands were brushing her breasts. She gasped as a flame of passion raced through her. She had never dreamed that loving a man could feel like this.

"Oh, Fenn," she whispered. "Tell me that you love me." As she spoke, she felt his hands pause for a moment in their exploration of her neckline.

"Dear, sweet girl," Fenn said lightly. "You're so deliciously innocent, how could a man fail to love you?"

He tried to kiss her again but she drew away, smoothing down her robe with hands that shook. She was being foolish, she told herself. Of course he did not love her; it was far too soon for that. Her Hussey blood had betrayed her and now she knew exactly what Mrs. Pegg had meant by her stinging remark about bad blood.

"I don't know what you must think of me," she said, unable to look at him. "I have never behaved this way before, please believe that."

She waited for him to speak, very much aware of his heart pounding uncomfortably close to her own body as his arm went round her.

"I do believe you." He spoke softly. "But there is nothing wrong in showing you're human. It is good and natural to feel desire, so don't try to fight your instincts."

"It is only right if you are respectably married," she replied softly. "Oh, I know it is far too soon to speak that way." She forced herself to look at him. "But there's a bond between us and that I can't deny."

"Nor can I." He leaned forward and briefly kissed the tip of her nose. "Now perhaps you had better return to your room. The servants will be abroad shortly."

Seranne rose to her feet at once. She resented the sudden feeling of dismissal his words evoked and yet she knew he was being sensible.

She ran up the stairs quickly, telling herself that nothing had changed, she was still the same Seranne Hussey she had been yesterday. But she lied. She was tingling from head to foot with desire. Her arms ached to hold Fenn once more and her lips felt bruised by his kisses. She was like a sleeper coming awake and the sensation was almost painful.

It was only a few minutes later that there was a sharp rap on her door and Mildred entered the room, her face fresh and rosy from washing. Her glossy hair was pinned back and she looked very attractive in a rose-colored gown cut higher over the breasts than was usual for her aunt's taste.

"Now, my dear." She sat down in a chair near the window and studied Seranne. "You are going to be sensible, aren't you?"

"Sensible?" Seranne replied. "I don't know what you mean, Aunt." She wondered for a fleeting moment if Mildred had found out about the little episode in the drawing room with Fenn, but her aunt's next words allayed that fear.

"About Dervil, I mean of course, dear. Now I happen to know he is looking for a wife. Someone with breeding and taste, a wife who will be a help to him in his career.''

''His career?'' Seranne echoed, but her thoughts were still of Fenn.

''I told you he's at the Foreign Office,'' Mildred said impatiently. ''He has no need to work at all; he could just as well live on his very substantial means.''

''His brother, Fenn, what about him?'' Seranne spoke carefully but Mildred was not fooled.

''Seranne, for heaven's sake forget about him. Turn your attention to Dervil before it's too late.''

''Why doesn't Dervil find a bride in London?'' Seranne knew she sounded petulant but she simply could not help herself.

''That's precisely what he will do if you do not listen to my sound advice, my dear,'' Mildred said forcefully. ''But he is here at this moment, free and unattached. Try to be a little more responsive to him, won't you?''

''How can I be responsive to him?'' Seranne asked quietly. ''I don't think he even notices I exist. In any event he has not so much as addressed a single remark to me that I can recall.''

''That is not to be wondered at,'' Mildred replied acidly. ''You have made sheep's eyes at his brother ever since the two of them arrived here.''

Seranne sighed. ''Don't let's quarrel, Aunt. I promise I will try to talk to Dervil. I suppose I have been rather rude to him. I'll do my best to make up for it, I promise.''

''Good.'' Mildred got to her feet. ''Now, dress quickly and we can go for a ride before lunch. The sunshine is quite brilliant this morning.''

When Mildred had left the room, Seranne put her

head in her hands and closed her eyes. Her aunt was clever at getting just what she wanted.

"But not this!" Seranne said out loud. How could she encourage Dervil to declare an interest in her when her whole being cried out in longing for Fenn?

3

The green fields sped away under the pounding hooves of Jody, the chestnut mare, and Seranne felt exhilarated as she guided the animal over the familiar countryside. She remembered the look of surprise that had spread over Mildred's face as she had watched her niece handle Jody with the ease of long practice.

"You are an excellent horsewoman, my dear," she had said. "But then there is a great deal of your father in you."

Fenn smiled warmly, his fair hair blowing back from his face. That he admired her in her close-fitting skirt and coat of clear green velvet was apparent. He did not have to say anything; his eyes spoke volumes.

Dervil was his usual uncommunicative self. A brief smile touched his mouth as he stared at her, and she wondered at his ability to make her feel like a spoiled and pampered child.

Still, she was determined to enjoy the balmy spring

weather and she would not allow anyone as unimportant as Dervil Cornwallis to spoil it for her. She urged Jody to go even faster, flinging back her head, reveling in the touch of the wind on her face and hair.

She became aware that there was a rider drawing level, traveling neck and neck with her before easily passing by.

It was Dervil. Seranne stared at his back, at the long dark hair sweeping the collar of his coat. He was increasing the distance between them; compared to him she was a mere dilettante at riding.

Gritting her teeth, she kicked at Jody's flanks with more ferocity than she'd intended. The startled animal reared up, head jerking at the reins. Seranne saw the blue of the sky merge with the green of the grass before she landed heavily on the clumpy ground.

"Come a cropper have you?" Dervil had returned and was staring down at her with open amusement in his silver-gray eyes. "You might learn to ride, given time. Until then I'd be more careful if I were you."

She scrambled to her feet, brushing the grass from her skirt. Her cheeks were red with anger.

"You enjoy ridiculing me, don't you?" she challenged and Dervil smiled with infuriating good humor.

"Do I?" he said, his eyes unreadable.

"Are you all right, my dear?" Mildred rode up alongside Seranne, her face full of concern. "Oh thank goodness you haven't hurt yourself." She rested back in her saddle. "It would have been awful if you'd had to miss the little dinner I've arranged."

Seranne looked gratefully at Fenn as he led Jody toward her. He was the only one who had any real thought for her welfare. She smiled up at him warmly as she slipped her foot into the stirrup. She ached all over and she wanted nothing more now than to return to the privacy of her own room. She was silent on the ride back to the Hall, brooding over the way Dervil had humiliated her.

Once indoors, she hurried up the wide staircase, without a word to anyone. It was good to have a little solitude, at least for a while. Dervil Cornwallis had made her so angry. He had positively enjoyed her discomfort.

She stood before the window and stared out at the river, flowing like a ribbon of greenish-blue between the lush banks. The sun was sinking now and a twilight haze was stealing over the countryside.

She sighed, knowing she would soon have to decide what she would wear for the dinner Aunt Mildred had arranged. Goodness knows why she was making such a fuss. It certainly would not be anything like the glittering parties she was used to giving in London.

Seranne moved across the room restlessly and stared at herself in the oval mirror hanging on the wall. No doubt the local gentry whom Aunt Mildred thought so important would look down their noses at the changes which had taken place at the Hall. She smiled to herself in a sudden flash of rebellion. Well, they would all find that she was greatly changed too. Gone was the dowdy, unfashionable girl she had once been. She would wear her most daring gown and shock them all.

She sank onto the bed, her spirits ebbing away. The only person she really wanted to impress was Fenn, and except for the brief interest he'd shown when he'd returned Jody to her this afternoon, he had been rather cool during the last few days. Seranne imagined that Mildred had been talking to him—telling him, perhaps, of her plan to marry Dervil to her niece. Well, Aunt Mildred would just have to accept the fact that there was nothing between Dervil and herself but dislike. Seranne could not envisage marrying such a man. He was so opinionated and arrogant he would make a martyr of any woman who loved him.

It was strange how much her life had altered, she reflected, ever since she had first seen Fenn Cornwallis standing in the hall in a shaft of sunlight, looking like a prince.

In a sudden spurt of impatience, she decided to put both men completely out of her mind. She would concentrate on the pleasant task of dressing for dinner.

The gown she finally chose was one of soft blue satin. The high waist and square neckline framed her white breasts, emphasizing the curves of marble flesh. The hemline was folded and decorated with silver braid in deference to the latest trend for military embellishments. As a last touch, Seranne pinned a piece of white lace to the braid at the back of her head, standing back a little from the mirror to see the result of her efforts.

She was suddenly uncertain about the wisdom of appearing in somewhat staid Devonshire company in a gown so daring. She sat down, careful not to crush the satin of her skirt, and thought about the guests on Mildred's list.

Thomas Hunkin and his wife would no doubt stare at her in open disapproval, comparing her unfavorably with their own two daughters, Grace and Beatrice. Their son Jonathon on the other hand would be inclined to admire her audacity. From the little Seranne knew of him, he appeared much more broadminded than his parents.

Then there was Captain Jennings. Mildred had only approached him because she had believed him to be an eligible widower. She had quickly found to her dismay that the Captain had acquired a new wife, but by then the invitation had been given and it would have been obvious bad manners to have withdrawn it.

Seranne almost lost her courage and rose from her chair, half intending to change into one of her old gowns, but her door opened suddenly and Mildred bustled into the room.

"Ah good, you're ready, dear." She tweaked at the piece of lace on Seranne's hair, rearranging it to her own satisfaction. "Captain Jennings has arrived early. I might have known the man would have breeding. You must go down and entertain him and that ghastly wife of his. I shall join you shortly."

Seranne opened her mouth to speak and then closed it again. Her aunt would simply fail to understand Seranne's misgivings about her appearance. She left her room and obediently made her way downstairs.

In the drawing room, Captain Jennings was seated next to his wife. He was obviously infatuated with the rather plain, plump young woman who smiled at him fatuously. He rose to his feet politely as Seranne entered the room and his graying eyebrows lifted a fraction before he recovered his wits.

"Charmed to be asked to Hussey Hall, Miss Seranne," he said, trying his best to raise his eyes above the neckline of her gown.

She forced a smile, feeling the color rising to her cheeks. Captain Jennings's wife leaned close to him, whispering something in his ear.

"Oh, may I introduce my dear Teresa?" he said quickly, and Seranne was confronted by an impudent scrutiny that bordered on rudeness.

Seranne murmured something in an effort to be polite, but her thoughts were muddled. She wondered how she would appear to Fenn against the background of her own neighbors. Would he see her as a dull country girl trying to be something she was not?

To her relief, she heard the sound of voices out in the hall and she realized the other guests had arrived. At least now she would be saved from trying to make conversation with the besotted Captain and his dim little wife.

Mildred arrived on the scene in time to usher her guests into the dining room with an ease that spoke of long experience. Seranne was seated opposite Fenn and next to Dervil and she knew that her aunt had planned it that way, determined to make it quite plain that Seranne was spoken for.

The food was served amid a buzz of conversation but Seranne was miserably aware that her choice of gown had been the wrong one. The other ladies present, with the exception of Mildred, were discreetly clothed in gowns that concealed more than revealed. Seranne felt entirely out of place.

Jonathon Hunkin, however, smiled at her admiringly, ignoring his father's scowl of disapproval. She returned his gaze, aware of Fenn talking animatedly to the plump Teresa and seemingly enjoying himself.

Dervil leaned forward and whispered in her ear: "You seem to have lost your tongue. Are you really as miserable as your appearance would suggest?" His silver-gray eyes held amusement and Seranne flushed.

"I feel unsuitably dressed, if you must know," she said flatly.

Dervil leaned to one side, openly studying her gown. "You look very charming," he said. "And I for one would like to see a great deal more of you."

She knew he was making fun of her and an angry retort rose to her lips. But she forced herself to remain silent, the sharp words dying unspoken. She would not squabble with Dervil; she was sure to lose.

"Come along, try to smile," Dervil whispered in her ear. "If I have read your aunt's intentions clearly, this is meant to be a gathering where the locals can admire the catch you've made."

Seranne could hardly believe the evidence of her own ears. She leaned toward Dervil, careful to keep her expression pleasant.

"If you are a good catch then I would gladly throw you back," she said, and was amazed when Dervil, after a moment's silence, laughed in genuine amusement.

Mildred smiled sweetly, obviously well-pleased with the way Seranne and Dervil seemed to be getting along so well together. She positively glowed with pleasure when Thomas Hunkin praised the new furnishings in the Hall and then went on to speak enthusiastically about the food on the laden table. Not knowing him very well, she missed the way he was staring into her neckline. In any event, Mildred would have considered him far too old for her; his son Jonathon, at about thirty years of age, was far more to her liking.

By the time the long meal was finished, Fenn had the plump Teresa eating out of his hand. She was staring at him with large blue eyes to the obvious dismay of the Captain.

As Mildred ushered everyone toward the drawing room, Fenn took Teresa's arm and whispered something to her. She giggled a little and slapped him lightly on his hand.

Seranne watched the little scene with jealousy flowing through her like a fire. It was even worse when Grace and Beatrice Hunkin joined the pair, standing gazing at Fenn with open admiration. The two girls may have been dressed discreetly but their conduct was bold enough as they both attempted to catch Fenn's attention.

"I think I had better have a word with Fenn," Mildred whispered in Seranne's ear. "It's all right for him to flirt with those simpering Hunkin girls but I believe the Captain is quite angry with the way his wife is being charmed under his very eyes."

Jonathon Hunkin appeared at Seranne's side. He smiled down at her. "You are fortunate in your choice of a husband," he said a little ruefully. "Dervil Cornwallis seems a fine man. Though I would have offered for your hand myself, if ever I'd been given the chance."

Seranne was at a loss; she could think of nothing to say. To protest that she and Dervil were simply acquaintances would be almost offering herself to Jonathon like a cast-off glove. For her part she had no interest in anyone except Fenn, and he, it seemed, was quite content to ignore her very existence.

"When your father was alive, he kept you almost completely to himself," Jonathon was saying. "I don't believe I've ever managed more than the briefest of conversations with you."

"My father was very protective," Seranne agreed. "I think he still considered me very much a child even when I reached my sixteenth birthday."

"He would be proud if he could see you now."
Jonathon's eyes glowed as he looked down at her and
Seranne stepped back.

"Forgive me," she said lightly. "I had better pay
my respects to Mrs. Hunkin. She seems a little ne-
glected, sitting there alone as she is."

Jonathon smiled. "My mother is hoping that one
of the girls will catch a husband tonight," he said. "I
don't think she expected Grace and Beatrice to take
up the idea with such enthusiasm though."

Before Seranne was halfway across the room, Dervil was at her side, taking her arm.

"Apparently we make an ideal couple," he said,
and when she looked up at him sharply Seranne saw
that his eyes were alight with laughter.

"What do you mean?" she asked in bewilderment.

He slid his arm around her waist. "Well, aren't we
supposed to be betrothed? I've just been receiving
some hearty congratulations on gaining such a beautiful bride."

"You enjoy making fun of me, don't you?"
Seranne challenged. "I suppose I appear dull com-
pany compared to the ladies you are accustomed to in
London."

"I do not always choose feminine company for
their wits." Dervil was looking meaningfully down
into Seranne's neckline and she bit her lip, longing to
strike out at him.

"You are so clever," she said in a low, fierce
voice. "I think I am beginning to positively dislike
you."

He stared at her in silence for a moment, his arm
tightening around her waist. "At least that's better
than indifference, I suppose," he said lightly.

"And that is what you feel for me, I presume,"

Seranne said, drawing away from him in a sudden spurt of anger. He was intolerable, never missing an opportunity to embarrass her.

Fenn was still the center of an adoring circle of females. On an impulse Seranne went over to him, slipping her hand through his arm.

"Come along, Fenn, it's about time you talked to me a little. I'm becoming quite jealous!"

"Oh, that's not fair." The protest was from Grace Hunkin. She pursed her narrow lips until they were almost a straight line in her sallow face.

"What do you mean?" Seranne asked, still holding on to Fenn's arm.

"You have a gentleman of your own," Grace said. "So I don't see why you should wish to monopolize Mr. Fenn Cornwallis."

To Seranne's chagrin, Fenn agreed with Grace. "Quite right," he said, his voice light. "You must not be greedy, my dear sister-in-law to be."

Grace laughed and rested her hand on Fenn's arm for a moment, as though laying claim to him.

"Oh, Mr. Cornwallis, you are so witty! Come, do tell us more about your travels, I am quite fascinated by your exciting work for the Government."

Seranne found herself being slowly excluded from the conversation. She listened miserably as Fenn described his duties as a Consul.

"Principally, I have to insure that there is fair trading between the countries," he said. "Sometimes I have to spend time abroad, and not always in comfortable surroundings, I assure you." He smiled. "But nowhere have I met such beautiful ladies as in Devonshire."

His eyes were resting on the Captain's wife as he

spoke and she simpered up at him, her doll-like face flushed with pleasure. Obviously Mildred's attempts to separate Teresa from Fenn had met with failure.

The Captain rose to his feet, his face red beneath the graying hair.

"It's time we were leaving," he said loudly. "Come along Teresa, I wish to go home."

She pouted and without taking her eyes away from Fenn she waved her hand toward her husband. "Oh, but I'm enjoying myself far too much. Don't be an old grouse."

The Captain's reaction was startling. He moved forward in one bound and caught Teresa by her plump arm.

"I said we are going home." He gave Fenn an angry look and raised his fist menacingly.

"You, sir, deserve a good thrashing—and I might just be the right man to administer it."

Fenn returned his gaze steadily. "I would not advise you to try," he said coldly.

Dervil moved forward and took the Captain's arm. "There's no need for any unpleasantness before the ladies," he said smoothly. "I suggest that you leave at once. My brother meant no harm, I'm sure."

The Captain pulled away sharply. "Very well, I shall be satisfied with an apology. The man has made sheep's eyes at my wife all night."

Fenn smiled suddenly. "You have my apology," he said at once, as if bored with the proceedings. "Good night to you both."

As if by a signal, the party came to an abrupt end. Mrs. Hunkin seemed relieved to have her husband take charge of their unruly daughters, ordering them outside to the waiting carriage.

"Good night, Seranne," Jonathon said softly, holding her hand a moment longer than was strictly necessary. "I hope we shall meet again before too long."

As soon as the rumble of wheels died away in the distance, Mildred turned on Fenn, her face flushed with anger.

"Why do you always have to be the center of attention?" she demanded. "If it hadn't been for Dervil's intervention there could have been quite an ugly scene."

"Don't take it upon yourself to reproach me, Mildred," Fenn said coldly. "You are not my mother, remember."

Mildred was speechless. The situation would have been funny if Fenn's tone had not been so fierce.

Fenn gave a curt bow and left the room and Mildred sank into a chair, fanning herself with her hands.

"I'm going to my room," Seranne said in a low voice. She felt suddenly dispirited, as though everything in her life was turning upside down. She hurried up the stairs and into her bedroom, tears glinting on her eyelashes. What if Fenn decided to go back to London? How could she bear to be separated from him now?

It was some hours later, perhaps two or three in the morning, that Seranne found herself walking along the corridor toward Fenn's room in a mood of quiet desperation. She didn't dare to think what would happen should she be seen. Aunt Mildred would be the first to condemn her; she would never believe that Seranne simply wanted to talk to Fenn. She would beg him, if need be, to stay just a little while longer so that they might sort things out between them. Her life was her own and Seranne was determined to make Fenn understand that.

She stood uncertainly outside his door, trying to summon enough courage to enter the bedroom. She hesitated, trembling. What if he should reject her completely? The thought was almost enough to make her turn and run back to the safety of her own room. But no. She must see Fenn; it was no use at all to stand alone in the silver moonlit corridor in a mood of indecision.

She knocked quietly and, without waiting for a reply, gently turned the handle of the door. She was inside the velvet darkness of his room then and her heart thudded so hard she thought it would burst.

"Fenn!" She whispered his name into the darkness and the very air seemed charged with emotion. She heard the rustle of sheets and then she sensed, rather than saw him, standing beside her.

"What are you doing here, Seranne?" His hands grasped her arms, warm through the thin silk of her robe. Seranne shivered.

"I had to see you." Her voice was a whisper. "I've been so miserable." She leaned forward until her head rested in the hollow of his warm, naked shoulder.

"I'm not made of stone, you know." The words were almost a groan and then his arms were around her, holding her close. She clung to him, closing her eyes with the sheer joy of being near him.

"I want *you*, Fenn," she said softly. "Not Dervil."

"You're so beautiful." Fenn's hands were caressing her shoulders, sliding down her back, pressing her close to him. "You are driving me crazy with desire."

He touched her breasts, lightly at first, and when she raised no protest, his hands became bolder, outlining the shape of her nipples with the tips of his fingers.

She drew a ragged breath. The strangest sensations were racing through her body. She was suddenly aware of every part of her being; her skin seemed to glow under his touch.

"Oh, Fenn, I love you so very much." Her hands were cupping his face, trying to see his expression, but the darkness was too intense.

"Seranne," Fenn said thickly. "How can I send you away now?" His hands moved downward over her body and Seranne clung to him even more closely.

"I'll prove that I love you," she whispered, pressing her hot face against his chest.

He drew her onto the bed, his arm around her, and Seranne knew that now there could be no turning back.

Very gently, he removed her nightgown and a sigh escaped from his lips.

"You feel like satin—the most beautiful thing I've ever seen. . . . Yet there is a fire inside you, I know it." His mouth touched her mouth and then her breasts, his lips teasing her nipples.

She lay unmoving. She was frightened and yet the sensations stirring within her could not be denied. Fenn continued to caress her, his hand gliding over her smooth stomach and then, gently, he was pushing her legs apart, his fingers moving delicately as though tuning a sensitive instrument.

She gasped, responding to his touch, moving in a rhythm of passion that seemed to sweep over her like a tide. He took her hand and placed it on his body and she was startled for a moment by the size and hardness of him.

"I won't hurt you, my darling," he whispered. "Just trust me."

She was almost delirious with desire for him and when he swung himself over her, kneeling between her legs, she arched herself toward him.

As he pierced her, she felt pain and great joy. Fenn would make a woman of her, and with their joining, she would become his forever.

He thrust inward and she stifled a cry. At once Fenn withdrew, waiting a moment before continuing with his movements. The sensations were almost unbearable and Seranne pressed her face against Fenn's golden body stifling cries of pure happiness.

His movements were quicker now, growing increasingly forceful. Suddenly Fenn was arching his body forward as though he would penetrate into the deepest recesses of her being.

She felt herself sweeping along on a dream of pulsating responses that shuddered through her so that her mind became blank and all she was conscious of was her body and his within her, pushing her to the very heights of ecstasy. She thought she cried out his name but she couldn't be sure, and then at last it was over and Fenn was lying beside her, his arm flung across her breasts, his eyes closed.

She gave a moan and curled against him. It had been the most wonderful experience of her life. It was like nothing she could ever have imagined in her wildest dreams, perfect, because Fenn had shown how much he loved her and needed her.

His fingers caught in her hair and in the dimness she saw that he was looking at her, a smile on his face.

"Happy, darling Seranne? Are you glad you came to my room tonight?"

She kissed him. "Fenn, I love you so much I'm almost afraid. I'm terrified that something will happen to part us. You won't allow that, will you? Promise me you won't."

"You are sweet, Seranne." Fenn lifted himself up on one elbow and looked down at her. "The most beautiful girl I've ever had, I swear it."

"You love me, don't you, Fenn?" She was almost begging for reassurance, and Fenn smiled, kissing her brow lightly.

"Of course I love you—who wouldn't? Now, don't you think you should get back to your room before our little secret is discovered?"

She suddenly felt chilled. "But Fenn, don't you want everyone to know we're in love with each other?" Her voice rose a little.

Quickly Fenn put an arm around her. "I'm only thinking of you, my sweet," he said softly. "Just imagine your aunt's wrath if she found out about tonight. We must be careful, you see that, don't you?"

"I'd better go now." She told herself that Fenn was trying to be sensible but his attitude hurt her deeply. She picked up her crumpled nightgown and slipped it over her head.

"Good night, Fenn, darling." She wanted him to take her to the doorway, to watch her return safely along the corridor but he didn't move.

"Good night, my sweet," he said.

And then she was outside his door, running along in the darkness, wanting the shelter of her own room.

She lay under the sheets, hugging herself to stop the shivering that had seized her. Hot, bitter tears flooded into her eyes, and in the loneliness of dawn, she began to cry.

4

It took Seranne several days to realize that the experience she'd shared with Fenn had not changed the world. At least, not his. She'd expected some sort of sign from him, an acknowledgement of the intimacy they'd shared. When there was none, her mood alternated between anguished uncertainty and almost rapturous delight.

Longing for him became like a fever in her blood, and even the smallest show of tenderness on his part would have lifted her to the heights of happiness.

The pain became unbearable as the days passed and Mildred was quick to notice the change in her niece. In her usual forthright way she demanded an explanation.

"What ails you, Seranne?" She was sitting at the head of the table, undisputed head of the household. "You're as pale and peaky-looking as the day I first arrived. Come along, my dear, there's something wrong isn't there?"

Seranne wished she could run and hide but escape was impossible. She held up her head, small chin jutting forward.

"Nothing's wrong, Aunt, except that I've been indoors too much. Perhaps today I'll take a walk along the river and watch the brigantines come in." She was aware of Fenn's quick glance.

"That's an excellent idea, I think I'll come with you." He rose from the table in a quick lithe movement. "If you've finished your luncheon, we could go straight away while the weather holds."

Seranne stared at him in confusion. She felt she should refuse Fenn's company, punish him a little for the misery he'd inflicted on her these last few days, but somehow she couldn't.

"Yes, all right," she found herself saying and then, before Mildred could protest, Seranne moved toward the door.

As she stood outside the Hall in the brilliant sunlight, waiting for Fenn to follow her, she leaned over the parapet that bordered the terrace and looked down into the river. She wondered what he would say to her when they were alone. Excitement was like wine inside her. Then Fenn was touching her shoulder, smiling down into her eyes, and the whole world seemed to take on a new brilliance.

"Let's get away from here," he said softly. He took her hand, leading her away from the Hall, along the winding drive and out onto the rough road that led down to the river.

She wanted to demand an explanation, to tell Fenn how distraught she'd been these last few days, but with her hand clasped in his, her courage failed her. How could she bring herself to spoil the magic of the moment?

The grass was lush and green under her feet, the sun hot on her bare head, and in the delight of the moment, Seranne found herself laughing out loud.

"I expect Aunt Mildred is having a fit," she said. "Did you see her face when you said you'd come with me? I'm sure she thinks it most improper for us to be alone like this."

"It is," Fenn said. "But there's no one to see us now, my sweet." He bent his head toward her but Seranne turned away, hurrying to the edge of the water, staring out at the golden ripples lapping near her feet.

"Look at the castle," she said as Fenn came up behind her. "Doesn't it seem like something out of a fairy tale, perched on the edge of the river like that?"

"Nothing so romantic." Fenn put his arm around her shoulder. "It serves as an assembly point for the local yeomanry while the war with Napoleon continues—didn't you know?"

Seranne was a little dismayed at the derision in Fenn's voice. He had sounded just like Dervil then, ready to read her a lecture at the drop of a hat.

"Let's walk toward the trees." Fenn slipped his arm around her waist, his tone coaxing now.

She could not help the thrill that ran through her at his touch. She looked up into his face, her eyes shining, the color running into her cheeks as she read desire for her in every line of his body.

He led her toward the green shade of the trees and the sudden coolness was welcome after the heat of the afternoon sun. Seranne felt a pang of misgiving as they plunged deeper into the woods, but Fenn was holding her hand tightly and she couldn't draw back even if she wanted to.

At last they came to a small clearing. The grass was

soft and lush and the overhanging branches formed a canopy against the sky. It was as if they had found a magic, secret world in which only the two of them existed.

Fenn flung himself to the ground and looked up at Seranne, smiling a little, though his eyes were hot as they rested first on her breasts and then on the curve of her hips.

"Sit beside me." It was a softly spoken command and Seranne felt weak as she obeyed, the grass rustling against her skirt.

He kissed her, long and lingeringly, but Seranne, aroused though she was, held back a little. She simply must talk to him, to find out once and for all if he really cared for her.

"Please, Fenn." She held him away. "Allow me a moment to think." She rubbed her face with the tips of her fingers, trying to put her thoughts into words.

"Do you love me at all?" she said at last, her heart beating so rapidly she could hardly breathe. His eyes were half hidden under his lashes and for a moment she wondered if he had heard her question.

"Of course." He drew her down until she was resting against him. The sun shone through the leaves of the trees, making bright patterns on his face and hair, and she so much wanted to believe he was speaking the truth. "I wouldn't be here with you otherwise."

She placed her hands on his face and kissed his mouth. His passion aroused a ready response in her and she knew that she had no strength to resist him. Slowly, he opened the buttons of her bodice and she closed her eyes, her lips parting under his.

When she was completely naked, he stared down at her, his eyes alight. She knew by the look on his face

that he found her beautiful, and she took a shuddering breath as he drew her close. He *must* love her, she
told herself reassuringly.

He was rougher than in their first lovemaking and
she welcomed the added vigor of his thrusts. She
sighed with joy as she lay on her bed of soft grass,
feeling his hands holding her breasts and wanting
him to fill her body with his. He withdrew, tantaliz-
ingly, and then pushed forward again and she cried
out in an ecstasy of delight. He moved and twisted
within her, sending shuddering sensations racing
through her thighs and stomach, reaching out like
fingers to every part of her body. It was as though
she was riding a stormy sea, lifted up until she was no
longer in command of herself. She closed her eyes,
feeling the orange sun dazzling through her lids. She
wanted the ecstasy to go on and on. She could have
spent a lifetime in the haven of green and gold where
they lay. But then it was over and, twined in each
other's arms, they rested.

They bathed in the sparkling water of the river,
laughing like children, and Seranne thought her heart
would break with love and happiness. She could not
imagine life without Fenn now. It was as though he
had always been there, waiting to bring her to life.
His body lay beside hers in the water, bronzed and
lithe, and then he turned and made for the shore.

She followed him, anxious now, hoping fervently
that no one would come along until she was safely in
the shelter of the trees again. But it was as though the
world was theirs alone on that silent golden day.
When they were dressed, they sat on the bank, waiting for the sun to dry the damp strands of Seranne's
hair.

*   *   *

It was late afternoon by the time they made their way
back through the trees in the direction of the Hall.
Fenn was silent and Seranne held onto his arm, feeling the whipcord strength of him, trying to preserve
the feeling of closeness between them for as long as
possible.

The world seemed to be at peace, dreaming in the
heat of the afternoon. Not even the merest trace of a
breeze disturbed the trees surrounding the gardens.

As they neared the large doorway to the Hall,
Seranne felt suddenly conscious of her untidy hair.
Aunt Mildred's suspicions would be immediately
confirmed unless there was a way of avoiding her
eagle eye.

Mrs. Pegg was mounting the stairs, carrying a tray
of iced water, and she clucked her tongue when she
saw Seranne, though she seemed not to notice her
disheveled appearance.

"Your poor aunt's resting," she said. "Seems real
out of sorts, a martyr to pains in the head so she tells
me. That's what comes of living in the city, I say."

Seranne hurried to her room and quickly stripped
off her crumpled gown. Relieved that she would not
have to face Mildred immediately, she washed her
hot cheeks in the water from the jug on the wash-
stand and combed the grass from her hair. Why was
it, she wondered, that greatly though she enjoyed
Fenn's lovemaking, afterward she felt so guilty and
dispirited?

When she left her room a few moments later and
made her way downstairs, it was to find Dervil alone
in the drawing room, a brandy glass in his hand.

"Do you want a drink?" he said abruptly. "You
look as though you need one." She shook her head

just as Fenn entered the room. The two brothers stared at each other.

"You both enjoyed your little outing, I take it," Dervil spoke with his usual sarcasm and Fenn flushed, a frown creasing his brow.

"It was very pleasant, thank you." Seranne spoke quickly, seating herself on the sofa. The last thing she wanted just now was for the brothers to quarrel. Somehow, it seemed that they were always at each other's throat.

Dervil helped himself to another brandy from the decanter on the sideboard. His eyes held a glint of irony as he stood beside Seranne, looking down at her.

"How would you like to keep me company tomorrow?" he asked. "I imagine you are fairly liberal with your time."

She returned his gaze, trying to fathom the meaning behind his words. Was he making her a proposition? The rich color flowed into her cheeks.

"I'm afraid I shall be rather busy tomorrow." She saw that Fenn was staring out of the window; he seemed remote from her, as though they had never lain under the sun together.

"Not with Fenn, you won't," Dervil continued. "He has plans to return home tomorrow, didn't you know?"

Seranne's heart contracted with despair. She started to rise and then sank-back again as Fenn's face told her all she needed to know.

"I didn't realize you had arranged to return to London so soon." Her voice was surprisingly strong, with no sign of the anguish she was feeling.

"My plans are not certain yet." Fenn spoke coolly. "But I shall have to leave the Hall within the next few days. I do have my career to think of."

Dervil put down his glass on the table and gave Seranne a mocking bow. "Do excuse me, both of you, I'm sure you would like to talk in private."

Seranne almost hated him in that moment. He had deliberately set out to let her know of Fenn's intentions and he was amused by the situation. Her fists were clenched and she made an enormous effort to keep herself in check until she heard the door click shut behind him.

"You can't be leaving just like that!" The words were torn from her lips as she rose to confront Fenn. He shook his head as though surprised by the intensity of her anger.

"But why not?" He stared at her as though she were a stranger, and for a moment she was speechless.

"You ask me that after what we've been to each other?" she demanded incredulously. "Didn't our love-making mean anything to you, Fenn?"

He crossed the room and put an arm around her shoulders. He kissed the tip of her nose and his smile was as charming as ever.

"Of course it did," he said softly. "You are a very beautiful young woman. But you *wanted* me to make love to you, don't forget that."

Seranne felt crushed and humiliated. She tried to draw away but Fenn held her fast.

"You mustn't try to rush things, my darling," he said lightly. "It's true I shall be away from time to time but I'll come down to see you at the Hall whenever I can."

"I care deeply for you, Fenn." She made one last effort to appeal to him. "Do you think I'd have allowed you to make love to me if I wasn't sure of my feelings?''

"You're very sweet and very young," Fenn said. "But there's a great deal you have to learn about life, yet."

"In other words I've allowed you to use me," she said in a small voice. "How could I have been so stupid?"

She turned and left him and a great weariness filled her as she climbed the stairs to her room. She felt as though she was living in a nightmare. She had made herself believe in Fenn's love, but now she knew the truth. She had nothing more than an hour's amusement.

She stood before the window, looking out at the quiet countryside. She had no one to blame but herself for what had happened. Aunt Mildred had given her a more than adequate warning about Fenn's fickle ways. Yet, even now, she loved him with a fierceness that hurt. She wrapped her arms around her body as if to hold the torment at bay, but the hot bitter tears ran down her cheeks and into her mouth and she knew she would never be the same again.

Later that evening, Seranne went downstairs to dinner with no outward sign of the anguish she had endured in the past few hours. She sat next to Fenn without glancing at him, surprised to see Mildred at her usual place at the head of the table and smiling warmly at her.

"My dear girl, it seems hours since I saw you." She showed no sign of the headache she had complained of earlier. On the contrary, her skin was glowing and her eyes were bright.

"Are you feeling better, Aunt?" Seranne asked politely and Mildred gave a tinkling laugh.

"Oh, my headache, you mean? That's quite vanished, my dear. I feel wonderful. I simply needed a rest, that's all. The weather has been intolerably hot today, don't you think?"

It was a strain for Seranne to endure the long, lavish meal as though nothing was wrong and it was with a sense of relief that she saw Mildred rise at last from the table.

"Come along, my dear." Her aunt linked arms with her. "We shall leave the men to their brandy and go into the drawing room, it's much cooler in there."

When they were alone, Mildred turned to Seranne, searching her face with anxious eyes.

"Now, dear, tell me what is on your mind. I know something's wrong and I want to help you in whatever way I can." She smiled encouragingly, and suddenly Seranne found the words pouring from her.

"Did you know Fenn intended to return to London tomorrow?"

"Yes, I did know. What is more, I heartily approve of him going, he is much too disruptive. I hadn't realized quite how difficult he could be."

"But I thought he would marry me!" Seranne couldn't keep the anguish from her voice. "I love him, Aunt, can't you understand what I'm trying to say?"

Mildred regarded her steadily for a moment. "You mean you have allowed him to make love to you? You silly, silly girl and after all I said to you about him." Her face hardened. "Well, now you must forget him. Is that clear?"

"How can I forget him?" Seranne asked bitterly.

"He must care about me a little, mustn't he?"

Mildred shrugged. "My dear, a man will take his pleasures where he can find them and love does not always enter into it."

"You make me feel like a harlot." Seranne's voice was low and Mildred caught her arm in a strong grasp.

"That's enough of that, my dear. There's no need to be sorry for yourself. You are a Hussey and all the Husseys have backbone; you'll get over all this. Now, dry your eyes. Nothing is irreplaceable."

"What do you mean?" Seranne looked at Mildred in sudden hope; perhaps she would find a way to make Fenn remain at the Hall a little while longer.

"There is still Dervil," Mildred said firmly. "He's the better catch of the two, my dear—haven't I told you that from the beginning?"

Seranne stared at her aunt aghast. "I could never care for Dervil," she said.

"Nothing is impossible, my dear." There was an edge to her aunt's voice. "It may be that Dervil doesn't realize how far your romance with Fenn has gone."

"Oh, he realizes," Seranne said bitterly. "He knows everything and he doesn't hesitate to show his scorn. No, Aunt, Dervil would never consider me for a wife, even if I was willing to marry him."

"You underestimate my determination, my dear," Mildred said softly. "If there is a way, I will find it, don't you fear. Ah, I do believe the men are joining us."

It was the longest evening Seranne had ever endured. She drank several glasses of fine brandy without even tasting it, and was relieved when at last Mildred rose to her feet.

"Time we were retiring to bed, my dears," she said genially. "I at any rate need my beauty sleep."

In the darkness of her room, Seranne lay curled under the sheets. She could find no relief from her tortured thoughts. She had fallen into Fenn's arms like an apple ripe from the tree. Could she really blame him for taking what was so freely offered? Well, she had learned her lesson painfully. She would never trust another man as long as she lived. Yet even as her lids drooped into an exhausted sleep, she knew that if Fenn should come to her at this moment and tell her he loved her, she would welcome him with open arms.

When she woke, it was from a troubled sleep and for a moment she thought she was still dreaming. There were voices under her window and the sound of wheels on the cobbles. In an instant, Seranne was out of bed, drawing back the curtains with unsteady hands.

The sun poured into the room, blinding her for a moment, then she saw her aunt handing some light baggage to Fenn. He stowed it away inside the coach that had the Hussey crest emblazoned on the door. Mildred climbed inside, Fenn following her, and the horses were stirred into movement. The large coach rumbled away from the Hall, the clatter of hooves growing fainter.

Seranne could hardly believe what she had witnessed. She pulled on a robe and went to the door. "Mrs. Pegg!" she cried. "Come here at once!"

The housekeeper mounted the stairs as quickly as her voluminous skirts allowed. Her face was full of concern and she was gasping as she reached the landing.

"What's wrong, Miss Seranne?" she asked breathlessly. "Are you sick? You sounded like a banshee! I swear the hair stood up on the back of my neck when I heard you call."

Seranne made an effort to speak calmly, "Where's my aunt going? What's happening, Mrs. Pegg?"

"Oh Lordy me!" Mrs. Pegg mopped her brow. "She's gone off to the city. She said to tell you she'll be back in a few days' time. She didn't want to wake you but she said you're not to worry about a thing."

As the housekeeper stopped speaking, Seranne became aware of Dervil standing at the foot of the wide staircase. His face was unreadable.

"Well," she demanded. "Aren't you going off to London too? I shouldn't think there's anything to keep you here now."

His silver-gray eyes seemed to look right through her as he answered slowly.

"Not a great deal, I must admit, except that I made a promise to Mildred."

"What sort of promise?" Seranne asked warily and she was flustered when he laughed openly at her.

"Simply that I would remain here until she returned." He paused. "I am the guardian of what she sweetly refers to as your chastity. Poor Mildred, she really is misguided."

A sense of pure hatred rose within Seranne and for a moment she couldn't even see his amused face for the mists of anger that rose before her eyes.

"Damn you!" she said loudly. "Damn you to hell, Dervil Cornwallis!"

5

The days that followed Fenn's departure were ones of sheer misery for Seranne. She missed him so badly that she could not give her mind to anything. The worst part of it all was the realization that he was not worth her anguish. Fenn Cornwallis was selfish and shallow, everything she should have despised in a man.

But her treacherous body cried out for his touch. In the dark hours of night, she twisted and turned in her bed, watching the daylight streaking the sky through her window. And she yearned to be possessed once more by her lover.

To add to her unhappiness, she found that the days were long without Mildred's no-nonsense presence in the Hall. She had become used to leaving household matters in her aunt's capable hands and now Seranne found it irksome to have to concern herself with accounts and the daily menus.

As for Dervil, she had barely acknowledged his existence ever since the moment when she had stood on the stairway cursing him. She blushed whenever she remembered the way he had laughed at her puny efforts to scratch the surface of his self-control. He was a man made of steel. His heart was as gray as his eyes, and as cold. He would not hesitate to crush her underfoot if she crossed him, she felt sure of that.

As though conjured up by her thoughts, Dervil strode onto the terrace where she was sitting watching the flow of the river. He stood against the late afternoon sunlight so that it appeared as if he had an aura of gold around him. She could not see the expression on his face but her heart lurched when she saw the letter in his hand.

"Don't allow yourself to become over excited," he said. "This is not a message from Fenn, it's from Jonathon Hunkin." He paused, turning the letter over in his hands. "I'm not sure that I should let you have it. I am your guardian for the moment, am I not?"

Her heart had sunk at his first words and she did not really care who the letter was from if not from Fenn. She shrugged and turned her face away from him.

"You can please yourself what you do," she said. "I simply have no interest in the letter."

He sat down beside her and tore open the paper. In spite of herself, Seranne felt annoyed at Dervil's intrusion into her privacy.

"Ah, he wants an assignation with you, alone. An astute young man, this Jonathon Hunkin."

Seranne felt the rich color run into her cheeks at the inference he was making. She snatched the letter and rose swiftly to her feet.

"What I do is none of your business, so kindly stop prying into my affairs."

In a moment, he was standing beside her, his hands gripping her arms so tightly that she flinched.

"You are not going to meet this man," he said lightly. "I gave my word I would look after you, and in spite of your inclinations, I am not letting you play the flirt while I'm around."

"How dare you!" Seranne's hand swept through the air, catching Dervil a glancing blow on his cheek.

He jerked her against him, then his mouth was upon hers, bruising, crushing, a gesture of scorn more than passion.

Seranne managed to free herself from him. The back of her hand was across her mouth and she felt sick with anger as she saw Dervil's eyes sparkle.

"If you need a little diversion, my dear Seranne, you can always count on me to provide it." His tone was insulting and she wanted to strike out at him once more but she didn't dare.

She turned and ran away from him, into the shady coolness of the Hall. She lifted her skirts and hurried up the stairway toward the sanctuary of her room. Only when the door was closed and she was leaning against it did she pause for breath.

The man was a monster, unfeeling and dissolute. It was apparent that he would stop at nothing in his efforts to make her humiliation complete. She wished never to set eyes upon him again. She sank down onto her bed and stared at the letter still crumpled up on her clenched fingers. Perhaps Jonathon Hunkin could help her in some way. Without pausing to think, she began to change into her riding clothes. She would show Dervil Cornwallis that she had a mind and will of her own.

If the young groom thought it strange that his mistress should be riding out alone, he gave no sign of his feelings. He obeyed Seranne's orders with alacrity, saddling up Jody and helping Seranne to mount the little mare.

Only when the Hall was left well behind her did Seranne feel a sense of relief at having escaped from Dervil's unnerving presence. In spite of some faint misgivings, she was determined to meet Jonathon in the little glade high up on the hill above the river as he had suggested in his note. He was the only friend she had and, although she realized her knowledge of him was slight, she felt he admired her and would help in any way he could.

He was at the meeting place before her and he looked extremely handsome as he smiled up at her in welcome.

"Allow me to help you dismount." His hands were on her waist, lifting her from Jody's back. "It's good to see you, Seranne, though I hardly expected you to arrive so promptly."

Seranne watched as Jonathon tied the little mare securely, swinging the reins round the rough bark of the tree. She tried to read the expression on his face and was disappointed to realize that he was after all a somewhat dull young man. Nevertheless, he would make an excellent friend and confidant, she felt sure.

"Let's sit down in the shade," Jonathon said, smiling at her. "Why not take off your coat? Here, let me help you, it's so hot this evening."

"I suppose I really shouldn't have come," she said quickly. "Aunt Mildred would heartily disapprove if she knew."

"Oh, I doubt it." Jonathon smiled. "It was your aunt who suggested we meet. She told me she was leaving the Hall for a few days, and she asked me not to neglect you. She felt you might be in need of company."

"As indeed I am," Seranne replied.

Jonathon smiled. "Your aunt is very persuasive. I felt I just had to get in touch with you as soon as my work allowed me any free time."

Seranne was silent for a moment, wondering what her aunt had in mind. Why should she scheme to bring Jonathon Hunkin into her niece's life?

She felt Jonathon slip his arm around her shoulder and she was uneasy. He was smiling down at her with open admiration in his eyes.

"You are unhappy, I can tell," he said softly. "Would you like to talk about it? You will find me an excellent listener."

Tears stung her lids and she was touched by the unexpected display of sympathy. She looked down at her hands. She simply had to talk to someone.

"I have never met anyone like Fenn Cornwallis," she said quietly. "It was all too easy to fall in love with him."

Jonathon rubbed her shoulder gently. "You are a beautiful and spirited girl; you need a man to love. It's perfectly natural."

Seranne sighed, leaning her head against Jonathon's broad shoulder. He was very kind and he was indeed a good listener. As she explained her feelings to him, a little of the bitterness seemed to leave her.

"I suppose I acted foolishly," she said. "Fenn wasn't right for me. Aunt Mildred did her best to warn me about him, but I didn't listen."

"You deserve a much better man than him." Jonathon was turning her to face him, and too late Seranne saw the look of lust in his eyes. He was pressing against her, bearing her backward to the soft ground.

"*I* would never leave you, my dearest," he said, his face flushed. "I would be good to you." He kissed her mouth. "Just let me love you. I need you so badly."

His hand was inside her bodice and as she tried to pull away from him the soft fabric of her gown tore, revealing her white breasts.

"You are so beautiful, Seranne," he said thickly. "I know what a girl like you needs, so don't worry. You won't find me lacking in experience."

Anger and outrage rose inside her and she pushed against Jonathon in a futile effort to free herself.

"How dare you!" she said in a low voice. "Let me go at once, do you hear me?"

"You don't mean it, my sweet," Jonathon whispered, his lips down in the hollow of her torn bodice. He was heavy upon her and Seranne struggled beneath him but her efforts only served to inflame him more.

She lay still for a moment, gathering her strength for a fresh attempt to break free. Jonathon was pushing up her skirts with one hand while the other was pressed against the firm flesh of her breasts.

Suddenly he was lifted bodily from her and, to her amazement, she saw a fist strike him on the temple, throwing him backward to the ground. Above him stood Dervil, a riding whip in his hand. It was lifted and then flicked with deadly accuracy.

Jonathon yelped and clambered to his feet. With one look at Dervil's strong, lithe body, poised to attack once more, he turned and darted through the trees.

"A very courageous lover," Dervil sneered. "You don't seem to be a very good judge of masculine character." He looked down at her as she lay with her skirts above her knees and her bodice torn and then he smiled, casting the whip to the ground.

"Jonathon Hunkin is a bungler. I can see he has not yet managed to have his way with you. As for my brother, he could never give you a son. In that respect he is as useful as a barren woman. I think it is about time you learned what a real man is.'' His hand went to his breeches before Seranne realized the meaning of his words.

''Don't touch me,'' she said in a whisper, trying desperately to cover her breasts with the remnants of her gown. She stared at him as he straddled her body, still unbelieving, and then his hand touched her breast.

''Feel that, it's a man's hand.'' He tightened his hold until she cried out in pain. She saw the darkening sky above his head and heard a whisper of a woodland creature and then, even as she tried to remove her mind from what was happening, Dervil was deliberately removing her clothing. She did not struggle; she knew that she could not fight him, he was too strong and too cruel. The more she protested, the more painful the experience would be.

He forced her bare legs apart and stared down at her body with cold scrutiny. Then his hands were beneath her, forcing her against him and she felt pain as he pierced her flesh.

There was no tenderness as he drove into her again and again. Then she found that her body was forced into an unwilling response. She began to move with him. Time ceased to exist as Dervil invaded her body and her mind. She was unconscious of everything but the searing heat in her thighs and the shuddering sensations that coursed through her entire being.

He moved with even more violence and she found herself clinging to him. She pressed herself up to meet him and then flung her head back, crying to the darkening sky like a wild creature at the final climax of delight.

He rested beside her, and when she made to rise, he pressed her back against the earth. She obeyed his touch from instinct rather than reason and when he pulled her close to him once more, she abandoned herself to him, not daring to think, simply living for the delight he was giving her. Dervil's passion lasted long into the hours of darkness, and Seranne's desire matched his own. At length they fell asleep on the carpet of moss and leaves, Seranne's head resting upon his shoulder.

It was almost daylight when Dervil awoke her. Without a word, he drew her to her feet and pulled her coat around her torn gown.

She remembered little of the ride back to the Hall. She was dimly aware of Dervil pushing her in through the door, toward the stairs.

"Go to bed," he commanded. His tone was cold, as though they were strangers—and indeed they were. She knew his body, oh yes, she knew every inch of him. But his mind and spirit, they were lost worlds to her and no doubt always would be.

Suddenly, it was as if the whole house had come alight. Seranne saw figures descending the stairway. She recognized with surprise Aunt Mildred, her dressing gown billowing away from her legs as she hurried downward. Behind her was an elderly man, tall, distinguished. They must have arrived at the Hall sometime during the night.

"What on earth has happened to you, child?" Mildred put down her candle and held Seranne at arm's length. "Why, my dear, your gown is torn to pieces!"

Seranne shook her head, unable to speak. She was bone weary and her mind refused to function properly. All she wanted was to fall into bed and sleep. But Mildred had other ideas.

"Come and sit down, my dear, tell me all about it." She led Seranne into the drawing room and poured her a generous measure of brandy. "You look awful, my dear. Now come along, drink this."

Obediently, Seranne took the glass. The brandy was hot against her throat, bringing tears to her eyes. She coughed a little.

"Please, Aunt, I just want to go to my room," she said in a whisper.

"Oh, my dear, how can I help if you won't confide in me?" Mildred turned to the gray-haired man who was standing in the doorway. "Lord Cornwallis, what shall I do? It's obvious the dear girl has been attacked."

Seranne took a deep breath, trying to clear her confused thoughts. This man was Dervil's father—how could she speak the truth in front of him?

At that moment, Dervil himself strode into the room, his face expressionless. He stood directly in front of Seranne.

"I suppose you told them you were forced," he said. "But I doubt if you have been completely truthful." He turned to Mildred. "I won't go into all the sordid details, not with you and my father present, but your niece got from me exactly what she deserved and wanted."

He left the room quietly and Seranne put her head in her hands, the hot tears burning her eyes.

Lord Cornwallis spoke for the first time. "I suggest we get the girl to bed, Mildred," he said mildly. "This can all be sorted out in the morning when everyone is calmer, don't you agree?"

Seranne flashed him a look of gratitude and, before her aunt could ask any further questions, she hurried out into the hall, wanting only peace and quiet and the safety of her own bed.

Seranne slept like one dead, and when at last she opened her eyes, it was to find that the whole pattern of her life had been changed.

She no longer felt any love for Fenn. On the contrary, she seemed to have lost the ability to care very deeply about anything at all. Dervil had taken her body, purging her memory of Fenn's lovemaking, leaving an emptiness that perhaps would never now be filled.

She remained in bed all day, refusing all offers of food and drinking only what was necessary to ease the ache in her throat. Her room was a refuge where she could close her eyes and shut herself off from the reality of life.

Aunt Mildred was not one to allow such nonsense to go on for any length of time, however, and at last she bustled into Seranne's room, her arms akimbo as she stood near the bed.

"Come along, my dear," she said in the hearty voice she usually reserved for people with slower wits than her own. "There is no need to remain here alone any longer. Lord Cornwallis has returned to London, and Dervil with him." She sat down and smiled coaxingly at her niece. "Do tell me what happened, my dear. Perhaps talking about it will help."

Seranne struggled to sit up, pushing the heavy hair from her face. The pain of suppressing her feelings was becoming too much to bear.

"I went to meet Jonathon Hunkin," she blurted out suddenly. "He . . . he seemed to think he could take advantage of me. He tore my gown and—"

"Oh, my dear, how awful!" Mildred said quickly.

"I thought a rival for your affections would make Dervil realize your true worth. I meant well, believe me."

"It's not your fault," Seranne said. "Dervil is inhuman. He drove Jonathon away with his riding whip, and then he . . . he . . ." She faltered a little as Mildred stared at her, almost with impatience.

"*Dervil* forced you? I can hardly believe that. He could have any woman he chose."

"He wanted to prove what a man he was," Seranne said bitterly. "It was his intention to teach me the error of my ways in choosing Fenn as a lover, and then Jonathon, in preference to himself." She lay back against the pillows. "I never want to hear the name Cornwallis ever again." She closed her eyes, feigning sleepiness, and after a few moments she heard Mildred leave the room.

It was several weeks later when Seranne, walking in the shade of the garden with Mildred, suddenly felt faint. Her aunt immediately sent for the physician and Seranne listened to his searching, personal questions, her cheeks hot, her heart beating swiftly in apprehension. When he left, she met her aunt's eyes, knowing what Mildred was going to say even before she opened her mouth.

"You are with child, my dear, but you are not to worry. You can leave everything to me."

Seranne folded her arms over her slender stomach and closed her eyes as though in pain.

6

Mildred lost no time in organizing Seranne's future. That Dervil had made love to Seranne even under such unusual circumstances seemed something of an omen. She was certain that the marriage of Lord Cornwallis's elder son and her niece was destined to take place.

Dervil had balked at first; that was only to be expected. But Mildred could be very persuasive, and once she had convinced him that the child Seranne carried must be his, he made up his mind with satisfying speed.

The large fortune that Seranne would bring her husband was in itself an inducement, but Mildred guessed that Dervil's main concern was to legitimize his offspring: he needed an heir. If he was to get one sooner than he had anticipated, then there was no one to blame but himself.

Seranne had taken to resting during the afternoon and now Mildred, peering into her room, decided to leave her niece sleeping. There was a great deal of work to be done on the marriage gown but the seamstress would simply have to manage without a fitting for today.

One of the spare bedrooms had been set aside for sewing and Mildred opened the door to find pieces of material spread across the carpet.

"How are you managing, dear?" Mildred asked the small, faded woman who was crouched over her work with complete dedication. "Nearly finished the oyster silk jacket, I see."

"Yes, Mistress Hussey." The woman peered at Mildred as though her eyes accustomed to tiny stitches could not focus at any distance. "The pink mousseline de laine is shaping very favorably. It will be cool should the weather be warm."

"Excellent." Mildred fingered the softness of the silk with satisfaction. Seranne would look sweet and becoming, a bride any man would be proud of. "When is the final fitting, dear?" she said, allowing the silk to slip through her fingers.

The seamstress put her head on one side. "The gown will be ready later today," she said at last. "But I'll not sew on the last button until the wedding day, for 'tis bad luck to finish the garment lest the marriage never takes place."

Mildred clucked her tongue. "*This* wedding will take place—you may be sure of that, dear."

She smiled to herself as she left the seamstress to her work. Yes, indeed, she would see her niece safely installed as the future Lady Cornwallis, and then perhaps she would return to London. Life in the country was all very well but she craved the excitement of the town. Her brief visit there, a month or two ago, had left her restless and bored with the slowness of Devonshire society.

She walked aimlessly along the corridor. Perhaps she would take a leaf out of Seranne's book and rest. She needed to be fresh because the next few days before the wedding would tax her strength and patience to the limit. She paused for a moment outside Seranne's room and then, with a small shake of her head, walked on past.

Seranne was not asleep. She had slid beneath the sheets when she heard someone at the door, not wishing to talk. She was tired and listless, her energy sapped by the preparations for her wedding. And yet she could not really believe that any of it was happening.

She sighed and pushed the sheets back again, her hand resting lightly on her stomach. It was difficult to imagine there was a young life within her—the result of that night when Dervil had taken her, time after time, teaching her that her body was treacherous, and she had responded, even while she hated herself.

And now she was to be his wife. The day after tomorrow would see her standing at his side in the little chapel at the edge of the gardens, taking vows that would bind her to him forever. She felt she couldn't go through with it. And yet what was the alternative? She shuddered and closed her eyes tightly, knowing she would never countenance bringing a bastard child into the world.

They had not communicated, she and Dervil. There had been no pleasantries exchanged, not even so much as a glance had passed between them. They were strangers, yet soon they would be sharing their lives together. It was arrant foolishness.

She forced her eyes to remain closed. She would try to sleep, to forget everything that was happening around her. Ignore the fact that her husband-to-be had traveled back from London and was under the same roof. It was the only way she could keep her sanity. At last, in spite of everything, she slept.

Her wedding day when it dawned was one of brilliant sunshine. Everything seemed to take on a startling clarity. As Seranne entered the chapel, she stared round her as if seeing it for the first time.

The dark oak beams reached like four arms across the domed ceiling, meeting in the middle and supporting a heavy candelabra. The walls behind the polished altar were a soft blue, decorated with white ornamentation like icing on a cake.

The stained glass window with its picture of the Good Shepherd holding a lamb reminded Seranne of her childhood when, to relieve her boredom during longwinded sermons, she had gazed up at the brightly colored glass, her thoughts flying beyond to the fields outside.

She glanced at Dervil, standing at her side. He was a stern stranger. He wore a gray swallow-tailed coat, and beneath it a waistcoat of the same oyster silk as her own jacket. A nice touch, she thought ruefully, carefully planned by Aunt Mildred.

The beautiful words of the service touched her deeply. It was as though she were under a spell, almost believing that this was a love match.

She must have made the correct responses, because at last Dervil was slipping a gold ring on her finger. She saw it gleaming in the sunlight and then, as the organ music swelled, filling the chapel, her eyes were blurred with tears.

This was a mock marriage, she reminded herself, to a man who cared nothing for her. This should have been the happiest day of her life and instead it was nothing but a charade.

The brilliant splash of sunlight on the flags of the pathway dazzled Seranne as she stepped outside the chapel on her husband's arm. Mildred, resplendent in a blue brocade gown with a black jacket, was the first to step forward. She enveloped her niece in her arms with genuine affection.

"My dear! You look so lovely I could cry." She

leaned closer and whispered in Seranne's ear: "Do try to be happy. You know love sometimes blossoms, if you only give it a chance."

"I'll do my best." The words were meaningless, empty of emotion, but she could not bring herself to disappoint her aunt, childlike in her faith that dreams could be realized.

The long table in the dining room gleamed with polished silver and crystal glassware. Roses and lilacs filled the flower bowls and the glittering sunshine shafted through the French windows, adding to the color and light of the room.

There were few guests. Lord Cornwallis and several of his nieces and nephews made up the main body of the gathering. For Seranne's part there was only Aunt Mildred.

The talk was slow, as if everyone sensed the undercurrents of tension between the bride and her taciturn groom. Seranne glanced at Dervil and his silver-gray eyes seemed to look right through her.

"Do you hate me so much?" she whispered through stiff lips, and he gave a derisive smile.

"Hate? That implies strong emotion. No, I don't hate you. Why should I?"

If he meant to be insulting, he achieved his aim. Seranne sank back in her chair, feeling the color drain from her face. At her side, one of Dervil's cousins made some inconsequential remark and she did her best to respond politely.

The time seemed to pass with painful slowness and Seranne's neck ached with the effort of holding her head upright. But at last the ordeal was over. The guests who were staying overnight retired early in order to be fresh for traveling, and Seranne felt she could relax a little.

She kissed Mildred's smooth cheek. "Good night," Seranne said softly. There was a great deal more she would have liked to say if only she could find the words. She wanted to thank Mildred for caring about her and for working with such zeal to make the wedding day a success. After all, it wasn't her aunt's fault that the bride loathed her new husband. Mildred had merely done what she thought best.

Slowly, Seranne mounted the stairs. The silent house seemed to breathe around her. She went into her old bedroom and sat there in the darkness, staring out at the night sky studded with myriads of stars. This was her childhood refuge, a place to hide from hurt. But her place was no longer here in the small, peaceful room. Tonight she must sleep beside her husband in the freshly decorated master bedroom.

"I thought I might find you here." Dervil was standing in the doorway, a lighted candle in his hand. Above the flame, his face was unfamiliar, more saturnine than ever, and Seranne shuddered. "Come along," he said sharply. "You need not think you can shirk your duty as a wife. Our marriage bed is ready—or had you forgotten?"

She rose to her feet. "I have forgotten nothing," she said coldly. "But I didn't know you were so eager for my companionship."

"It's not your companionship that makes me eager," he said.

She felt her cheeks flame as she followed him along the corridor into the main bedroom. The silk covers were drawn back from the huge bed and Seranne took a deep breath as she tried to imagine sharing it with Dervil.

"Undress quickly." He was already unfastening his breeches. "I am waiting."

She felt a sudden searing anger flare up inside her. He was treating her in a way that she could not tolerate. Not even the lowest harlot deserved such scorn.

"I am a woman, not a slave," she said coldly, clenching her hands to her sides to stop them from trembling. "Please treat me with a little courtesy and we shall perhaps succeed in living together in some sort of peace."

He turned and caught her tightly, slipping the neck of the gown from her shoulders so that one of her breasts became exposed.

"Do not lecture me, madam," he said. "Now, take off your clothes before I tear them. Do you understand?"

"No!" Seranne cried.

But Dervil was holding her close to him, his strong fingers pulling the seams of the gown apart. He dropped the soft jacket to the floor and, with one movement, wrenched the undergown from neck to hem.

"You animal!" Seranne hissed, but as he lifted her onto the bed, her breathing became uneven. She felt him kiss her throat and then his warm lips moved to her breasts. She tried to resist him but her body was betraying her as his fingers gently slid between her thighs.

Her whole body waited to receive him. She lay, head flung back against the pillows, arms spread out, and when she was almost ready to faint from desire, he entered her flesh. She could have cried with ecstasy of his body joining with hers. She moaned as his hands clasped her waist, as if to draw her downward, making his penetration more complete.

But he was more restrained than he had been that first night when he had taken her under the stars. She sensed his exercising control and she knew that he was considerate because of her condition. She felt a soft, tender feeling flooding through her that enhanced her delight, and when the shuddering climax to their lovemaking swept her to the heights, there were tears in her eyes. She admitted to herself then, as she lay against him in the afterglow of emotion, that he had awakened something within her that Fenn, though her first lover, had left undisturbed.

It was a shock when Dervil rolled away from her and lay staring up at the ceiling, a derisive smile on his face.

"You are so predictable," he said. "I believe you would couple with any man and find delight. You have the instinct of a harlot, my dear wife."

She drew on the blue brocade gown that lay across a chair at the side of the bed.

"I *hate* you, Dervil Cornwallis," she said in a fierce whisper. "I have never despised any man so much."

"Liar," he said smoothly. "Now go to sleep, it's been a long day."

While there were guests in the house, Seranne had felt able to retain some measure of equilibrium. That first morning she had made a good pretense of being a happy newlywed wife, and if Dervil's glances were heavy with sarcastic amusement, she felt it possible to ignore them.

It was after the rush and bustle of the departure of the Cornwallis family, en masse, that she experienced a sinking of her spirits.

The house was large, yet Seranne found it increasingly difficult to avoid her husband. If she hadn't known better, she might have imagined he was seeking her company.

If Aunt Mildred had remained behind, at least for a while, the situation would have been easier to handle but Mildred, with a coyness that was absurd in the circumstances, had insisted on leaving the couple alone. Though she tried to change her aunt's mind, Seranne had been forced to see the sense in Mildred having the benefit of the company of her old friend Lord Cornwallis on the journey home.

She sat now in the shade of the trees on the terrace, staring down into the softly flowing river. She had been aware of a strange pain in her side for several days but she had dismissed it as a natural effect of her condition. Today, however, it was more intense and she wished there was someone in whom she could confide her fears that all was not well with her pregnancy.

A shadow fell across her hands as they rested in her lap and she looked up to see Dervil standing beside her. If only their marriage had been a real one then she could have talked with him, told him of her fears.

"Idle, as usual, madam," he said tersely. "I declare I've never met a woman more inclined to dream away the hours. Shouldn't you be occupied with the affairs of the home?"

She felt her hands curl into fists. "We have servants to attend to that sort of thing," she said with icy calm. It wasn't what she had meant to say at all. She was well aware of her duties and responsibilities but she felt so ill that she had allowed most of the burden to fall onto the shoulders of Mrs. Pegg since Aunt Mildred's departure.

"I see." His voice was colder than ever. "So, you see your future as one long round of pleasure, is that it?"

She shook her head as if the action could ward off his anger. She had no strength to quarrel.

"Please, just leave the subject alone for the moment. If you wish me to take a more active part in the running of the house then I shall try to do so." She forced herself to rise and bit her lip as a pain cramped her side.

"Don't walk away from me," Dervil said with casual authority. "I am tired of following you about the place whenever I want to speak with you."

Anger seared Seranne with a suddenness that brought rich color into her cheeks.

"You have me in your bed at nights," she said fiercely. "What more do you want?"

He gave a short laugh. "I suppose to ask for intelligent conversation is too much." He caught her arm, his fingers biting into her flesh. "We have to live with each other, and I tell you now, I will not endure a sullen wife."

"I am not sullen!" Seranne said quickly. "I obey you in the marriage bed every night."

"And are you trying to tell me you do not like that state of affairs?" He smiled. "Come now, I know you too well for that."

"Oh, leave me alone!" Seranne pulled away from him and hurried through the house. She had to escape. She needed time alone to think. Could she go on like this, under the same roof as Dervil? It might be better if they were to part now, before the child was born. Her heart sank. But then Dervil would never be prepared to give up his own offspring, he was not that sort of man.

She found herself at the back of the house, close to the stables. Her mare Jody nuzzled her hand and Seranne leaned her cheek against the animal's warm flank.

On an impulse she led Jody out into the yard. She was not dressed for riding; her gown of watered silk was entirely unsuitable for anything other than sitting in a comfortable chair, but the need to escape was strong.

She would simply ride at a leisurely pace across the fields: it could do her no harm. Jody was a gentle creature, obedient in spite of being spirited. Seranne waited no longer; she was up on Jody's back and heading away from the house before she had time to think.

The sun was on her face and the freshness of the breeze lifted her hair from her shoulders. It was a sparkling day, one when she should have felt it good to be alive. Why then did she have this heavy sense of foreboding?

She followed the line of the river, allowing Jody to amble at will, bending to eat the lush grass. She blotted out all thoughts from her mind and simply enjoyed her temporary freedom from her husband's uncomfortable presence.

The harsh sound of a hunting horn shattered the stillness of the afternoon. Seranne looked up, over Jody's suddenly plunging head, and saw hounds and riders bearing down on her. Before she could grip the reins, the little mare, startled into movement, bolted, mane streaming.

Seranne felt the hard jolt of the ground beneath her and then she was rolling helplessly, over and over, stones cutting into her ill-protected body in the silk gown.

She came to rest at last in a heap and as she lay, catching her breath, the hunt passed over her, unaware of her presence.

When she tried to move, the pain in her side brought a moan to her lips. She lay quietly, trying to ease the ache that was slowly spreading through her entire being.

All was silent once more except for her own harsh breathing. She turned her head and saw that Jody was but a few feet from her, ears up, eyes wide and frightened.

"Jody, come here," she called. The effort sent waves of pain from the pit of her stomach, spreading out like ripples to encompass her back.

Seranne turned on her side, her knees drawn upward. She felt the warmth of her lifeblood and knew that she was losing the baby.

The grass beneath her head was soft and fragrant and as she closed her eyes, Seranne wondered if she would die alone in the fields like a stricken animal.

There was a sound in her head that she thought was her heartbeat. It grew louder and she recognized it as the galloping hooves of a horse.

She tried to call out for help but her voice was faint on the soft air. She called again and Jody, sensing her distress, whinnied loudly.

The rider was turning, coming in her direction. Seranne sensed rather than saw the figure hurrying toward her. Then she was being lifted in strong arms, and the sky arched blue and clear over her head before she slipped into a deep unconsciousness.

7

"So there will be no child, after all?" Dervil was leaning against the fireplace in the large bedroom, whip tapping against the soft leather of his riding boots. His tone was not unkindly and Seranne felt hot tears burn her eyes.

"No."

The word was indistinct, and Dervil stared across at her with sudden sharpness.

"You are sorry?" he asked, and she could not meet the silver-gray eyes as they seemed to look deep within her.

"Yes." How could she explain to him that the child had begun to become a reality to her? It had seemed something apart from the both of them, a gift rather than the natural result of their passionate but loveless coupling.

"You are young and strong," he said. "There will be ample opportunity for motherhood." He moved briskly to the door as though he felt he had said enough. "Rest, regain your strength. The physician tells me that in a week at most you will almost be your old self." The derision was apparent in his voice now and Seranne flinched.

"I will do my best not to lie idle for too long, you may be assured," she said pointedly. As he opened the door, she sat up. "Dervil." It was strange speaking his name. "Thank you for coming after me. I might have lost my life if you hadn't."

"Fortunately the stable boy saw which direction you took so I was able to follow you with little difficulty." He stared at her for a long moment in silence. "Didn't you stop to consider that riding in such a delicate condition was inadvisable?" He seemed curious rather than concerned, and Seranne turned away from him, lying back against the pillows.

"I suppose I *am* a foolhardy woman," she answered with a flash of defiance. "Otherwise I would not find myself married to you."

"I will not quarrel with you now," he replied evenly. "But we both know who stood to benefit most by our little arrangement. You, Seranne. However, we are legally married now, and if you have any notion of trying to change that, I would advise you to forget it."

He left her, shutting the door quietly behind him, and Seranne closed her eyes against the threatening tears.

Her strength returned quickly, as the physician had predicted, and Seranne was out of bed and taking the air in just over a week. In an effort to please Dervil, she involved herself more closely in the running of the household and found a certain satisfaction in his approval.

Since the day he had found her lying helpless under the hedge, Seranne had felt a sense of obligation to her husband. In any event, it was easier to appease him than to be continually at cross purposes.

He seemed a little more mellow lately, as though making allowances for her distress over her miscarriage of his child. He was a man of unpredictable moods so when he strode into the drawing room where she was sewing, a dark look on his face, she felt herself grow tense.

"We are to go to Russia," he said without preamble. "You'd better insure we have a good supply of warm clothing; the weather in St. Petersburg is vastly different to ours."

Seranne stared at him speechless. Had he gone mad? She rose from her chair near the open French windows and bit her lip in agitation. Dervil sat down at the desk and drew a sheet of paper toward him.

"Aren't you going to explain?" Seranne found her voice at last. "You can't simply tell me we are setting out for a foreign country without giving me a good reason."

He stared at her levelly. "Fenn has fallen sick. The poor climate has apparently affected his constitution. You and I, my dear wife, have been elected to bring him home."

Rich color flooded into her cheeks when she heard Fenn's name. No wonder Dervil was in a bad humor. It was asking a great deal of him that he go to the aid of his wife's lover, even if he was his brother.

"Perhaps it would be better if I remained here," she ventured diffidently.

"You are coming with me." Dervil spoke decisively and Seranne could see that to argue with him would be useless. He stared at her over the top of the desk. "Aren't you anxious about my brother?" he said coldly.

She was flustered, not knowing what he expected of her. She walked slowly out onto the sun-splashed terrace and leaned her hands against the warm stone of the surrounding wall. She had hardly thought about Fenn at all since her marriage and now she wondered at her gullibility in falling into his arms as she'd done.

That he was dashing and handsome was undeniable and she shivered as she remembered the golden body lying naked beside her. She had been attracted to Fenn, he had swept her off her feet, and what was more important, he had awakened her to womanhood. Regret swept through her and she wished, quite suddenly, that Dervil had been the first man she'd known.

"I do apologize for disturbing your reverie." Dervil was beside her, his expression difficult to read. "But we have little time for dreaming. I have replied to my father's letter giving my word that I'll set out from English shores within the week."

"That's impossible!" Seranne gasped. "There's so much to arrange. I will need clothes—you said yourself that the climate in Russia was inclement."

"All the more need to hurry then." He was very close and Seranne was aware of the warm masculinity that emanated from him. He was a tall man with whipcord strength and a strong sexuality that stirred her even when she was most angry with him.

"Be careful, Seranne," he said softly. "Your lustful thoughts are beginning to show in your expression."

"I have no lustful thoughts," she denied quickly.

Dervil took her slowly and deliberately in his arms, holding her close, his hand twined in her curls, pulling back her head so that she was forced to look up at him.

"Your eyes tell me a different story." His mouth came down on hers, hard and demanding and she felt the strength drain from her.

"Do you have to taunt me?" she whispered against his lips, aware that her heart was racing.

He silenced her with a kiss and his hand was in the small of her back, pressing her against his masculine hardness.

"Don't," she said raggedly, trying to draw away

from him. "Someone might see us."

"We are properly married," he replied. "But if you feel a little shy, why not come with me to the privacy of the bedroom?" His hand slipped into her bodice and his fingers closed around the fullness of her breast. She drew a sharp breath. They had not been together like this for some time and she was torn with hunger. Ashamed, she forced his hands away from her body.

"You were just telling me I must make preparation for the journey," she said, avoiding his eyes. "So please excuse me."

"Aren't you at all curious?" His words halted her as she made to hurry from the room. She looked back at him in bewilderment.

"I don't know what you mean," she said shortly. "Curious about what?"

He smiled with maddening slowness, taking his time before giving her an answer.

"Why I am taking you with me to Russia, of course," he said at last. "You didn't think it was for the charm of having your company did you?"

She was conscious of the hot color running into her cheeks as she faced him, hands clenched, forcing herself to be calm.

"What is the reason, then?" she asked, her voice level and controlled.

"Simply this, my dear wife, I do not trust you to be alone during the months I'll be abroad." The words were spoken softly and it took Seranne a few minutes to digest their meaning.

"How dare you?" she said furiously and Dervil smiled though his eyes were unreadable.

"How dare I speak the truth about your lack of chastity? I dare anything Seranne, remember that. In any event it suits me to have you with me. If my brother needs nursing then I am not as well equipped as you to minister to his needs." He paused. "Just so long as you do not minister too enthusiastically."

Seranne felt near to tears as Dervil walked from the room, leaving her clenching her fist in impotent fury. She took a deep breath. She must now allow him to upset her. He was merely goading her for his own amusement. Soon, she felt more composed and ready to deal with the immediate task of choosing the correct clothes for the journey.

She hurried up the stairs, calling for Ellen to come and help her. In the bedroom, she flung open the cupboard and stood back to examine the contents, wondering, even as she drew out a warm, fur-lined cloak, how she would react when she was forced to meet her former lover again.

Ellen came into the room behind her, staring in open curiosity as Seranne placed a hat box on the floor. The young maid plucked at her apron, obviously longing to question her mistress.

"Mr. Cornwallis and I are to travel abroad," Seranne said and, even as she spoke, excitement rose on a crest within her. She knew that in spite of her protests, she had to go with Dervil to Russia.

"Abroad, miss?" Ellen's eyes were wide as she repeated Seranne's words. "What foreign parts are you visitin' if I may ask?"

"That's not important, Ellen." Seranne examined a heavy velvet gown which, though a little old-fashioned, might serve very well in a cold climate. "And do remember that I'm married now. I'm no longer Miss Seranne. I'm Mistress Cornwallis."

She sat down on the bed, the velvet falling in shining heaps at her feet. She had realized in a moment of crystal clarity that she was beginning to enjoy her married state. Was it possible that her feelings toward her husband could be softening a little?

"Is there somethin' wrong, mistress?" Ellen said in her slow voice, and Seranne smiled.

"Nothing serious, Ellen. Now come along, please help me to sort out my wardrobe and fetch the black box from the attic. I do believe it will be just the thing for storing my clothes aboard ship."

As Ellen hurried from the room, Seranne heard the sound of crisp hooves echoing around the courtyard outside her window, and looking out, she saw Dervil riding away. It was just like him to leave the Hall without giving her any reason for his going. He was a law unto himself. It concerned him but little that if he should return late supper would be kept waiting. She felt a momentary anger at his lack of courtesy and then she shrugged and continued to sort through her clothing.

In any event, Dervil returned within the hour while Seranne was combing her hair before the mirror in their bedroom. He took the stairs two at a time and she heard the quickness of his footsteps as he came into the room.

"I have booked us a passage," he said, his face whipped with color from the wind. "We are to leave from Bassets Cove in six days' time." He looked at her hair spread over her shoulders and his fingers lifted a strand, examining the golden curls as though seeing them for the first time.

Seranne sat in silence, unsure how to react to his touch. She searched his face for a sign of his feelings but Dervil was a man who gave nothing away.

"Captain Porter will not wait for us, so we must be on time. I take it you have begun your preparations?"

"I have chosen clothes I believe suitable for the journey," she said. "I took the liberty of glancing through your own wardrobe and I feel you're in need of a good topcoat before we leave."

"Very thoughtful of you," Dervil replied, allowing her hair to fall back to her shoulders. "I have a more than adequate stock of clothing in my London home. I shall take the mail tomorrow and fetch them."

"Shall I come with you?" Seranne asked diffidently, although she hated to appear anxious for his company.

"I don't think so," he said briskly. "I shall make the most of the opportunity to visit some old friends."

Seranne felt suddenly cold. She was excluded from his life in London as though he was ashamed of her.

"I see," she said icily, turning her face away so that he wouldn't see the color that had risen to her cheeks.

His hands were resting on her shoulders then and he was drawing her toward him, forcing her to rise to her feet. "It's a long time since we made love," he said with a hint of laughter in his voice. She knew that he was quite aware of her annoyance and he was setting out to antagonize her further.

"Is that what you call it?" she said waspishly. " 'Love' is the last word I would apply to your attacks upon my body."

He slipped her gown from her shoulder and his mouth was warm as it touched the hollow of her neck. She remained passive in his arms, neither responding nor repulsing him.

"Don't try to be the little ice maiden, my dear Seranne," he said, his eyes suddenly looking into hers. "I know how hot-blooded you really are, so what's the use of pretending?"

She refused to answer him and suddenly he swept her up into his arms and set her across the bed, his heavy weight upon her.

"Very well," he said, "if you wish to be coaxed then I am prepared to humor you, a little." He gave a short laugh and pushed her legs apart with his knee. "I shall make you beg me to love you," he said as he slowly began to undress her. "You know you can't resist."

"You flatter yourself," she said, trying to ignore the way her blood was stirring as he drew off her petticoat.

He stood up from her and looked down at her nakedness and there was a smile of derision on his face as he unbuttoned his breeches. She could not draw her eyes away from his lithe body. His shoulders were broad, his waist small. His thighs were strong-muscled; he was every inch a man. Seranne tried to look away as he lay across the bed at her side, his hand touching her breast so gently that a shiver ran through her.

"You see?" he said, smiling. "You are responding to me already." He bent over her, his lips warm on her eyelids. He kissed her mouth, briefly, and moved lower to her breasts.

Her determination to remain indifferent to his caresses was weakening. It was her Hussey blood, she told herself, bad blood that was betraying her yet again. She stifled a moan as Dervil's fingers brushed the softness of her stomach. She hated herself even as her hands reached out to draw him to her. She closed her eyes, her neck was arched and she whimpered as he drew away, teasing, tormenting her.

"I told you I would make you beg," he said softly. "Come along, Seranne, tell me you want me."

"Please!" The word was torn from her. Like a conqueror, he grasped her in his arms, holding her hard as he thrust into her with a suddenness that made her cry out.

It was more wonderful than anything Seranne had ever experienced. She longed to speak words of joy and love to Dervil. Yes, love. She could not deceive herself any longer. She loved her husband.

The climax came like a huge wave dashing against rocks, fragmenting into tiny pieces that ran through her body in flames of relief. She clung to him, her face buried in the strong warm neck, and was engulfed in tenderness for him.

She sighed as he drew from her. She heard him pulling on his robe but she kept her eyes closed. She wanted to preserve the feeling of happiness and fulfillment for as long as possible.

She felt him sit on the bed beside her and then, abruptly, he spoke.

"Well, how do I compare with my brother?" he said harshly. The question was so unexpected that Seranne sat up, staring at him in alarm.

"You will be seeing Fenn again in a few weeks," he continued, his face hard as though carved from granite. "Will you fall into his arms once more and plead with him for love as you pleaded with me?"

"No!" Seranne covered herself with one of the sheets. "What sort of woman do you think I am?"

"I think you are the sort of woman who needs a man between her legs—whoever he might be." Dervil ground out the words as though he hated her.

"That's not true!" she cried. "You are mistaken in me if you think that."

"The facts speak for themselves," Dervil said. "First you allow my brother to make love to you and then I find you in the woods with that poor fool Hunkin. Now you are happy to have me in your bed."

"I did nothing to encourage Jonathon Hunkin—and if it is wrong to feel passion then you are as guilty as I am," Seranne said hotly. "Can you deny you enjoyed making love to me?"

"I deny nothing." Dervil moved away from her. "But a man can enjoy whoever happens to be available. A woman in a bawdy house can be more tasty than a wife, especially a wife who is, shall we say, a little well-used?"

He left her and went into his dressing room, closing the door with a click of finality. Seranne beat against the pillows in anger and pain. She had almost told Dervil that she loved him: she must have been crazed with passion.

"All right, Dervil Cornwallis," she whispered. "If it's warfare you want, then you shall have it in full measure."

The day of their departure from the Hall proved cloudy and dismal, the hot sunshine suddenly vanquished by a flurry of rain. Seranne stared around her, drinking in the familiar sights, knowing with a sinking of her spirits that it would be many months before she saw her home again.

Dervil was standing watching her, the usual ironic

smile curving his mouth. Seranne hurriedly climbed into the coach that was to take them to Bassets Cove and tried to hold back the tears threatening to overflow.

She looked through the window, her face turned away from Dervil who had seated himself beside her. She thought she saw a movement behind the curtains but she could not be sure. She was leaving home with complete lack of ceremony, as though merely spending a day out at market.

The coach jolted into motion and the sound of the horses' hooves echoed against the wet stones of the driveway. Seranne leaned back in her seat, closing her eyes, uttering a silent farewell to the familiar house and estate.

She did not wish to talk, so she feigned sleep. She found the jogging of the coach soothed her and the soft rain outside fell with monotonous regularity. Soon her pretense became reality and she slept.

She was completely unaware that she had fallen against her husband's shoulder and that he was staring down at his young bride with an expression of bewilderment as though wondering how this soft creature at his side was stealing into his blood like a fever.

When Seranne woke, the journey was over. She could hear the calling of the seagulls overhead, and as she alighted from the coach, she smelled tar on the salt breeze.

The rain had stopped and the harbor shimmered in a haze of heat as the sun broke through the clouds. Tall, elegant houses fronted the cove which was dotted about with fishing nets and small boats.

On the full tide bobbed a ship, high masts pointing skyward. She felt suddenly afraid.

"Come along." Dervil took her arm and led her forward. "It's time we went aboard." He gave an order over his shoulder for the boxes to be brought and then they were crossing the frail bridge between the harbor edge and the ship.

"Your timing is good, sir." A tall, heavily built man greeted Dervil, pushing back his hat over grizzled gray hair. "Welcome to my ship."

The two men shook hands and then the Captain pointed to the sea.

"She is a little troublesome today." His voice was heavy and guttural, with an accent Seranne could not place. "But my vessel is built for deep waters, so no need to worry."

"You have my full confidence, Captain Porter," Dervil said, placing his arm around Seranne's waist as the deck seemed to roll beneath their feet.

"Excuse, if you please." The Captain made a sharp bow and moved away, giving orders in a loud voice to his men.

In spite of her fears, Seranne felt excitement rise within her as she stared around the vessel. All seemed movement, urgent and quick, as the sails billowed above her head, flapping as they filled with wind. She experienced the sensation of flying through the air like some graceful bird as the skies raced above her equal with the sea in restlessness.

"You appear to be enjoying yourself," Dervil remarked. "I was afraid I would have a victim of seasickness on my hands."

Seranne looked at him levelly. "I never was the sickly kind," she said shortly.

"Just as well," he replied. "The journey might prove somewhat trying."

"I trust you will not find me an encumbrance."

Seranne would have moved away from him but his arms were tight around her waist.

"You are a fiery creature," Dervil said with a smile. "You take every word of mine as a criticism of your behavior."

"Am I wrong, then?" she asked, her heart pounding as though his answer was of the utmost importance.

"Sometimes," he said. The ship swung suddenly and his arms closed around Seranne, holding her close.

"Dervil," she said quickly, before her courage could fail, "please will you pretend we have just met and there's no bitterness between us? Let's try to forget what's past and make a fresh start."

"We can try," Dervil said softly. "We can try."

8

As the ship sailed eastward, the winds became fresh and it was not pleasant to venture on deck unless wrapped in the warmest of clothes. The ocean stretched in endless, swelling troughs; sometimes not even a speck of land could be seen. It was as though the world had become composed of sea and sky and the only life was that aboard the small ship.

Seranne kept to the small cabin a great deal and therefore it was a relief to her that Dervil honored his word to forget any past bitterness and behaved as though their marriage was not simply one of expediency.

She still could not fathom the depths of her husband. Dervil was a man who sometimes sat close to her in the tiny cabin, yet as far away from her in spirit as though he had remained in England. But she learned that he could be humorous when he chose, and beneath his controlled exterior there was a passion and a capacity for loving that she was beginning to wish she could exploit to the full. It was apparent that any woman who received Dervil's wholehearted trust and affection would be greatly privileged.

Sometimes, in the evenings, Captain Porter would invite them to eat supper with himself and his officers. Seranne was amused and flattered by the attention paid to her on such occasions, well aware that as the only woman on board she was bound to be something of a novelty. But there was one man, a Mr. Borisov, who made her feel uncomfortable; he did not trouble to hide his disapproval of her. He was a thin, swarthy-faced man who spoke with the same guttural accent as his Captain, and Seranne had been aware from the first moment she'd set eyes on the man that he did not like her.

When she told Dervil of her feelings, he simply laughed, resting his hand reassuringly on her shoulder.

"It's considered bad luck, by some, to have a woman aboard," he explained. "Probably Borisov is the superstitious sort."

It seemed a reasonable enough explanation and yet Seranne wasn't entirely convinced by it. She felt that the man had something personal against her. However, she tried to dismiss it from her mind; after all, they would only be on the ship for a few more days, then they would be landed at Stockholm at the end of the first stage of their journey. From there, they would take a fresh ship to Russia.

Suddenly the weather turned sour and the rain set in. Dervil became moody. The confines of the cabin irked him and he was short with Seranne, talking in the clipped hard way he had when disturbed.

They turned in early on the first night of the rains and Seranne was disappointed that, yet again, Dervil went straight to his own bunk on the other side of the cabin. Since the journey had begun, he hadn't come to her bed once, and she wondered with a feeling of misery if he was tiring of her.

She fell asleep at last to the sound of the wind rising and the rain lashing the ship and her dreams were troubled. She was not aware of the extent of her restlessness until she woke, sweat beading her face, to find Dervil standing beside her.

"What's wrong?" he asked abruptly.

She reached up her arms to him, wanting and needing his touch. She knew, suddenly and quite clearly, that however little affection Dervil might have to offer, she would be grateful for it.

She hid her face against his warm, bare shoulder. "I feel a strange sense of foreboding. I'm being silly, I expect."

"It's just the heavy weather frightening you," Dervil said easily. "Move over, I'll sleep with you tonight. Don't worry, you're quite safe."

She wasn't sure if he meant safe from the storm or from his advances, but she clung to him, feeling the long length of him against her body through her thin nightgown. She shivered and this time it was not with fear.

"Dervil." She clung to him, her lips pressed

against his neck and soon she felt him begin to respond. Excitement filled her as his breathing deepened, mingling with her own. He wanted her, it was obvious by the way his body had hardened. His arms tightened around her.

"I thought you wanted us to act as though we'd just met," he murmured thickly in her ear. "Well, that was just manageable when I was sleeping alone, but you surely know that celibacy does not appeal to me."

Seranne pressed closer. "Nor to me," she whispered. "Oh, Dervil, love me, please love me."

She smoothed his face with the tip of her fingers. Everything about him was so familiar to her, so beloved—how could she ever have thought him cold? Even more impossible, how had she ever believed herself to be in love with Fenn? She could see now she had felt nothing more than infatuation for him. He had come into her cloistered life and swept her off her feet, but he had not cared one jot about her; he had just used her. She had been ignorant of men and easily duped.

"Dervil, I don't care what you think about me, my darling, but I must tell you how much I've grown to love you." She hid her face against his chest.

He leaned over her, kissing her mouth, forcing her lips apart, his tongue probing hers. His hands were busy opening the buttons of her gown, slipping it over her shoulders. He touched her breasts, his fingers teasing the nipples until they stood up firm and hard. Then his lips moved downward, his hand holding each breast in turn while he caressed the firm flesh with his lips.

She was aflame, her body moving against his of its own volition. She flung back her head and gasped as his fingers searched between her thighs.

"I love you, Dervil." She closed her eyes, muttering the words like a chant, knowing nothing except the ecstasy of her sensations. She was alive with desire, wanting with almost impossible impatience for him to penetrate her body.

"Now, Dervil!" She lifted herself up as he slid his hands beneath her and then, when the moment of joining came, she almost screamed out loud with the delight of it.

He moved slowly at first, taunting her almost as he withheld his passion. She moaned softly, and he went deeper, so that she felt they would be inextricably bound together forever in the joy of their union.

Then, together, they moved with increasing speed and passion, rising to the heights. Seranne caught him close, holding on to him as the shuddering climax came, almost tearing her apart, then she fell back and lay panting against the pillows.

"Promise me one thing, Dervil," she whispered. "Don't sleep in your bunk any more on this trip. I want you close to me, always."

He smoothed back her tangled hair. "Go to sleep," he said. "Forget the sea and the rain."

As she snuggled against him, Seranne wished for one thing more: that Dervil would tell her he loved her. But that, she supposed, was asking too much. She loved him enough for both of them and she would have to be content with whatever affection he chose to give her.

It was some hours later that Seranne felt herself being woken. Dervil was standing by the bunk, fully dressed. She sat up quickly, her heart beating uncomfortably fast.

"There's nothing to be alarmed about," he said quietly. "But I want you to get dressed. Come along now, put on your warmest clothes."

As she stepped out of the bunk, she felt the floor of the cabin heave beneath her feet and she became aware that the whine of the wind had risen to a roar like the breath of some demented animal.

"I just knew something would go wrong," she said, struggling to find her clothes in the light of the flickering candle Dervil was holding for her. "Are we in danger?"

"I doubt it." Dervil shielded the candle with his hand. "We're being driven toward the coast of Russia, but that could be advantageous to us. We might even be able to persuade the Captain to let us disembark at one of the small ports on the northern coast instead of taking us to Stockholm."

Seranne pulled on her high-waisted coat, its heavy collar edged with fur, shivering a little in the night air. As yet the weather in Russia would be warm, it being high summer, but now with the cold easterly wind and rain lashing the ship, Seranne had a taste of what the winter might be like.

"Wait here," Dervil said. "I shall see Porter, find out exactly what's happening." He took her face between his hands and kissed her. "Don't look so worried, we'll be all right." His very kindness was unnerving.

When he had gone, Seranne leaned against the door, biting her lip. The ship rolled violently and she fell against the bunk, clinging onto it desperately. She heard the swish of water on the deck and shouts from the men as they battled to keep on course and she knew that her sense of foreboding had been justified.

"Dervil!" Her voice was lost in all the noise as the ship creaked and groaned beneath her, heaving with the swell of the sea, almost threatening to turn turtle as the waves crashed downward on the deck.

One of the sailors caught her arm, leaning forward, shouting into her face. The words she could not understand. But she knew by his gestures that he wanted her to return to the cabin.

"My husband," she said. "Have you seen him?" She tried to make the man understand but her voice was too weak and he shook his head, pushing her gently backward.

An enormous wave towered over them for a moment, hovering, a monster with silver wings. Then stunningly it crashed down on the ship, snapping the mast as though it were a twig.

Seranne felt herself being thrown backward. A scream was torn from her as through the rush of the choking water she saw the sailor pinned beneath the heavy wood of the mast. She was swept against the outer rail and she clung to it desperately, almost being sucked overboard into the boiling sea. How she had the strength to hold on she didn't know. She hung like a ragdoll for a moment before dragging herself back on deck, her coat heavy with water, clinging to her body. She struggled free of its hampering folds, and made her way back toward the door to the stairway. The sailor was dead, his neck broken by the mast. She felt sick.

She crawled on all fours up the slope of the deck and tried again to call for Dervil. The ship shuddered and seemed to rise up in the middle before falling into the trough of the waves. Suddenly, to her horror, the deck planks were splintering beneath her grasping fingers.

Then hands were lifting her and she sobbed as she saw Dervil, his hair plastered over his face in wet, black strands. He dragged her to the stump of the mast and began to lash her to the jagged wood.

"You'll be safe here," he shouted. "At least you won't be washed overboard."

"What about you?" Seranne clung to his hands. "Stay with me—*please*, Dervil!" She felt the bite of the rope as it tightened around her waist and then the mountainous sea was rising above them again.

Seranne heard herself scream. The ship seemed to be snapping into pieces. There was noise all around her; it seemed even to penetrate into her head. She tried to hold on to Dervil but water filled her mouth, blinding her eyes. She was drowning. She pulled against the ropes but they held her fast, and then she was sinking into blackness, down into the very depths of the ocean.

When Seranne opened her eyes once more, they were stinging fiercely and her vision was blurred, so that it took her a few seconds to realize she was floating in comparatively calm water. She was still lashed to part of the mast. She began to cough and a rough hand turned her head sideways and she found that the position helped her to expel the water she'd swallowed until at last she could breathe freely. Her vision slowly cleared and she looked round her, unsure of what had happened.

"You live then." The guttural voice of Borisov brought her back to reality sharply. "You looked like you dead but I tie you to my raft anyway."

She raised her head and saw him silhouetted against the predawn sky, kneeling on a partly submerged piece of decking. It appeared to be holding up mainly thanks to the support of the stout column of the mast to which she was bound.

"Where are the others?" she said quickly. "My husband, have you seen him?"

The man shrugged carelessly. "Drowned, perhaps. I know not." He made a sweeping gesture with his hand, toward the empty seas. His expression was laconic, as though accepting his fate without question.

"Dervil!" Seranne cried sharply. "We must look for him, *please*! I have money, you will be well rewarded."

"No good to look," he said. "We drift with the wind too far from the wreck." He pointed. "Land is over there—my land, Russia. We make for coast, near St. Petersburg. There we find help."

"No!" Seranne cried hysterically, tearing at the stout rope that bound her. She wanted to dive into the sea, to search for Dervil and if she could not find him to let herself sink below the waves and drown with him. But he had tied her too securely and she could not free herself. The knots, soggy with water, refused to budge under her desperate fingers. At last, exhausted, she fell back against the wood of the mast, her eyes dry and staring, the strength drained from her. She could not think anymore, or feel; she was numb with shock and horror.

She had no clear recollection of arriving on Russian shores. She felt Borisov cut the ropes with a knife and then he was hauling her out of the cold water and up onto the beach. She watched in a stupor as he lit a fire and stared at her over the flames, dislike in every crease of his face.

"Come, warm yourself," he said disdainfully. "Dry your clothes, if you please. Otherwise you catch lung fever."

She just sat there looking at him, her teeth chattering, and with a shrug he threw some branches on the blaze. The warmth reached her and she lay down, face against her hand, staring at the burning wood. She imagined she was home at Hussey Hall; she thought of the way she and Dervil had stood at the altar together, exchanging vows of fidelity even though love had been absent. And now she had lost him to the sea, just when she realized how much she really cared for him.

The dawn air was bitterly cold, and she felt Borisov throw a coat over her. She wished he would not bother; she did not care if she lived or died. She lay staring into the fire until at last her eyes closed and she slept.

When Seranne woke it was to a feeling of utter despair. She sat up, the damp coat Borisov had thrown over her falling to the ground and stared round her. She was quite alone on the empty stretch of coast and it was as though no one existed in the world except herself. It seemed that Borisov had abandoned her.

The fire still flickered dimly and she put a few more logs over the flames, watching them flare and she wondered what she was going to do. She couldn't simply sit here for the rest of her life. She got to her feet feeling stiff and weary, looking round in confusion.

She began to walk toward the sea. It was calm now, with no sign of the cruel, heaving waves that had wrecked the ship. She could see pieces of wreckage brought in by the tide but there was no sign of survivors, though she strained her eyes to see along the rim of the water.

"Oh, Dervil, my love," she whispered. "Come back to me, please come back."

There was nothing to break the silence except the restless surge of the sea against the coast and the sucking sound of the tide receding.

She sank down on her knees, her head in her hands, and wept.

The sound of voices distracted her and Seranne rose to her feet, staring dully at the band of men on horseback riding slowly toward her. In the forefront was Borisov, his thin figure jerking as he walked ahead of the riders. He pointed at her and a sudden fear gripped her as he drew nearer.

The men dismounted and crowded round her, staring in open curiosity. They were swarthy men, dark of countenance, with black hair long to the shoulder. All of them wore bright gaudy shirts with full sleeves, and Seranne saw the glitter of steel from under the sashes tied around the men's waists.

Borisov stared at Seranne unblinkingly. "You go with Cassell," he said. "He leader of gypsies. Be nice and he keep you for his own."

"Please, Borisov!" Seranne said in anguish. "Don't leave me with these men. Take me to St. Petersburg. My brother-in-law, Fenn Cornwallis, is a personal friend of Tsar Alexander. He will see you are well rewarded."

A thin smile spread over Borisov's face. "Is that so?" he said. "But I am well paid now." He held out his hand to the tall bearded man who seemed to be the leader of the band and the man thrust some gold pieces toward him impatiently.

Borisov moved back a pace as the leader spoke sharply to him in Russian. He seemed suddenly afraid and replied meekly, nodding his head vigorously.

"*Please* help me, Borisov." Seranne made one last desperate attempt to reach the man.

"I not help," he said thickly. "I had pale wife like you once, she cheat on me."

"But that's not my fault, Borisov, and my countryfolk will be very angry if they ever find out what you've done."

He moved so that he stood between herself and the band of men. "Give me that." He pointed to her wedding ring. "I will take it to the Tsar and we shall learn if you speak the truth."

As she hesitated, Borisov grasped her hand and drew off her ring, pushing it into his pouch.

Cassell spoke again, with quiet authority, and Borisov immediately moved away, disappearing quickly over a low headland. Seranne watched him go with dismay, feeling her last link with safety was gone. Even though she had disliked the man, he had at least had some vestige of civilization about him.

Cassell made a gesture with his finger across his throat and one of his men set off along the bay after Borisov's retreating figure. Seranne felt sick as she realized the little Russian was to be put to death.

She felt a hand grip her arm and she looked up into the gypsy leader's face.

"You English?" he asked. Fearfully, she nodded. He smiled as though well pleased. "I speak a little of your language," he said. "I have some sailors from the sea many moons ago and they teach me."

His words gave Seranne a small hope. Maybe she could convince him it would be better to let her go. Before she could speak, however, he had swung her up into his arms and placed her on his huge stallion. He mounted the animal and his arms were around

Seranne's waist, his breath warm against her cheek. She tried to hold herself away from him but it was impossible.

They set off inland at a sharp pace and Seranne tried to look back to see if Borisov had managed to escape. But she could see nothing except a stretch of sand and the sea falling away into the distance.

The journey proved a short one. Within the hour, the band were riding into the heart of a large camp, the like of which Seranne had never seen before.

Fires burned in the form of a circle and surrounding the ring were row upon row of mushroomlike structures. As she drew closer, she saw that these were primitive tents made of freshly cut green wood that was bent over and covered with dried animal skins. From the interiors of the tents curious eyes stared out at her, though no one ventured forth until Cassell slid from his horse and shouted out crisp instructions in a loud voice.

Then the women emerged in silence and stood staring at Seranne. One of the women muttered something and there was a babble of voices.

Cassell smiled. "They say you are moon goddess," he explained. "Come meet Tribe Mother." He caught her wrist and drew her toward one of the largest of the tents. There, seated on a roughly cut chair, was an old woman who bore a striking resemblance to Cassell. Her cheek bones were high, her eyes like dark almonds. She took a pipe from between her lips before inclining her head.

"Kusha." She pointed a lined hand toward herself and Seranne nodded her understanding.

"I am Seranne." She repeated her name. "Seranne Cornwallis." She saw that the woman was struggling to pronounce the strange sounding words and her heart sank. It seemed she would have no help from the Tribe Mother; how could she, when they weren't even able to speak to each other?

"You go inside." Cassell gave her a small push. "You stay with my mother, then you be my woman."

Even as the meaning of his words sank into Seranne's mind, she found herself inside the Tribe Mother's tent. She bit her lip, looking around wildly for a means of escape. She would never submit to the gypsy leader; she would rather die.

The old woman spoke to her softly and then took her arms, pressing her down onto a spread of brightly colored blankets. Seranne saw that the tent was as weatherproof as any house. Strong branches formed an arch overhead and the covering skins overlapped each other so that no rain could penetrate. Heavy, ornate pots stood in a row along the wall and the gleam of copper showed the industry the gypsy woman put into her polishing.

Kusha came to her offering an earthenware bowl of chicken broth. Seranne shook her head and turned away, feeling sick at heart. She lay herself wearily down on the rough blankets, too numbed even to cry. She had no will or strength to fight; it seemed easier to accept whatever Fate had in store for her.

9

As night fell over the encampment, fires flared higher into the darkened sky, illuminating the raw-boned faces of the women sitting cross-legged on the ground. Kusha was at the center of the circle, her hair flowing free to her waist, her arms upraised, fingers pointing toward the heavens. Her deep, strong voice intoned strange words.

Seranne had been brought out of the tent and stood shivering in the shadows. It seemed that her presence was forgotten for the moment as the womenfolk conducted their curious ceremony.

Of the men there was no sign and Seranne was apprehensive. At least with Cassell watching over her she had felt safe from immediate danger. Now as she waited, not knowing what was to come, a sense of panic began to rise within her. She wanted to scream into the night that she needed freedom and solitude, a time of peace, so that she could at least come to terms with her grief over losing Dervil so suddenly and with such cruel finality.

She had sat for hours on the pallet in the candle-light of the tent and in closing her eyes had tried to close her mind also. She did not wish to think or feel. She had curled up into a small ball, feeling more dead than alive.

But this strange ceremony was something she had not expected. It gave her a sense of unreality to be standing in the darkness, involved and yet not part of the tribal rites. She looked up, startled, as the women on the outside rim of the circle stood up, silhouetted in the firelight like so many moving shadows.

Kusha beckoned to Seranne. It seemed futile to resist. She went forward to stand alongside the statuesque woman in the ring of blazing fires.

Two younger women came toward her, smiling, and gently but firmly removed her dress and then the tattered shift until Seranne was completely naked. She hid her embarrassment, holding her head high, trying to raise her mind above what was happening.

A vessel containing a dark thick liquid was placed at her feet and she was told by way of gestures that she must step into it. She did so and the sensation was one of softness and warmth.

Kusha handed her a cup and told her to drink. Seranne obeyed. At the same time, the women began to bathe her skin with firm strokes, rubbing her limbs until they shone. She was beginning to feel relaxed, even drowsy, and she wondered what was in the cup she'd drunk from so freely.

She realized dimly that she was taking part in some form of initiation. It was obvious that no harm was intended because, during all their ministrations, the women continued to smile at her, dark hair falling across swarthy skins, hands strong and skilful.

Her hair was washed and dressed with pungent oil and then, still naked, she was led to a large concave rock that stood directly in the center of the ring of fires. Kusha took her hand and, intoning strange words, forced Seranne down onto the rock, placing her arms and feet in specially made crevices of the stone so that she was spread-eagled. Strangely, she felt no distaste for what was happening; she merely accepted the ceremony as essential to her well-being.

The woman began to chant. The moon was directly above Seranne, falling in a shaft of light between the oiled, shiny whiteness of her thighs. It was as though the large orb in the sky was penetrating her body and Seranne felt an almost sensuous joy.

Long minutes passed while the moonlight spread over her entire body, encompassing her until she felt drawn into the silver light. Then the ceremony reached its climax: as Seranne watched, the women of the tribe began to dance.

Drum beats pierced the stillness of the night and the women chanted in monotonous unison, feet stamping on the dry earth, arms extending to the sky. The dancers bent gracefully from the waist, fingers touching soil, then rising slowly to touch thigh with breast. Seranne supposed that the tribe was invoking some god of fecundity and that she was to be the recipient of the fruits of their prayers.

Abruptly, the dancing ended and Kusha was helping her to rise from the stone. She clapped her hands and a young beautiful girl knelt on the ground before Seranne, offering her a gown of exquisite silk.

Seranne would have dressed herself but the girl shook her head and placed her hand on her breast and then on her forehead as a token, Seranne guessed, of her subservience. She dressed Seranne as though she were a helpless child.

The tribe was seated on the ground and bowls of food were being passed from hand to hand. Kusha led Seranne to the center of the ring of women and the young girl followed at a discreet distance behind her.

"Natasha." Kusha pointed to the girl, who quickly bowed her head, holding out a bowl that contained chicken pieces spiced with pepper. It was apparent that Natasha was to be her servant and Seranne nodded her thanks as she took the food.

After the meal was finished, the women sat in silence, hands idle in their laps, apparently waiting. Seranne was surprised at the feeling of peace that descended on her as she waited with them—though for what, she had no notion.

There was the sound of galloping horses and the women rose to their feet. It was obvious that the return of the men marked the start of the festivities because, amid shouts and laughter, cups of wine were passed around and music filled the air.

Seranne saw Cassell coming toward her. He was smiling, his long curling hair swinging back from his shoulders as he walked. He took her hand, kissing her fingertips, and cautiously Seranne inclined her head in his direction, acknowledging his salute but unable to think of anything suitable to say.

"You are one of us now, Silver Princess," he said softly. "I welcome you and I ask permission to court you." He spoke as though expecting no reply. Seranne remained silent. "We will marry when the new moon is conjunct Pluto with Venus rising," he continued. "I will be good master to you and give you many sons. The tribe shall love you, you will be one of us, but if you disobey our laws, you will be punished like any other."

Her hand lay passively in his. Broad-shouldered and muscular, he was a strong man, a leader in every respect, and Seranne sensed a hardness hidden beneath the gentleness he now displayed. He would be a dangerous man to cross.

"Come now." He drew her toward the center of the ring where some of the tribe had gathered, standing in groups, looking toward Cassell as though awaiting some sign from him.

"You dance with me," Cassell said to Seranne. "It

will seal our courtship in the eyes of my people. They will accept you then as the chosen bride of Cassell.''

Seranne tried to resist but he was too strong. He drew her to him, his arm closing round her waist so tightly she could hardly breathe.

She wanted to explain that she could not dance with him, could not agree to be his bride. She had loved Dervil, and she had lost him; never again would she lie in the arms of any man.

Cassell swirled her round so suddenly that she was dizzy. Her skirts flared out behind her and the flames of many fires danced before her eyes. The people of the tribe were stamping their feet and clapping their hands in appreciation, and she realized she could not stop dancing and humiliate Cassell before his people.

She matched her steps with his, swinging round, the stars overhead moving crazily as if they, not she, were dancing. Her hands were caught up in the column of Cassell's neck to keep herself from falling, and with a sudden, ear-piercing shout, he lifted her bodily off her feet, holding her high in the air, as though in triumph.

When he set her down once more, the other couples joined in the dancing and breathless, Cassell led her to the entrance of his tent.

"Sit, Silver Princess," he said. "You are so pale, so fragile, I fear you might break."

She could not catch her breath. She was still weak from her ordeal in the sea and it took her a few minutes to compose herself. She tried to think of a way of convincing Cassell that she could not marry him. But when she looked up at his dark face, as hard and stern as if it had been carved out of rock, her courage failed her.

Seranne didn't know how she endured the rest of

the night. The feast of food and wine continued into the small hours of the morning. Men lay entwined with their womenfolk around the dying embers of the fires. They had coupled openly, under the starlit sky, and fallen asleep like children.

"Come." Cassell caught her waist, lifting her up. "You sleep now, and when sun rises, Tribe Mother and Natasha will teach you your duties."

He led her inside the tent where a single candle had flickered down to a stump, the grease spilling over onto the copper holder. The smell was so familiar that Seranne felt a wave of homesickness sweep over her.

"You have small body." Cassell put both hands on her hips, feeling her bones with probing fingers. "But you are wide enough here to carry my sons." He smiled, his hand moving downward and inward to her thighs. Seranne flinched but remained still. "We shall make together a tribe of silver-heads and they will be the most sought-out studs for many miles around." His eyes flashed and Seranne trembled, wondering if he meant to take her there and then but he moved away reluctantly. "Sleep now."

She sighed with relief, sinking down onto the pallet piled with blankets. Her mind was racing as she tried to think of a way to escape. But even if she managed to leave the camp, how could she reach the Tsar in St. Petersburg? One thing she was sure of: she could not and would not remain a captive to Cassell.

Homesickness engulfed her and she pressed her eyelids tightly shut, covering her mouth with her hand, fearing she would cry out loud in her misery.

"Dervil," she whispered. "Why did I have to love you only to lose you?" She turned over on her back, her body aching for the touch of his hand. He had woken her to true womanhood and she could never give herself to another man.

Seranne must have fallen into a restless sleep at last, because when she opened her eyes again daylight was flooding into the tent. Outside, from the direction of the ever-burning fires, a terrible screaming was tearing the stillness of the air. It brought her to her feet with a feeling of terror, as though she were in the grip of a nightmare.

She crawled to the front flap of the tent, peering through it.

In the center of the circle stood a woman, young and beautiful, her hair hanging almost to the ground as she strained back against the ropes that bound her to a stake. Her clothes had been torn from her quivering body and her dark skin glistened with sweat. The sun was high in the sky, glaring down into the girl's face, and even from where she was crouched, Seranne could see the bite of the leather thongs that held the girl's arms above her head.

As she watched, Seranne saw one of the women pour water over the thongs and the girl screamed, begging to be released, as the leather tightened. Seranne shivered, wondering what crime the girl had committed. Suddenly Cassell appeared and pushed her aside, entering the tent.

"Be silent." He held up a warning hand and Seranne obeyed. "This is not for your eyes to look upon. It is not good for you to see the punishment."

But Seranne could not tear her eyes from the unfortunate girl. As she watched, the leather thongs dried in the sun, tightening inexorably around the girl's slender wrists. The blood-curdling shrieks turned into a constant pitiful groaning.

"She has disobeyed the rules of our tribe." Cassell spoke without emotion. "She knew she did wrong when she crawled into the bed of another woman's mate and now she must pay."

Seranne heard the finality in his voice and shuddered; it seemed the tribal retribution was swift and brutal, with no room for mercy. She retreated further into the tent but still she could hear the girl's low, agonized moans.

"You will do no work, today," Cassell said. "Because of this trouble we are to have a day of prayer in readiness for the execution."

Seranne turned slowly, the blood draining from her face.

"Execution?" she echoed. "Do you mean that young girl out there is going to be slaughtered? How can you let such a thing happen? It's inhuman."

Cassell drew himself up to his full height and his eyes glittered darkly as he looked down at Seranne. He did not speak for a moment. He seemed to be searching for the right words to explain to her.

"My laws are different from yours but they are just. The girl was caught in her sin. She carries a child of shame."

"She is going to have a baby?" Seranne felt lightheaded with horror. "But that makes it even worse! The girl should be cared for. You should protect her unborn child."

"No." Cassell shook his head. "You do not understand. The infant will be malformed, have two heads or shortened limbs. It carries the evil of sin and must be destroyed." He spread his hands wide. "No more talk. We will slowly teach you our ways and then you will come to understand us. Until then, you must guard your tongue well."

Seranne slumped onto the pallet; there was no point in saying any more. She could not help the pathetic creature outside.

"What will happen to him?" she asked. "The father of the child, will he be punished too?"

Cassell looked incredulous. "Punish? Of course we will not punish. He is a weak man and was led astray by the cunning of the woman. You cannot blame him." He shrugged. "Men are governed by their bodies, women by their heads. It is simple, is it not?"

Seranne remained silent, staring down at her clasped hands. The ways of these strange people were unfamiliar and frightening. Cassell touched her cheek.

"You must begin to learn my language," he said. "Then you will truly be one of us, Silver Princess."

She nodded, but her whole being was in revolt. She did not wish to be one of the gypsy tribe. She wanted to be free, to return to civilization.

She rubbed at the oil which still clung to her skin. She longed to bathe, to wash her hair free of the sickly aroma of spices and honey.

"Why you be sad?" Cassell drew her to her feet and she was held against the brilliant red silk of his shirt. "I will put many boys in you and we will have new tribe. And I will not visit the lodges of other women."

His hands slid from her waist to cup her breast, and his breathing quickened. Seranne, obeying an instinct she didn't understand, pushed him away fiercely. She was afraid for one moment that he was going to strike her; his brow was furrowed and his black eyes almost closed as he towered above her, his

long hair hanging in an unruly mass around his
strong face.

"I'm sorry," she said breathlessly. "But you must
wait until we are married before you touch me."

"Is this the way of your people?" he demanded,
and Seranne, grasping at straws, nodded emphatically.

"Yes. And my laws mean as much to me as yours
do to you."

He shrugged his huge shoulders and the red silk
clung to his rippling muscles.

"I want you." His statement was simple, direct,
and Seranne knew that if Cassell chose to take her by
force there would be little she could do to stop him.

"But you don't know anything about me," she
protested, wondering if she could appeal to his better
nature, persuade him that she was unsuitable as wife
to the leader of the tribe.

He took her hand, staring down at the small white
fingers. He smiled and pressed his lips into her palm.
He was far too close for comfort, his dark head
almost touching her breasts. Seranne inched away
from him and he let her go reluctantly.

She drew back, but to her dismay Cassell followed
her. She was growing tired and didn't know how long
she could go on playing his game of cat and mouse.
She sank down onto the pallet covered with bright
blankets, hoping he would realize how weary she was
and leave her alone. Instead, he stood over her, large,
almost menacing, his dark eyes bright as polished
pebbles.

His gaze fell to the roundness of her breast beneath
the richly colored cloth of her bodice and she could
feel herself shrinking away from him. She knew she

could not bear his touch; she wanted no man to know her body as Dervil had. Cassell crouched down, his eyes alight.

"Do not worry, I will not dishonor you. I wait until wedding night. I will make you love me, my Silver Princess." He rose swiftly: "I shall leave now." He pushed back the curtain and stared out at the camp.

"Now it is noon. You will eat and afterward you will rest. Tonight, the girl meets her punishment." He sounded almost regretful and Seranne rose to her feet, her eyes wide as she looked up at him.

"Is it not possible for you to show mercy?" she asked breathlessly. "You are the leader, your word is law."

"Nothing can be done," he explained. "What of the wounded wife? And there is her man, he could be tempted once more. Do not meddle in what you do not understand."

Seranne crouched at the entrance to the tent, watching Cassell vanish into the distance. Somehow she had to escape from him—but she couldn't leave without at least trying to help the girl. She pushed back her long hair and tried to think. If she waited for darkness, she could perhaps cut the girl free. No one need ever know who had helped the prisoner to escape. Her breathing quickened, she was badly frightened by the prospect of taking such a drastic course of action. Yet even now the girl was suffering from sun blisters on her face and body and Seranne could hear her moaning softly.

It seemed a long time before the sun set in a flaming orange orb behind the hills. Even as dusk crept around the encampment, Seranne hesitated, not knowing exactly when the ritual execution would take place. Then, quickly, she seized the knife lying by the platter of food Natasha had brought her earlier. She would have to act quickly before her courage failed.

The space between the tents and the girl seemed endless as Seranne crept forward, her heart in her mouth. She clutched the cold steel of the knife firmly and when she reached the spot where the girl was tied to a pole, she was so frightened she could scarcely think straight.

Quickly, Seranne sawed through the tough leather thongs that bound the girl's wrists. She'd expected an attempt at flight or perhaps a show of gratitude but the girl sank to her knees, her thin shoulders bowed, shaking her head from side to side.

"Go," Seranne urged. "Run for your life." She pushed the girl's shoulders gently but still she just crouched in a position of utter dejection, not making any attempt to move.

"What is this?"

It was Cassell. He was standing over them in the darkness, his eyes glowing red in the light from the fires that flared on the perimeter of the camp.

"Return to the lodge," he ordered, his voice fierce.

Seranne obeyed, running on her bare feet as fast as she could. Only when she reached the doorway of the tent did she stop. Cassell was tying the girl back in position.

It had all been for nothing; she had risked her own life and the girl had not seemed to wish to escape. It was past understanding.

The moon slid out from the clouds and, as if on a given signal, the center of the clearing became alive with women. There was not a man in sight; even

Cassell had disappeared like a shadow into the darkness.

The women ranged themselves around the place where the prisoner was tied and Seranne wondered what was going to happen next. She shuddered, determined not to watch but then Kusha was at the door, beckoning her forward.

"What do you want?" she said. Kusha did not answer; she took Seranne's arm, indicating that she accompany her.

Seranne reluctantly went outside, trying to control the shaking of her hands as the bright moonlight fell like a wash of molten silver over the upturned watching faces of the women.

Kusha placed her hand over Seranne's lips, apparently warning her to remain silent. Then she led her to the center of the circle, where Seranne was seated on a huge chair.

She was not clear what was happening. There was a great deal of chanting and then a woman stepped from the crowd and made a mark over the head of the girl. This was presumably the wronged wife; she looked sorrowful rather than angry as she droned a strange dirge. She raised her arm high and sharply brought her hand down to her side. Two milky white horses were led into the clearing. They were halted alongside the girl who was almost paralyzed with fear.

The prisoner was released from the pole and then her ankles were grasped and spread wide, one being tied to each of the horses.

Seranne tried to remain impassive as a whip was placed in the hands of the wife, who stood quite still and silent, her head bowed, while the girl lying on the ground moaned and writhed, her eyes wide and staring.

The whip cracked. The horses bolted in separate directions. A roar filled the air like the cry of a monster. Seranne, faint with horror, stood her ground through sheer effort of will, trying not to see or hear the girl's agony.

At last it was over and Kusha was leading Seranne back to the tent where she almost fell onto the pallet, staring unseeingly into the darkness, her emotions so torn and twisted that she believed she would never feel anything again.

10

Not many miles from the gypsy camp, along the golden curve of the beach, stood a small hut. Its wooden roof shimmered in the heat of the sun that had passed through August and into September with undimmed brilliance. And at the back of the building, fields of corn stood head high, rich and ripe, a golden harvest waiting to be culled.

On the outside porch, legs stretched bare and brown into the sunlight, sat a young Russian girl. Her face was elfin, eyes large and dark as she thought of the stories she'd heard of the looting and burning carried out by French soldiers. The army of Napoleon had crossed the countryside meeting no resistance from the inhabitants of the towns and villages they destroyed.

The stories did not worry her unduly. She knew her people; they would move when the time was right. In any case, she had other things to think about. She rose languorously and went inside. The darkness was striking in contrast to the hot sun on the porch.

Mon looked down at the man lying on the bed. He was dark and handsome, a gift to her from the sea. He had been weak and sickly when she'd found him, but now his wound was healing and his strength was gradually returning.

She had been walking along the beach, searching as always for anything the tide had to offer. It was obvious there had been a shipwreck by the large pieces of timber floating shoreward.

Mon had searched the coves with eagerness. Sometimes after a storm there would be a bolt of cloth or a keg of wine washed up on the rocks. Instead she had found him, her dark-haired god with silver eyes. But she had almost been seen returning homeward with him. There had been an ugly little man clutching the arm of a pale girl with golden hair. He had been bartering with Cassell, leader of the gypsies, exchanging the girl for money. She had cried out as she had been dragged away, but Mon had no time to worry about anyone else. All her energies had been directed into bringing her man home to the little hut.

Now as she brushed his curly hair back from his face, she smiled. He slept like a baby and now it was good sleep, sound and peaceful, not the feverish ravings that had so frightened her.

She had done everything she could for him, cooling his heated body with water the way her mother—rest her soul—had taught her. She had mixed him drinks from the wildflowers growing in the fields, administering the potions with patience and love.

There were some who had called her mother a witch, and for all Mon knew she herself might be branded with the same stigma, but she only tried to heal and to give people the peace of mind they seemed to crave and yet could not find.

For the most part she lived in seclusion, except for an occasional adventure with one of the local farm boys. Lately, though, there had been a restlessness she'd failed to understand—until the man had come into her life. And then she realized she wanted a real mate, someone she could love and respect.

He was over the crisis now, and when he woke from his sleep he would see her, really see her, and perhaps he would fall in love with her and stay forever.

She left his side and began to prepare a meal for him. There was a little rye bread and she had made cabbage pastries earlier that morning in readiness for his waking. She would have liked some chicken for a rich nourishing broth but she had been unable to barter any of her elixirs lately. It seemed that all the peasants were in good health because of the unusually long summer.

Suddenly she heard a sound from the bed. Lifting her head, she pushed back her dark hair, her eyes bright with anticipation. He was awake at last.

She went into the room and he was struggling to sit up. The eyes that had looked at her only in delirium were clear now, questioning. She smiled, nodding her head in encouragement.

When he spoke, his voice was still weak. The words were strange ones, not of her own tongue. His face wore an anxious expression and she sat beside him, easing him gently back against the pillows.

"Take care," she said in Russian. "You have been sick, very sick; you mustn't try to get up."

He shook his head and she saw that he did not understand her. She rose swiftly and brought him food and held some to his lips. He ate a little and then fell back, shaking his head.

She moved the bandage from the wound on his temple, pointing to it.

"Better now. My herbs have healed the cut, but your head aches a little, no?" She put her hand to her own head, wincing, and he understood the gesture.

He spoke again and by the tone of his voice she knew it was a question but the words were so strange she knew she would never understand them.

She brought him a drink. "It is good," she told him reassuringly. "Make you sleep again and when you wake you will feel stronger."

He drank thirstily and again she nodded her encouragement. He closed his eyes almost immediately and she remained beside him, taking his hand in hers, smoothing his fingers gently. She watched his mobile mouth as he smiled and she longed to press her lips against his, to feel him respond with the passion she felt sure he was capable of. He was a big, strong man; if he had been any weaker he would have died from the great amount of blood he had lost.

It was several hours before he woke again. The sun was setting in a red and orange sky and the heat of the day was giving way to a cool breeze.

"You feel good now?" Mon asked. "I have built a fire so you can sit up with me for an hour or two."

She sat on the bed and swung her legs slowly to the ground, indicating that he do the same.

He was stronger than she had imagined and with

very little help from her he was able to make his way into the other room, where he looked around as if trying to get his bearings. She pushed him gently into a chair kneeling at his feet.

"Mon," she said, pointing to herself. "And what is it they call you?"

He understood at once. "Dervil." His voice was thin from weakness but she liked the sound of it and smiled up at him.

"Dervil . . . You are my man now. You come to me from the sea and I gave your life back to you. We are bound together. Before winter comes we will gather plenty of wood from the forest. You can hunt for game, we will be cozy and safe through the snowy months."

"Mon." He said her name and pointed to the door.

She understood that he wanted to see what was outside and she shook her head. "Not now, it's nightfall; the sea winds are cold. Tomorrow perhaps." She drew a picture of the sunrise in the sand on the floor and he nodded his understanding.

He leaned over then and roughly drew a picture of a woman with long hair and above that the sun. He touched the sun and touched the figure's hair and Mon knew at once that he was asking about the girl who had been sold to Cassell.

"No!" She shook her head and jealousy was like a hot knife searing her. That girl must have been his woman; he was anxious about her. Well, in all probability she was dead now, or at best serving in the tent of one of the gypsy men. Soon the tribe would be moving onto fresh grounds, and though Mon would miss the occasional trade of selling the younger ones her love potions and elixirs, she would feel safe once they were on the move and the golden-haired one taken out of reach.

It was her guess that the tribe would leave the coast and travel inland sometime in the next few weeks, and she would do all she could to help them on their way.

That night, Mon slept as usual on the floor beside the bed, listening to the man's heavy breathing. She whispered his name to herself in the darkness. *Dervil.* It was like a charm. She sighed restlessly. In the morning she would give him one of the potions she had made from a special flower, which brought a dreamlike state and a feeling of well-being. He would be content to stay with her then; he would forget about the golden-haired girl.

It was a long time before sleep came and, even when it did, Mon suffered bad dreams that frightened her into wakefulness before the light of morning had come.

She rose silently and went outside. The sky was dark still, the horizon just visible, the trees appearing flat and colorless.

Mon had been so sure he was to be her man, a gift to her from the sea; hadn't she brought him back to life? Yet there had been such misery in his silver eyes when she had denied knowledge of the girl. Was she perhaps wrong in keeping the truth from him? She made up her mind to remain silent for a while, to see if she could make him happy; if not, then she must think again.

He was up and about when she returned indoors. He looked a great deal stronger now and she could appreciate for the first time what a tall man he was. He stood at least six feet tall in his bare feet, and his shoulders, though thin, were broad. He smiled when he saw her and Mon's heart danced with happiness.

"Hungry?" she asked. He shook his head, not understanding. She made a pantomime of eating and rubbed her stomach. He nodded, repeating the Russian word after her. She was delighted at his quickness of mind; he would soon learn her language and then they would really be able to talk to each other.

They spent the day quietly resting, he regaining his strength, she careful he did not tire himself, and when the sun fell behind the hills she made him understand he should go to his bed.

The next night she was careful to put the potion in his hot drink and he swallowed it without question. Soon, his eyes began to droop and she led him across to the bed, helping him to lie down. She crawled between the rough blankets alongside him and began to caress his body. She had come to know it so well; she had bathed him carefully every day, rubbing creams into his skin so that the bed would not cause him to suffer with soreness.

His arms slowly came round her and, though she knew that he was not in full possession of his senses, Mon thrilled to his touch. She would bring him peace and relief and he would feel more settled in her little home.

She ran her hand over the hardness of him, rejoicing in his virility and manhood. He would be a fine lover, and in turn she would make him happy and fulfilled.

He rolled over until his body covered hers, and she uttered a sigh as he kissed her with passion. In time he might come to love her as much as he now desired her. She wound her arms around his neck, pressing herself close to him, her eyes closed.

He was a master in the art of love. His fingers were filled with magic as they touched her innermost, secret places. He gave her a sense of excitement such as she had never experienced before. She was almost swooning as he kissed her small breasts, teasing the nipples with his tongue. He held her gently, reassuringly, as though she were a precious object to be handled with care.

Never in her quick, hurried bedding with local farm boys had she felt such passion. She put her arms around his broad back, holding him close. She uttered endearments in a low guttural tone, words she knew in the back of her mind he could never understand. In his turn, he whispered to her softly and she pretended his words were not prompted by the elixir she'd given him. He was still holding himself back, touching her, kissing her as though savoring every moment. She became impatient for him to join his flesh with hers and she stroked him into an ecstasy of desire.

When he did penetrate her softly waiting body, she whimpered, not in pain but in delight. He was every bit the man she'd thought him, his movements vigorous and intended to produce the utmost enjoyment.

She arched herself to meet his thrusts, wanting the moment to go on forever. She knew that, after this, she could never be content with the clumsiness of the youths with whom she'd coupled before.

Her whole being sang with joy; she felt that each thrust would tear her asunder. She clung to him, moaning like a demented creature of the forest, and when the final moment of ecstasy came, she found herself crying tears of happiness.

"My loved one," she murmured, touching his face. "I'll never let you go. You are mine now, and I am yours. We will find happiness, you'll see. You will forget everything but this joy we have in being together."

He fell over onto his side, his hand around her waist, his lips close to her hair.

"Seranne," he whispered. "My darling Seranne, I love you." His eyes were closed and his breathing became even and regular. He was asleep.

Mon silently left the rumpled bed. Her heart was like a stone. She recognized the name as the one he had called out many times in his delirium, and she knew with a feeling of anger and despair that it belonged to the girl with the golden hair.

Dervil would sleep now for an hour or two, and Mon suddenly made up her mind to visit the gypsy encampment and find out for herself what had become of the girl whose name Dervil called with such longing.

She packed her elixirs and a box of special powders, tying them in a leather bag around her waist. She would walk the few miles to where the tribe had set their camp. With luck she would be there before noon.

The day had blossomed into one of intense heat and Mon tied a scarf around her hair to protect herself from the sun's brightness. Her skirt was light and cool and her bodice open at the neck. She felt that the day would have been perfect if she could have ignored the existence of the one Dervil called Seranne.

The grass was drying and brown and it crunched under her feet as Mon made her way cross-country to the camp. She was filled with curiosity and wondered what sort of woman it was who could inspire love in the heart of a man like Dervil. She hoped that the girl had been given to one of Cassell's men. It would have to be an old man or a youth, because the strong men of Cassell's tribe already had women and the tribal customs forbade a man to take more than one woman.

The acrid-smelling smoke from the camp fires that were lit day and night, even in hot weather such as this, drifted skyward. Mon began to walk more quickly now that her destination was in sight.

All was quiet in the camp; it seemed caught in the dreaming sunshine. Mon guessed that the inhabitants of the mushroom-shaped tents were resting from the heat of the sun.

She approached the big tent belonging to Kusha, Tribe Mother, knowing that her permission must be sought before Mon could make her way through the camp peddling her medicines. Fortunately for Mon, most of the tribe were born on Russian soil and so spoke her native language as well as their own strange tongue.

As she neared the tent, a girl emerged from the entrance, her skin very white in the bright sunlight. Mon saw the swinging golden hair and knew that this must be the woman who had captured Dervil's love. She was pale as a flower, her skin delicate and smooth, and her deep violet eyes were filled with sadness.

Mon spoke but the girl had no understanding of her language and retreated into the tent. Kusha emerged, greeting Mon with a smile.

"Welcome, my child," she said warmly.

When Mon's mother was alive, she had made friends with Kusha, meeting with her every spring, spending days at the camp with her child at her side, discussing remedies with the Tribe Mother who herself was something of a healer.

The girl with the shining hair had disappeared into the back of the tent and Mon took the opportunity to question Kusha about her, doing her best to appear only casually interested.

"Who is the woman?" she said. "The one with the yellow hair."

Kusha smiled proudly. "She is to be wife to my son. We shall have golden-haired boys to rule our tribe." She paused. "Now, what have you brought to show us? Have you a remedy for the bone ache I know will come upon me once winter falls?"

Mon knew that nothing more would be said about the girl, at least not by Kusha who could be tight-lipped when she chose. She would have to use her cunning and find a more willing informer.

Just then, as though in answer to Mon's thoughts, Natasha came from behind the curtain, carrying a bowl of scented water in her hands.

"I have attended Silver Princess." She bent her head low. "Shall I return to my tent now?"

Kusha nodded almost absent-mindedly, dismissing the slim young girl with a wave of her hand. But Mon had caught the flash of resentment in the dark eyes as Natasha left the tent.

She talked for a while to Kusha but saw no more of Cassell's bride. Perhaps she was resting; she looked delicate, too skinny and pale to be a red-blooded mate for any man.

The moment she left Kusha, Mon made directly for the tent of the girl Natasha. It was clear that her duties included serving the English girl and she would not be as reluctant to talk as Kusha had been.

Natasha was in a difficult mood, however, and it took all Mon's guile and the promise of a love potion to get any information at all from her.

"The wedding will be soon," she said truculently. "It is I who should have been Cassell's bride. He had eyes for no one but me until *she* came along." She spat on the floor, showing her venom, and Mon reached out a restraining hand.

"Anger is no good," she said. "Not unless you direct it to a purpose."

Natasha stared at her. "What do you mean? What could I possibly do to the bride of our leader without being terribly punished?"

Mon smiled. "You know more about your customs than I do. Is there not some way you can turn Cassell against her? What if she were to be found in the lodge of some other man?"

Natasha shook her head. "That's not possible. None of the men would take such a risk. And the girl is interested in no man, not even Cassell."

"She does not wish to become his bride?" Mon asked. "But why?"

"She had a husband," Natasha explained. "But the sea took him and she grieves for him still. Sometimes when I sit beside her as she sleeps, I hear her cry out his name."

"Perhaps you could make use of this," Mon said thoughtfully. "Can the girl be made to refuse Cassell at the wedding ceremony, before all his people?"

Natasha looked up quickly. "She would be executed," she said abruptly.

"What is your choice?" Mon asked. "A lifetime spent with another, lesser man than Cassell. Worse still, you could be given to an old one or a young green boy. You, who were once destined to be Tribe Mother.''

Natasha bit her lip thoughtfully and Mon suppressed a smile, knowing the girl was won over.

"Don't worry," she said. "I will give you my help." She emptied the leather pouch and selected a small earthenware jar, offering it to Natasha. "Here is a love potion. Use it well and at the right moment."

Natasha's eyes brightened. "If I can make Cassell sleep with me he will be honor-bound to take me as his bride before the whole tribe."

Mon smiled cunningly. "But you will have to get rid of the girl first. She has bewitched him with her pale beauty."

She left the thoughtful Natasha and made her way round the camp; it would not do to arouse suspicion by leaving before she had offered her elixirs to the rest of the tribe.

Dusk was falling when Mon at last returned to the small hut at the edge of the sea. A candle was lit just inside the window and her heart warmed as she thought of Dervil there waiting for her.

He looked at her long and hard as she came in through the door and she held out the bag, showing him it was empty, hoping he would understand that she had been about her work. He nodded, and she seated herself near to him, crouching at his feet, holding her hands up toward him. Suddenly he gripped her wrists, hurting her with his clenched fingers. He said something in the quick angry voice and when she shook her head, not understanding, he let her go so abruptly that she fell sideways on the floor.

He pulled the bag from her waist and shook it in her face. She realized that he guessed she had administered some potion to him and that he was angry with her.

"For sleep, that is all," she said and showed him what she meant by closing her eyes and resting her head on the floor. "Sleep," she repeated. He shook his head, his anger suddenly leaving him. He went and sat on the crumpled bed and rested his head in his hands.

"Damn you, Seranne," he said in his clear English voice. "Why can't I forget you?"

Although Mon could not understand the words, she knew instinctively the meaning of them. He was consumed with guilt because he had lain with a woman not his own. She must tell him it was all right; yet perhaps it was in his land, as it was with the gypsies, a crime punishable by death.

She pulled his arm. "Look." She drew a picture in the sand. It was of the sea with the figure of the girl under waves. "She must be drowned," she said urgently, believing that the lie would ease his conscience.

He closed his eyes as though still weak from his sickness, and he lay back on the bed.

Mon smoothed his cheek and he simply lay there, not responding but not pushing her aside, and she was satisfied that she had done the right thing. In time he would forget his past; he would recover and live for the future, taking the woman who was near in the place of the one he had lost. That was the way of men. They might love and mourn with their hearts but a true man like Dervil needed a woman to assuage the hunger of his body. And she, Mon, would be on hand. She had experienced the love of his body once and now inside her was a longing to lie with him again. He was the only man who could ever satisfy her and she would do anything to keep him.

11

Seranne sat in the firelight of the camp, her position on the left hand of Cassell indicating to all that she was his chosen bride and above reproach. On his right hand sat his mother and ranged around inside the circle of fires were the men of the tribe, their womenfolk behind them.

Cassell was giving directions to his people, telling them how to defend themselves if the French should reach so far north as to penetrate the camp.

It was doubtful that the army of Napoleon would be allowed within twelve miles of St. Petersburg where the Tsar Alexander waited in his splendid palace for news of victory over the enemy. It seemed that he waited in vain because the army of the French had already taken Moscow, sacking and looting, with no opposition until one angry merchant had set fire to the city.

The Tribe Mother had been given one of her visions, and she rose now to comfort her people, telling them in clear ringing tones what fate was to befall the enemy who had dared venture foot onto Russian soil.

"I have seen a long summer which will give way overnight to deep snows and treacherous winds."

She raised her arms up toward the eye of the moon. Her head was flung back and her eyes closed.

Watching her, Seranne shivered. She understood only a few of the words but the doom in Kusha's voice was clear.

"Winter will come with great teeth," she was saying, "teeth that will tear the enemy limb from limb. The soldiers along with their camp followers will try to outrun the old but they will not succeed."

Cassell leaned toward Seranne, whispering an explanation of his mother's words, and she felt his fingers brush her cheek. She edged away from him, hating his touch.

Kusha paused for a moment, as though trying to see further into the mists that now obscured the moon. Her hair hung below her waist and her bare feet were planted firmly on the dry soil.

"The victory will be ours and there will be no need to fear attack here, neither will the great Tsar Alexander be in danger. The French will be driven away and they will rue the moment they set foot on our land."

The moon was quite covered by clouds now and in the darkness Kusha sat down, her vision over. A sigh rose from the listeners, for the Tribe Mother was endowed with great wisdom and her words had the ring of truth.

Cassell got to his feet and Seranne, as she had been taught by his mother, stood behind him, her head bowed. She remained in this position until he had walked through the camp and entered his tent. Then and then only was she free to retire to her own bed.

She was very tired and yet she knew that, even when she was stretched out on her pallet, she would be unable to sleep for the thoughts that raced through her head, haunting, tormenting her. Thoughts of Dervil drowning in the swelling ocean and fears for her future if she should fail to make good her escape from the camp.

But now she had found an ally where she had least expected it. Natasha her servant had begun to teach her words, drawing pictures in the dry soil to illustrate her meaning.

Seranne had been suspicious at first, fearing the girl had been set to spy on her. Then she had learned that Natasha loved Cassell and was to have been his bride. It became clear then why the girl wanted to help her avoid the marriage with Cassell.

Seranne had been tempted to confide her plan of escape to the girl, but she held her tongue, afraid that once she made her escape Natasha would be punished. She had witnessed at close range the swiftness and barbarity of the tribe's rough justice and she had no desire to see Natasha suffer a similar fate.

So she made her plans secretly, watching the activities and habits of the tribe, learning that late afternoon was the time when the camp was almost deserted. The men for the most part were sleeping in the heat of the afternoon sun and the women busy with their domestic chores.

She had already wandered to the fringe of the camp on several occasions, aware that she was always being closely watched. Eventually, however, the guards on the camp perimeter had become accustomed to her presence. They would smile at her as she picked the wildflowers or petted the horses that were tethered in a line to the north of the clearing.

She formed a plan to bribe one of the guards to

allow her to ride a little way. But in the meantime she must act as if she was happy to be groomed and tutored for her role as Cassell's bride.

Kusha was dressing her now in the bridal finery that she would wear at the ceremony. She was to learn by heart the things she must say and the actions she must take that would bind her to the tribe leader for a lifetime.

Kusha knelt on the floor and measured the hem of the long, shapeless overgarment, satisfied at last that it hung well. It rested just above Seranne's instep and the hem was weighted with round, flat stones.

The gown itself was silvery, sewn with a shining metallic thread. It was scooped low across her breasts, revealing more than Seranne considered proper. Kusha apparently thought otherwise because she pulled at the soft silk, instructing the woman at her side to put some thread into the bodice in order to make the neckline lower.

She then pushed at Seranne's arms, indicating that she sit on the blanket. Some of her words were quite clear but much of what she said still was incomprehensible to Seranne. She had learned quite a lot of the language from Natasha but by no means enough to communicate properly.

"This Cassell," Kusha said and Seranne nodded, realizing that the Tribe Mother was taking the part of her son in her mime of the wedding ceremony. Kusha sat opposite her and took up a cup, pretending to drink from it.

"Cassell do this first," she said. "Then you take cup." She handed it to Seranne, speaking once more, far too quickly for Seranne to make much sense from what she was saying. She saw the Tribe Mother tip the cup and spill some of the liquid and then shake her head.

Seranne nodded but she was barely paying attention. Her thoughts were centered on making her escape before it was too late.

Kusha pushed at her hand and made her go through the motions of drinking from the cup and then she rose and placed a crown of flowers, crystallized by some mysterious process, on Seranne's head.

This, she guessed, was the culmination of the marriage ceremony. After the crown was placed then Cassell would presumably claim his husbandly rights. Perhaps he would do so in full view of the entire tribe.

She nodded her head as though accepting all that Kusha was telling her. She didn't like to deceive the Tribe Mother because she had grown to have a great respect for the older woman, but she couldn't allow herself to be forced into a marriage with Cassell.

Kusha called out loudly and, shortly after, Cassell came across the clearing to the tent. His mother said a few quick words to him and he laughed, catching Seranne's hand and drawing her outside into the sunshine.

Resigned, she followed him to the sacred stone in the center of the ring where she had been initiated. Cassell's dark eyes were full of mirth as he looked at her.

"We are to practice the coupling," he said. "This is something I like very much."

She felt herself grow cold as he placed her on the stone, her feet spread wide, her arms stretched outward. His hand went to the bright sash that held his breeches and Seranne took a deep shuddering breath, expecting him to push aside her skirts at any moment and attack her.

Kusha laughed and spoke chidingly to her son and some of the tribeswomen, who had gathered to watch, laughed too. Cassell shrugged his massive shoulders and then he was standing across Seranne's body, looking down at her with regret.

"My mother tells me to keep patience," he said. "We are only to pretend to lie together." He looked round the gathered circle of eager faces and pointed to himself, laughing. Seranne saw that he was greatly roused and she closed her eyes, feeling the rich color flood her cheeks.

Then he was upon her, his knees between her outstretched legs, his body, huge and smelling of oil, pressed hard against her. He bent his head and kissed her breasts. She tried to keep her revulsion from becoming apparent in her face. She must not arouse suspicion; she must pretend to accept Cassell's passion without question.

He was crushing the breath from her and then he was gently pulling the neck of her gown. Suddenly, one of her breasts became exposed and he leaned away from her, pointing at her, calling out something at which the womenfolk laughed uproariously. His hand closed around her and his mouth caught her nipple. Seranne thought she would faint from her efforts to remain still and quiet under his rough treatment of her body.

Kusha came to him at last, pulling him away. He groaned and put his hands on himself, turning to the women appealingly. He looked down at Seranne then and lifted her, holding her above him for a moment, before setting her on her feet.

She almost ran to her tent and quickly drew off her torn gown. She had to get away at once. She could bear no more of such humiliation. She dressed hurriedly and then, before her courage failed, left the lodge.

The sun beat hotly on Seranne's shoulders as she walked casually toward the rim of the camp. It was an extraordinary day, hotter than ever, and she could see the guard nodding sleepily as he sat beneath the shade of a tree. She smiled to herself. Perhaps he would not wake at all, and if he did, she was ready with a plausible tale of wanting to ride for a little while. She also had a piece of gold, stolen from Kusha's tent, hidden in her gown.

She spoke softly to one of the horses, her fingers busy untying the rope that tethered the animals between two trees. Her heart was beating swiftly but the guard did not move, his head was sunk onto his chest and she could hear his snores plainly in the stillness of the hot afternoon.

As soon as she had a horse free, she swung herself over the creature's back. It was difficult riding without a saddle but in her desperation she felt no fear of falling. She simply wanted to put as much distance between herself and the camp as she could.

Cautiously she urged the animal forward. Still the guard did not wake. She sighed with relief and gave the horse its head, elation rising in her as she galloped across the fields.

Her hair swung back from her face and she was almost crying with joy at the thought of her freedom. She had no idea where she was going; she simply rode on as fast as she could, clinging to the horse's mane.

She grew hot and weary as the ground sped away

beneath the animal's hooves. Her body ached and her eyes burned but determination gave her strength. Then, suddenly, the blue waters of the sea came into view and she realized she must be near the spot where Borisov had sold her to Cassell.

She eased the horse to a gentle trot and looked around for any signs of habitation. If only she could find someone to take her to St. Petersburg she would be safe, but until then she knew she could be recaptured at any moment and taken back to the gypsy encampment.

A small hut, standing on the edge of the bay, almost hidden among the trees, caught her eyes. She slid down from the horse and made her way toward the door. Her heart was beating swiftly; it would be all too easy to meet with hostility. She was a stranger after all, and dressed as she was now, in the gaudy clothes favored by Cassell's people, she did not look as though she would have two coins to rub together.

The door was opened by a Russian girl, dark and pretty, with strange-smelling bundles of weeds tied to her belt. She looked startled when she saw Seranne, her eyes going at once to the long golden hair as though she couldn't believe what she was seeing.

"I need help," Seranne said, holding out her hands in supplication. "I need to get to St. Petersburg. Please, is there anyone here who can show me the way?"

The girl gave a quick look to the closed door of the room behind her and put a cautionary hand over her lips, indicating that someone was in there, presumably asleep. Her eyes were dark as she stared at Seranne and then she seemed to make up her mind to help. She drew Seranne around the side of the house, into the shade of the trees. Her actions were furtive and Seranne guessed that the news of her marriage to Cassell must have spread to the inhabitants of the surrounding villages.

The girl, fortunately, seemed kindly disposed. She disappeared inside and Seranne waited impatiently for her to return, wondering if it was the presence of a heavy-handed father that disturbed the girl, or perhaps a jealous husband.

In a few minutes, she returned, carrying in her hands a cloth which contained some food. She held out a cup to Seranne, nodding her head, encouraging her to drink.

The heat had given Seranne a thirst and she realized that it might be some hours before she could find refreshment again, so she emptied the cup and handed it back with a smile of gratitude.

The girl said something and then took her arm, leading her forward but keeping out of sight of the windows. She gestured toward the horse, urging Seranne to remount. She obeyed, and the girl swung herself up behind, pressing the animal forward with a skillful kick of her heels.

Seranne wondered where they were going. They seemed to be turning back the way she had come. She tried to speak to the girl, ask her some questions, but her mouth was suddenly dry. It felt furred, with a taste of bitterness that lingered from the liquid she had drunk.

The horse was making steady progress, leaving the salt tang of the sea behind, heading inland and now Seranne was quite sure they were going in the direction of the camp.

"No." The word came out slowly, as though

Seranne had lost the ability to speak. "You don't understand . . . I want St. Petersburg. You must stop."

She felt herself slip sideways and she grasped the horse's mane, trying to steady herself. Everything seemed to swing in a terrible violent arc around her head. Her eyes refused to focus and the trees seemed not above her head but under her feet.

She felt she was falling and she had no strength or will to save herself. She plunged headfirst toward the dry grass. The last thing she remembered was uttering a thin scream that died in her throat as she hit the ground.

When Seranne opened her eyes, she had no idea where she was. She tried to sit up but firm hands restrained her. It was nighttime and a candle flickered at her side, dazzling her so that she could see but faintly the shadowy figures sitting around her.

As her mind began to clear, she recognized Kusha bending over her. The Tribe Mother's eyes were veiled and her expression revealed nothing.

Cassell stepped into her range of vision and his strong finger traced the line of her jaw.

"If I thought you tried to run from me, your punishment would be swift," he said. Seranne shook her head, unable to speak, and Cassell smiled. "But I feel you are innocent." He caught her chin in his hand, staring into her eyes, and she read a warning there. "You wanted to ride, to be alone, to think your English thoughts before you become Cassell's bride, is it not so?"

Seranne had the presence of mind to nod. She saw Cassell turn to his mother and speak quickly in his own tongue. Kusha inclined her head but her eyes were still lacking in warmth. She knew the truth, Seranne realized, but Kusha would hold her silence rather than anger her son.

"You sleep now," Cassell said. "We speak more in the morning." He ushered the shadowy figures out of the tent and Seranne fell back on the brightly colored blankets, her hand over her eyes.

Her attempt to escape had proved a dismal failure. Cassell had chosen to give her the benefit of any doubt he might have about her loyalty and that was fortunate. She shivered as she remembered the punishment.

Kusha was not so willing as her son to forgive, that much was obvious. The Tribe Mother would be watchful, on her guard; she was too shrewd to be lulled into a sense of false security by Seranne's show of meekness.

It appeared that there was no one willing to help her escape from the gypsy encampment. Even the strange Russian girl from the seashore had been her enemy. It was clear now to Seranne that the girl had given her a powerful medicine, something that brought a speedy loss of senses. She had no doubt received a reward from Cassell and was hand in glove with the gypsies.

Seranne sighed and tears of self-pity came to her eyes. She could see her life stretching out before her as Cassell's reluctant wife, nothing more than a slave and a means of begetting golden-haired children.

She sat up and peered toward the front of the tent. She sensed rather than saw a movement outside: she was being carefully guarded.

She returned to her pallet and stared at the wooden

struts of the tent. She was a prisoner, captive to a ruthless man whose revenge would be swift and barbaric should she make any further attempt to escape. The tears sprang from her eyes and ran down her cheeks and she curled herself into a ball, her shoulders shaking as sobs racked her body.

When she had ridden toward the long stretch of the ocean, she had been close, somehow, to Dervil. All the nights that she had forced herself to try and forget him were to no avail, because now the memories flooded back of the way her husband had held her, made her body sing with happiness, loved her as she had never been loved before. Perhaps his love was more of a physical nature than emotional but she had begun to believe in those long days aboard ship that a closeness could grow between them. The barriers had begun to crumble, and she had caught brief glimpses of the warm man Dervil might have been, given the right circumstances.

Now that was all gone. She was alone in her grief in a strange land and round her were people who simply failed to understand that she was not born to live the life of a primitive.

She slept eventually and through her troubled dreams she lived again her short experience of being Dervil's wife. She felt his hand upon her breast as if it were a reality, and when she woke her pillow was wet with tears.

Natasha came to her at first light and seemed unusually friendly.

She smiled and spoke to Seranne in Russian. Most of the conversation was too difficult for Seranne to understand but she caught the word for marriage and she grasped the gypsy girl's arm.

"When?" she asked. "When is the marriage to

take place?'' Her heart was beating rapidly as Natasha shook her head, not understanding her words. Speaking in stumbling Russian Seranne finally managed to make her meaning clear.

Natasha knelt on the ground and drew a picture of the moon with her finger. ''Tonight,'' she said.

''No!'' Seranne shook her head, tears of distress on her eyelashes. The Russian girl looked at her and picked up a cup. She made a pantomime of handing it to Seranne, then she threw it to the ground.

Seranne stared at her eagerly. ''If I do that I'll be refusing Cassell, is that it?''

Natasha repeated the gesture, once, twice, her face urgent, her eyes dark pools in her raw-boned face.

''What will happen then?'' Seranne said quickly and bit her lip as she realized the girl could not understand. She spoke a few tentative words in Russian, and for a moment Natasha stared at her without comprehension. Then her face brightened.

She made a pushing gesture with her hands as though sending Seranne out of the tent. She spread her arms wide and Seranne smiled.

''Do you mean that if I reject Cassell, then I'll be free?''

Natasha shrugged and turned away. It was obvious that Seranne could get no more information from the girl. She tried to read her expression. Was she giving good advice? Seranne had no means of knowing. Only one thing was certain: if she took the cup and drank from it, she would be the gypsy leader's bride. Cassell would place her on the sacred stone and take her in full view of the entire tribe. That was something she would not—*could* not—allow to happen.

She shivered and closed her eyes. ''Dervil,'' she murmured. ''Dervil, my love, if only we could be together again, I would never ask anything except to be with you.'' The tears came then, hot and bitter, and Seranne laid her head wearily on her blanket.

12

By late afternoon, the entire camp was seething with movement. Preparations were being made for the wedding feast that night. It was almost as though Seranne's short absence from the camp had spurred Cassell into action. He wanted the golden woman safely within his tent so that he could fill her with his child.

The women were engaged in cooking the food that was to be served cold after the ceremony. Chickens turned on spikes of wood, spitting into the flames as the meat browned to an appetizing crispness. In the heart of the fires, pastries filled with cabbage and herbs cooked to mouthwatering golden brown, while in the pots bubbled eggs that once boiled would be crushed and mixed with spice.

The mushroomlike tents had been brightly decorated with pieces of silk spread out on long branches. The bridal lodge was new, the skins still fresh, clean and unweathered. Within were spread colored rugs and the bed was made of a brush pallet covered with warm blankets.

During the day, numerous gifts were brought to Seranne's tent where she was being prepared for her wedding. Mostly food was given as a symbol of prosperity but cooking pots were favored, being greatly prized.

Seranne was thoroughly washed, her body carefully oiled, treated with a waxlike substance that made her limbs shine. Her hair hung down to her waist and was combed until it was soft and gleaming.

Seranne longed to escape from the nightmare of it all but she was not left alone for a moment. Giggling women and children surrounded her, touching her body with innocent curiosity, exclaiming at her whiteness. Lewd gestures were made, indicating what Cassell would do to his bride when he had her on the sacred stone.

Kusha remained at a distance from the proceedings. Seranne guessed she had not been forgiven for her attempt to run away; the Tribe Mother had not believed for one moment that Seranne had merely left the camp on an innocent ride. It was clear that she now doubted the wisdom of the match between her son and the white woman. Seranne wished she could talk with Kusha and beg her to intervene.

The women were standing round her in a circle now, watching her with bright dark eyes. Seranne stood naked before them, wondering what was going to happen next. The air was stifling inside the tent and perspiration shone like jewels on her skin. She tried to speak to the women but they giggled, shaking their heads, and she knew it was useless; her knowledge of their language was pitifully scant.

The ranks suddenly parted and an old crone entered the tent. She carried a live cockerel in her hand and its wings flapped violently for a moment as it attempted to get free.

The crone held out a none-too-clean hand and

waved it toward Seranne, indicating that she kneel down. She did so but her eyes were wary as they rested on the woman.

In a sweeping movement, the crone drew out a blade and, before Seranne could move, the cockerel was hanging limp, blood pouring from its neck. The woman held it aloft as though to sprinkle some of the still-warm blood on Seranne's shoulders. She leaped to her feet and backed away, feeling so sick she could hardly speak.

The old crone turned in amazement and spoke to one of the women. In the buzz of talk Seranne heard Kusha, her voice raised in authority.

She said something sharply to the wide-eyed women and slowly they left the tent. Then Kusha came and stood before Seranne, her strong hands grasping her shoulders so that the old crone was free to complete her duties.

As the blood trickled between Seranne's breasts, she felt her self-control snap. She pushed the Tribe Mother away with a strength she'd not known she possessed.

"Leave me alone!" she cried. "I've had enough of this barbarism!" She tried to stop herself shaking as she cleaned the blood away.

Kusha spoke slowly in Russian but Seranne was too angry to attempt to listen.

"I will *not* marry Cassell!" she said fiercely, flinging the soft gown to the floor.

Kusha looked as though the skin had shrunken away from the large bones of her face. She might not have understood the meaning of Seranne's words but her actions were unmistakable. She turned and left the tent and in minutes the entire camp seemed silent and empty.

Seranne pulled on a thin shift to hide her nakedness, wondering what was going to be her fate now
that she had spoken the truth about her feelings.

It was more than an hour later and Seranne was
almost convinced that no one was going to bother her
again when she heard footsteps outside. The curtain
was pushed aside and two of Cassell's men stood
there, dressed in full regalia, towering over her.

They did not speak but she noticed that one of
them carried a whip and tucked in the belt around his
waist was a long, evil-looking knife. She stared at
them, trying to pluck enough courage to speak, but
the words would not come.

The two men stood in silence, guarding the doorway. Seranne, self-conscious in her flimsy shift,
looked for something with which to cover herself.
Even as she bent to pick up a blanket one of the men
moved, his knife at her throat, and she recoiled in
fear.

He stood silent and impassive and she resigned
herself to wait for whatever was going to happen
next.

She was stiff and uncomfortable standing facing
the men but she was afraid to sit down. She hardly
even dared to breathe; the man with the whip looked
as though he knew how to use it. She was almost
fainting with tiredness and fear by the time Cassell
pushed his way into the tent.

He seemed gigantic in his tight breeches and full
flowing silk shirt. Around his head he wore a ban-
danna and from under it his dark hair hung loose at
his shoulders.

Looking at him quite dispassionately, Seranne
could not argue about his fine looks. He was a hand-

some masculine man, but there was no sensitivity in him. He was all male and she would never be more than a servant to him. In any case, how could she give herself to him when she still ached with love for Dervil? Even though she knew her husband was lost to her forever, she could not betray the feelings she still had for him.

Cassell came to her and caught a handful of her loose swinging hair in his big hand. He twisted it so that her head was forced backward and then he was thrusting her down onto her knees.

"You deserve death for the disrespect you showed Kusha." His voice was harsh. "I will show you what the alternative of marriage with me is. Learn this lesson well, for whatever happens you will never be set free. You have been initiated into the tribe. You are one of us now, and subject to our laws."

He dragged her outside into the brilliant sunshine and threw her on the ground.

"You will be taken to the lodges of all those men who do not have a woman of their own. You will be allowed to choose which man you will live with and then come to me and tell me your decision."

Seranne stared at him with hard dry eyes. She was afraid to speak. She did not want to make him even more angry, but she felt a sense of rebellion rising within her. She was growing more determined that, whatever happened, she would not spin out the rest of her life in the gypsy camp. By one means or another, she would get away, even if it meant risking her life.

"Take her," Cassell said to his men. "And take her servant with her so that there will be a woman present. When you have shown her what she is to see, bring her back to me."

She was pushed forward and she found her hands being twisted cruelly behind her back. Cords were secured round her wrists and she winced, feeling the bite as the rope was pulled, dragging her, stumbling along the uneven ground.

After a few moments, Natasha ran across the clearing to Seranne's side, her face softened a little with pity. She did not speak and Seranne wished she had simply followed the girl's instructions and refused Cassell at the wedding ceremony.

The tents of the old ones were situated on the perimeter of the camp. Seranne was dragged forward and pushed roughly to where an old man sat huddled over a fire. His hat was pulled low over his furrowed face and a large nose jutted beaklike from between half-closed beady eyes. Around his shoulders was a thick blanket, coarse and matted with age. When he looked up at them, he grinned a toothless smile and prodded Seranne as though she were a beast up for sale in the marketplace.

"Do you wish stay here?" one of her captors said, dragging at the ropes that bound her wrists. Seranne shook her head emphatically. Grinning, the big man with a whip drew her away.

"Go," he said and she found herself inside one of the tents, her eyes blinking in the sudden gloom. The occupant of the bed in the corner appeared more dead than alive. His skin was drawn tightly across facial bones so prominent that he looked like a death's head. Only his eyes moved, and Seranne shuddered.

"Take me to Cassell," she said humbly, and she almost cried with relief as the men drew her outside into the warmth and light of the day.

She had made up her mind that she would beg

Cassell's pardon, go on her knees to him if need be. Nothing could be worse than a life spent caring for an old man, not even marriage to the gypsy leader.

Natasha followed as the two men led Seranne stumbling over the uneven ground toward Cassell's tent. The eyes of the women met for a moment and Natasha was the first to look away.

Seranne wondered if the gypsy girl thought her foolish for not wanting to marry Cassell.

He was seated in a huge chair inside his tent, his feet resting on a footstool of soft fur. He spoke quickly to his men and they nodded, obviously explaining to their leader that the Silver Princess had begged to be returned to him.

"You see?" He looked at Seranne with triumph in his dark eyes. "I am much more to your taste than the old ones, is it not so?"

"Yes, it is so." Seranne's words were barely audible.

Cassell reached for her, gripping her arm and forcing her down to her knees before him. His eyes were bright as he reached out and ripped at the bodice of her shift, tearing it to the waist so that her breasts were completely exposed. She jerked away from him as one of the men behind her laughed.

With a sharp nod, Cassell ordered the two men out of the tent. They went quickly, pushing a hard-eyed Natasha before them. Seranne tried to remain calm but panic rose inside her as Cassell reached out both hands, grasping her breast with a cruel fierceness. It was an act intended to prove that she was the slave and he the master, and tears of pain and humiliation came to her eyes.

His breathing quickened and his face was flushed as his hands moved over her soft roundness. Seranne realized that Cassell was hot with desire for her, and revulsion rose within her.

"We will hold the ceremony as planned," he said. "And at the moment the moon shows her face we will be joined before the eyes of my tribe."

His mouth came down on hers, savage and passionate. He was brutish and arrogant and Seranne knew it was useless to fight him.

"There." He smiled as he drew away from her. "I knew you would prefer my vigor to the fumblings of an ancient one. I thought one glance at what your future could hold would change your rebellion into submissiveness."

His hand was reaching down to her thighs and Seranne moved away from him, speaking quickly.

"It would be better if we kept our coupling for the right moment." She looked down, pretending a passion she did not feel. "I want you as eagerly as you want me, but our union would not be blessed with sons if we did not choose the right moment."

She was playing on the superstitious side of his nature and she could see him hesitate. She rose to her feet, moving toward the entrance to his tent.

"I must make my peace with the Tribe Mother," she said. "But I will be waiting as eagerly as you for tonight."

He looked for a moment as though he would draw her back into his arms but then he opened the flap of the tent to allow her outside. She made her way quickly across the clearing, almost running in her panic, unaware that Natasha had seen her holding the torn bodice over her breasts and believed that Seranne had given herself to Cassell.

Natasha bit her lip, jealousy searing her. She had been sorry for the pale foreigner, almost inclined to help her get away from the camp before it was too late. But now her heart was hardened; let Fate take its course; the girl had only herself to blame.

Seranne went immediately to her own tent and drew off the torn remnants of her shift. She quickly washed herself in the bowl of scented water that stood on the floor, left by the women who had attended her earlier. She felt unclean, and she rubbed her breasts as though to erase the memory of Cassell's cruel touch.

Quickly, she dressed herself in a sturdy cotton skirt and a brightly colored bodice, wrapping a thick woolen shawl around her shoulders. These were the clothes that the gypsy women would discard when they dressed for the wedding ceremony and Seranne would know exactly where to find them. Once she had spurned Cassell, there would no doubt be a terrible outcry. In the confusion, she could make her escape. This time she would not head toward the shore but inland with the hope of reaching St. Petersburg before she was missed.

The flap of the tent opened suddenly and a few of the women came silently into the interior. There was no laughter now, no gentle teasing. The women simply attended Seranne with speed and dexterity, anxious not to incur the disapproval of the Tribe Mother by showing the rebel white girl any sign of friendship.

The preparations seemed endless. Kusha, her face hard, stood by, watching carefully, ready to pounce on anything that was not done to her satisfaction.

Seranne's head began to ache. Her mouth was dry as she thought of the ordeal before her. If she was forced to lie with Cassell she would never be free.

At last she was dressed in the gown with silver

threads running through it and the outer garment was hung around her shoulders. The final touch was the crown of crystallized flowers, carefully placed on her head. Then she was ready.

She was led outside and she could see Cassell among the other tribe leaders seated around the largest of the fires. He was magnificently clothed in bright silks and around his great shoulders was a fur cape.

He rose when he saw her and stepped forward to meet her. In the center of the ring of bright fires, they sat facing each other but not touching, waiting for the ceremony to begin.

There seemed to Seranne to be a great deal of chanting. Then she was raised to her feet and, one by one, her garments were stripped from her as on the night of her initiation.

Oil was brought and placed between them and this time it was Cassell who rubbed the sickly smelling perfume into her body. She stood quite still, trying not to show her repugnance. When he had finished, he himself was divested of his clothes, and he stood tall and magnificent in the firelight.

She took the oils and rubbed them into his shoulders and chest and down over his strong thighs. He smiled as she knelt and smoothed the oil into his strong legs. His hand rested for a brief moment on her hair, the first gesture of tenderness she had ever witnessed from him.

The cup of wine was brought and with great ceremony was handed to Cassell by the Tribe Mother. He drank from it deeply, then held it high above his head. After a few moments, he passed the cup to Seranne and said a few words in his own language which she could not understand. He was smiling at her encouragingly, but for a moment she was not sure what to do.

"You must drink too, my Silver Princess," Cassell said softly. "And when the moon shows her face we will sow the seeds of the future generations of my tribe. Together we will make a golden harvest of sons, so drink quickly, and I will lead you to the sacred stone."

She was nearly hypnotized into obeying him. All around her was the beat of primitive music and the chanting of many voices. Above her the moon was emerging from the clouds; when it did, Cassell would take her body and use her. She forced herself to think of how her future would be if she accepted him as her husband. A thin note of warning seemed to ring within her.

With a great effort, she lifted the cup of white liquid over her head and threw it downward. The cup tipped and the liquid spread over the dried grass sinking into the soil at once.

A gasp went up from the watching people and as Seranne poised herself ready for flight she caught sight of Cassell's face. He was ashen, his eyes almost staring from his head.

"You she-devil!" he hissed. "Your action has cursed me with the shame of childlessness. The liquid was a symbol for my seed and you have cast it to the ground. For that you must die!"

She tried to run but he caught her arm and spun her round so that she was facing him. He struck her once across the face and she crumpled, her senses reeling. He straddled her and she thought he was going to kill her there and then with the knife he suddenly held between her breasts. She tried to scream but her voice would not come, and then she was aware of Kusha, pulling at Cassell's arm, ordering him to control his anger. His hold slackened; he drew away from her staring at her as though she was abominable to his sight.

"You have done a great harm, this day." Cassell's voice was low but the venom in it frightened Seranne more than a noisy outburst would have done. "You have taken away my right of leadership and for that I will have my revenge."

Kusha held up her hand and spoke to the restless people who stood in groups, talking loudly.

Her words were in Russian and Seranne could understand but few of them. It seemed the Tribe Mother was trying to explain that Seranne was not fit to be Cassell's bride. She was saying something about infidelity but the words came faster and Seranne stopped trying to follow them.

Cassell looked down at her; he was ice cold, his eyes glittering, his strong jaw clenched. She lay impassive, wondering if death was going to come swiftly, but then Cassell spoke.

"Kusha tells me that you are not coming to me pure," he said. "She says you have lain with others of my tribe. If this is so then you cannot be bride to Cassell."

Seranne thought quickly; perhaps this was a way out of the unendurable situation she found herself in. She remembered then, with sharp clarity, the fate of the young gypsy woman who had lain with a man not her own—torn to pieces between two horses.

"It's not true," she said desperately. "I have been with no man. If Tribe Mother believes me unfaithful to you, why has she remained silent so long?"

Cassell exchanged quick words with his mother and she pointed toward the moon. Cassell nodded and then spoke to his men.

A man carrying a whip lifted Seranne bodily to her feet and pushed her ahead of him. He gave a sharp order which she did not understand and then the lash swung in the air, cracking loudly before winding itself around her naked body.

She felt nothing for a moment and then it was as if she had been cut with a knife. Blood oozed in a line around her back and stomach and she screamed in pain and fear.

"Cassell, please don't do this!" She saw him look back at her and then he shrugged.

"It is out of my hands now. Kusha has told me that the moon did not shine on you when you took the cup from me. That is proof of the guilt you bear."

The man raised the whip again and pointed to the perimeter of the camp. Seranne had no choice but to move forward on trembling legs. Horror sped through her as she saw she was being taken to the place where the gypsy girl had been tied before her execution.

She was tethered like an animal, arms jerked above her head, and then left alone. The clouds were chased across the sky by the cold night breeze and Seranne hung her head in misery. She was going to die.

She felt someone creep up beside her. To her surprise, she saw Natasha carrying a cloak. The girl spoke in a low voice, her eyes downcast. She wrapped the cloak round Seranne's shivering body and then, like a shadow, sped away into the darkness.

13

By morning, Seranne felt half-dead with fatigue and terror. The dark hours of the night had been the longest she'd ever known. In her mind, she had imagined herself being torn apart, her limbs tortured and broken, her body mutilated.

She hung now against the cruel leather thongs that bit into her wrists. Her legs were so weary she could hardly stand upright, and yet any effort to relax her aching muscles meant that her arms were almost pulled from their sockets.

Pale fingers of daylight began to spread through the camp and the sounds of morning came clearly to Seranne as the women of the tribe prepared the first meal of the day.

Natasha appeared, a bowl of gruel in her hands, held forward as though a peace offering. Beside her stood the huge gypsy who had tied Seranne to the post the night before. He held his whip in his hand as though ready to use it at any moment.

But, to Seranne's great relief, the man untied her. She sank to the ground, wanting nothing more than to rest her aching body upon the soft grass. Natasha again offered the bowl and Seranne shook her head, too weary to do anything but stretch her cramped body.

"Must eat." To her surprise the man holding the whip spoke to her in English. "Come, Lee will help you." He sat her up against the crook of his arm as though she were a child and began to spoon the gruel into her mouth.

The food revived her, and as the sun rose, warming her chilled limbs, she began to feel alive again.

"What will happen to me?" she asked.

The man shook his head, his arm still around her. "I think you will be captive until after the leader is wed," he said, and nodded to where Natasha was kneeling on the grass. "She will be bride in your place."

Natasha held out her hands, sensing what was being said. She spoke rapidly in Russian and the man Lee waved his hand at her impatiently.

"I am Romani, I speak little Russian." He grinned. "But I learned the English good from sailors, like Cassell our leader did."

Natasha spoke again, more slowly, and Lee shrugged. "She says tell you she sorry for what happen."

Seranne struggled to sit up. Her body ached as though she had been savagely beaten and the line around her body where the lash had caught her burned fiercely.

Lee saw her wince. "I too sorry," he said. "But I watch you now, see you do not run from camp. If you try . . ." He shrugged, touching the whip with a large brown hand and Seranne was in no doubt that he would use it.

Lee lumbered to his feet and gestured for Seranne to rise. He seemed to have remembered that she was merely a prisoner and he the leader's trusted friend.

"I take you to tent where you must stay quiet and obedient," he said. "If you need me, I be kind—understand?"

She was led to a tent that was a little way removed from the others. Once inside, Lee bound her hands loosely and wagged the whip in her direction.

"Don't try to run," he said warningly. "I not like hurting you but if I have to then I will."

He sat cross-legged on the rough mat of skins and stared at her in a way that unnerved Seranne. He was a huge, almost ugly man, his hair long and curling on his shoulders, his eyes dark, unreadable.

"What is going to happen to me?" Seranne asked him once more and he shook his head.

"You will be taken before the elders of the tribe," he said abruptly. "After that, I cannot say."

The flap of the tent was pushed back and Lee got to his feet, having to bend his broad shoulders and lower his head, being too tall to stand upright.

Kusha came into the interior, her dark eyes cold as they rested on Seranne. She spoke rapidly, directing her words toward Lee. He shook his head violently as though disagreeing with the Tribe Mother. At last he turned to Seranne.

"Kusha says you should confess," he said and somehow Seranne knew that the anger in his voice wasn't against her. "You must tell how you lie with other men of the tribe," he continued. "If you do this, you might be allowed to go free."

"No!" Seranne spoke fiercely. "I won't lie." She looked appealingly at Lee. "When could I have done these things? There has been no opportunity."

"It might go better if you agree," he said. "Tribe Mother is wise and knows what is best."

Before Seranne could reply, Kusha had moved impatiently toward the entrance. She spoke quickly to Lee and stormed out of the tent without stopping to look back at Seranne.

He shook his head. "You have angered her. I do not know what she will do now. When you cast the marriage cup to the ground you cursed our leader.

Now you must be proved an unworthy bride before he can remain head of the tribe.''

A woman came into the tent and gestured with her head for Lee to leave them. She held out a long heavy white robe to Seranne and nodded, her black eyes flashing as she began to draw off the tattered cloak. Seranne jerked away.

"I am quite capable of dressing myself," she said, and if the gypsy woman failed to understand the words, she knew by the tone that her action was unwelcome.

Quickly, Seranne dressed in the coarse robe. It was shapeless, hanging to her feet, but at least it was modest, completely covering her body.

Lee returned to the tent and with him the guard who had previously accompanied her to the tents of the old men of the tribe. His eyes were alight and his mouth twisted into a cruel smile as he looked down at her. She knew instinctively that this man was her enemy; unlike Lee, he would hurt for the sheer pleasure of it.

She was pushed from the tent and out into the clearing encircled by the ring of fires. Cassell was seated on a raised dais, shaded from the sun by a canopy of scarlet and gold. He neither looked at her nor acknowledged her presence in any way. He stared directly ahead, a harsh set to his face.

Kusha came toward the group. She was dressed in a long cloak of dark fur and on her head she wore a turban of the same skins. She appeared regal and indomitable and Seranne's courage almost failed her. Kusha was a formidable opponent and would have no mercy.

"Thal." Kusha called the guard to stand before her and he obeyed. She spoke to him slowly in Russian and Seranne caught one or two words and guessed that the Tribe Mother wanted the man to speak against her.

"The woman was a creature demented," he said slowly in halting English. "She beg me to take her. I am weak and she cast such a spell I could not help myself."

Kusha spoke to him again and he shrugged. "It happened when I took her to the tents of the old ones. On the way we saw a young boy and he too had knowledge of her body while I watched. She was a beast, a she-wolf; she lay with the old ones and I could not stop her."

Seranne stared at the man in growing disbelief. No one could believe the foolishness he was uttering. Kusha was turning to her people, repeating in their own language the things the guard had said, and a shout of anger went up from the women.

Kusha held up her hand for silence. She stood over Seranne and asked her a question; behind her, Lee translated the words.

"Tribe Mother wants to learn from you the truth," he said. "Have you done these things?" In a lower voice he spoke again. "It might be wise to say what Kusha wants to hear."

"No!" Seranne screamed the word. "I am not what you wish to make me. I have done nothing wrong, nothing, do you hear me?"

Thal stepped forward, a sneer on his face. His hand reached out toward her and Seranne stepped back in sudden fear.

"There is a mark on the woman's breast, over her heart," he said. "Shall I show it and prove I have known her?"

He tore at the coarse material of the robe and

pointed in triumph as her breasts were exposed revealing a small birthmark.

Seranne stared around her in a mixture of anger and fear. "But I was tied naked to the punishment post," she said. "Anyone could have seen the mark."

Kusha raised her hand as the crowd of onlookers began to talk excitedly, pointing at Seranne in accusation. It was clear that to the gypsy tribe the white woman's guilt was proven.

"You must beg Tribe Mother's pardon," Lee said urgently. "Then she may show mercy."

Kusha began talking and from the expression on her face Seranne knew with a shrinking heart that she was uttering words of condemnation.

Lee took Seranne's arm. "Come," he said sadly. "You are to be prepared for death."

She was taken to a tent a little way off from the others, set in a triangle of trees. The interior was lit with candles and a form of altar stood at one end. Crimson cloth decorated with gold and silver hung over the shrine and upon it was a skull that had been cleaned and polished until it shone.

"Can't you help me, Lee?" Seranne asked, sinking onto the soft skins that covered the floor. "You were present all the time I was being taken to the tents of the old ones, you know that none of those things I'm accused of are true."

"I cannot help," Lee said. "You will be watched at all times until the hour of your execution."

Seranne felt fear run through her at his words. She bit her lip, trying to control her panic.

"I shall be watched but *you* won't," she said. "Look, Lee, go to St. Petersburg, to the Tsar Alexander, tell him of my plight and he will send help."

Lee shook his head. "I fear for my tribe's safety if I do such a thing," he said slowly. "Some may be killed if the soldiers of the Tsar come. You do not know what you ask."

Seranne touched his arm. "Would you have my death on your conscience, Lee?"

"Very well," he said slowly, "Lee will go to the Tsar. I will be cursed forever if I let you die, knowing your innocence."

She looked into his face and then he turned away.

She knelt at the foot of the altar and closed her eyes. She did not know to whom she prayed: the customs of the tribe were foreign to her, but with eyes closed, she asked for strength to face the ordeal that must surely come.

The hours passed with excruciating slowness. Seranne saw the sun gradually fading from the sky and the stars begin to shine. Soon the moon would slide from behind the clouds. Was that to be the hour of her execution? Everything the tribe did was in accordance with the cycles of the moon, so it seemed likely that her death would take place some time during the night watches.

Suddenly she came to a decision. She could not simply sit waiting for her death. She crept toward the front of the tent and cautiously lifted the flap. A burly guard barred the way. At the sight of her, he took a knife from his wide sash and held it toward her menacingly. With a sigh of despair, Seranne retreated once more into the dimly lit interior of the tent.

She had to find a way out of the camp before it was too late. She could depend on no one to help her. Lee would not be in time even if he did reach the Tsar.

She walked toward the altar. There, lying on it, she saw a curved knife, the blade gleaming in the candle light. She could only believe that Lee in his compassion had tried to help her in the only way he could.

She took it in her hands and thought of the man standing guard outside: even with a knife, she could not hope to win a struggle against such a giant. She went down on her hands and knees and crept behind the altar. She was at the far end of the tent now, with only the covering of skins between herself and freedom. Perhaps she could cut her way out.

Taking the knife, she forced it through the toughness of the skins, finding it far more difficult than she had anticipated. Her arm ached with the effort of making a jagged tear in the coverings and her breathing was uneven as she glanced over her shoulder, fearing discovery.

Beads of perspiration ran into her eyes. She forced herself to rest for a moment, then again she attacked the covering of the tent with a fierceness born of terror.

At last there was a hole just large enough to crawl through. With a quick glance behind her, Seranne wriggled through the aperture, holding her breath with fear. She was out under the night sky then, in the shadow of the triangle of trees.

Keeping low, she made her way around the outskirts of the camp. She would try to steal one of the horses, for she would have very little chance of escape, barefoot as she was, over such rugged terrain.

There was a guard sitting near the line of posts where the animals were tethered. Seranne paused, wondering if she should try to distract him by throwing a stone into the woods. Then she saw the man make himself more comfortable against the bark of the tree, his eyes closed.

She remained crouched in the shadows for what seemed an age. At last her patience was rewarded. The man's head fell against his chest as he slept.

She inched her way forward, eyes wide, ears straining to hear the smallest change in the guard's even breathing. She was just about to stand up and untie the rope that held the restless animals when she heard a sound behind her. The man had woken as suddenly as he had fallen asleep. He rose to his feet, cursing in the darkness as he searched around for the knife that had fallen from his grasp.

Seranne moved between the horses, making her way further from the man with every step. She was in danger of being trampled but her fear drove her on. She almost fell into the shelter of the trees and she lay there gasping for a moment, trying to recover from her terror.

She would not risk another attempt at taking one of the horses. She would have to make her way across country on foot. If she were fortunate, she might encounter a Russian peasant who would be willing to aid her. In any event, she knew she must put as much distance between herself and the encampment as possible before her disappearance was discovered.

She set off at a fairly steady pace, trying to ignore the stones that cut into her feet. Overhead, the moon shone brightly and Seranne knew that by now someone would have gone into the tent and found she had gone.

She walked until a pale daylight streaked the sky and then, exhausted, she fell into the shelter of some leafy shrubs and slept.

The sun was high in the sky when she awoke and

Seranne guessed it must be around midday. Cautiously she looked around her, wondering how far she had traveled during the night. In the distance, she thought she heard the sound of horses' hooves and in panic she began to run.

To her right was a huddle of trees and she made for the green dimness, throwing herself into the long grasses that grew in the shade. Her heart was beating so fast she had difficulty in drawing breath and her mouth was dry with fear.

The riders were in sight now and Seranne saw the brightly colored shirts and the wide bandannas of the men of the gypsy tribe. They must have discovered her escape almost at once and been searching for her since daylight. It was probable that Cassell would have led his men in ever-widening circles around the camp, realizing that Seranne could not have gone far on foot.

She lay quite still as one of the men rode into the trees, beating the ground with a long stick. He passed so close that she could hear him breathing, and she closed her eyes tightly, praying she would not be seen.

She remained where she was hidden by the grass until the last sound of hoofbeats had died away on the still, hot hair. Then, and only then, did she venture out into the open once more.

Too late, she realized that she had fallen into a trap. From four sides, riders advanced upon her. There was nowhere she could run.

Cassell himself caught her up roughly, flinging her across the saddle in front of him. His anger was apparent and she knew with a sinking of her heart that she was doomed.

"You enjoyed your taste of freedom?" he said

acidly. "You gained for yourself one more day of life but you shall suffer all the more for it, believe me."

It seemed little over an hour before they arrived at the encampment. Seranne ached in every limb from the jolting she had received on the journey. Cassell disappeared among the tents, leaving her hanging across the saddle, and it was Thal who caught her in his arms and placed her none-too-gently on the ground.

He raised his hand and slapped her, his hand stinging her cheeks so that tears came to her eyes. Another blow knocked her backward and she fell to the hard ground, gasping with fear.

She was aware of hands on her body then, like so many crawling insects, as she was divested of her torn robe. She struggled to rise, but with a harsh laugh Thal bent and caught her ankles, jerking them upward so that she fell on her back once more. Her legs were wrenched apart and Thal leered down at her as he tied a cord around her legs. He said something and made a lewd gesture and the other men laughed coarsely.

Two horses were led toward where Seranne lay and were placed tail to tail. The two ends of the bond that held Seranne's legs were tied one to each saddle. Half crazed with fear, she tried to wrench the leather thongs from her wrists but they would not budge.

Thal knelt across her body, his hands fondling her breasts. He smiled down at her, his body wriggling against hers.

"I could make it easy for you," he said, and he drew out a knife, placing it between her breasts and pressing lightly. A trickle of blood ran down her body and Seranne shuddered.

"I would rather die now," she said fiercely, knowing that even if she let the gypsy do what he liked with her, he could not save her from the execution.

She heard the voice of Kusha ring out and Thal moved away from Seranne quickly. It seemed that the ceremony of death was about to begin.

Seranne's head fell back against the earth; she tasted the dryness of the soil and looked up at the darkening sky, knowing that after the next few agonizing minutes she would never see or feel anything again.

Then Seranne became aware that the pounding she heard was not her own heart. It was the sound of hoofbeats echoing against the ground beneath her head.

Suddenly, into the clearing rode an army of men, sending swirls of dust rising into the air around them. Shots were fired and there were screams of terror from the women. Confusion broke out and figures were running in all directions. From the corner of her eye, Seranne saw Thal advancing stealthily toward her, and in a moment of dread she knew he meant to spur the horses into action.

He raised his arm, but even as she screamed, Seranne saw him arch backward, mouth open. He toppled with a terrible slowness to the ground, a knife plunged into his back.

Lee stepped over the guard's prone body and pulled the knife free. He came to Seranne and cut the cords that bound her, smiling as he helped her to rise. She saw blood on both his hands and then a great blackness swept over her and she knew no more.

14

It was becoming apparent to Mon that she was losing her battle to keep Dervil with her. As his health and strength returned, so his restlessness increased, and it was only a matter of time before he took his leave.

She had grown to love him in a way she had never loved before. She wanted his devotion as much as she wanted the sweet delight of his body, but his thoughts were centered always on this golden-haired one he called Seranne and she knew he would not rest until he found her.

After that time when he had lain with her in a state of drug-induced passion, he had been angry. But his natural needs had grown too strong for him and he had soon become her constant lover. He had given her such joy that Mon could not bear to think of life without him. She would have fallen on her knees and begged him to stay if she thought it would do any good. But the time was fast approaching when he would leave her, and in her heart she knew what she must do.

She would go back to the camp and learn what had become of the English girl. She was no doubt married now to Cassell and firmly entrenched in the gypsy way of life. She might even be filled with child. If this was so Mon would tell Dervil; then perhaps he would forget this Seranne. But she knew there was a risk: Dervil might try to take the woman away from Cassell, and the gypsy leader would not let his woman go without a fight.

She heard movement from the bedroom and placed

the pot of eggs over the flames of the fire.

Dervil entered the room, his broad chest naked and browned by the sun. His face was covered by a thick beard and above it his mysterious silver-gray eyes stared at Mon as if searching her very soul.

"There is something wrong?" she said and he nodded slowly, his hands resting on her shoulders.

"But you have been good to me, Mon." He could speak her language quite well now. She had spent long evenings teaching him the words and his quick mind had enabled him to absorb everything she told him.

"I am only good to those I love," she said simply. "I would die for you." She turned away from him. "I will go look for your woman, the one you call Seranne. I have heard stories of her and I will learn the truth for you."

His face was suddenly alert, eager, and it pained Mon to have such clear proof of his feelings. He caught her arm, turning her round toward him.

"What have you heard, Mon? Tell me!"

She shrugged. "I know only that there is a stranger in the camp of the gypsies. It may be she, it may not. But I must go alone." She spoke firmly. "You would not be welcome and no one would talk if you were with me."

He went to the door, his hand resting on the handle, the hot sun shining onto his face as he stepped outside. He walked along the front of the hut and stared out toward the sea and Mon slowly went after him.

She rested her cheek against his warm back, her hands around his waist. Hot tears burned her eyes as she tried to speak.

"If I find her and she still wants you, I shall do my

best to return her to you." It cost her a great effort to
say the words that would sever her life from Dervil's,
but she knew deep inside her that they had to be
spoken.

He turned, taking her in his arms, his chin resting
on her head. "Find her, Mon."

She eased herself away from him and went inside
the hut. She picked up her bag of herbs, tying it to
her belt, hardly able to see for the tears in her eyes.

She left him still staring out to sea and slowly
walked away, her steps as heavy as her heart. All she
could hope for now was that the woman had made a
new life for herself with Cassell. He was a handsome
man and as his wife she would have everything she
wanted—women to wait on her, the best food and
wine, the reverence of the rest of the tribe. She had
enough. It was unjust that she should have Dervil
too.

Mon sighed. But then this Seranne had tasted Dervil's love, and any woman would be foolish to give
up such delights, whatever might be offered in their
place. She could not believe that the golden-haired
girl would prefer to live in the gypsy camp; she would
want to return with Mon once she heard that Dervil
was alive. She wondered at her own foolishness: what
had happened to the Mon who cared only for herself?

It was Dervil who had changed her. She had
learned through him what it was to really love another human being. Even if she should lose him now,
she would not have changed the last few weeks.

The sun was hot overhead and her footsteps
dragged through the dusty soil of the track. She was
unusually weary, her pace slow. It was as though
summer was never going to end this year and yet Mon

knew from experience that winter could come down with terrifying suddenness. The sky could change from blue to gray almost in moments, the bitter easterly wind sweeping white thick snow over the land, smothering everything and making journeys such as this one an impossibility.

Her spirits lifted. If this girl should be with child then she would be compelled to stay in Cassell's tent at least until the little one was born. In such circumstances, Mon would be justified in telling Dervil that his woman was content. If she could keep Dervil with her in the little hut until the snows started, she would have him for the entire winter months. Who knew what could happen in that time?

At last the encampment came in sight. There seemed to be a great deal of activity around the perimeter and Mon paused for a moment, unsure of what she should do next.

She heard loud cries and then a booming noise pierced the heat of the day with a suddenness that frightened her. She could hardly believe what her senses told her. There was a battle going on at Cassell's camp.

She hid behind the trees, making slow, cautious progress over the ground, determined to learn more even though her heart was pounding with fear. There was a shout of pain and before her startled eyes a man in soldier's uniform fell to the ground, clutching his chest from which jutted a large evil knife.

She crouched down among the dry bracken and long grass, her hands clinging to the warm bark of a tree. The soldier's limbs continued to twitch uselessly for a moment before he became suddenly still.

She could not understand what was happening. Why should soldiers attack Cassell's camp? She forced herself to go forward and she cursed as she fell over a stump of a tree, grazing her arms as she hit the ground.

She lay there for a moment, winded, and the action saved her life because a small party of soldiers rode right past her, sabers raised, horses plunging through the undergrowth near her.

She lay panting for a few minutes, fear making her mouth dry. When the soldiers vanished into the distance, she dragged herself forward, inching nearer the camp.

The battle must have been a fearful one. Mon could see that many of the tents had been put to the flame and smoldered even now. Some men had been killed and their women wept over them. The fighting seemed to have taken place in the hours of darkness, and it was apparent that the soldiers had claimed the victory.

Gradually, the soldiers were leaving, mustering a short distance from the camp. Mon realized it was best to remain hidden until the last soldier had left the camp. She would see then if she could help in the nursing of the injured.

She gasped as she saw a big, deep-chested soldier with gold on his uniform, leading a woman toward the tethered horses. She had long flowing hair that shone in the sunlight, and Mon recognized her at once. Her heart sank. So the golden one still lived. Bitterness filled Mon's breast as she saw the girl lifted onto a horse; from the slimness of her body, it was obvious she was not with child.

Suddenly, the impact of what she was seeing hit her with such force that her head was spinning. Everything would be all right. She could go back to Dervil now and tell him the truth: the woman had disappeared, no one knew where.

When the last of the soldiers had ridden away Mon went forward, still cautious, and looked round her. The camp was in an utter turmoil and it would take many days to restore order.

She saw Kusha emerge from her tent, one of the few not burned to the ground. Mon went forward quickly, her hands supporting the shaken woman.

"Retribution has come upon us," Kusha said. "It is the curse of the English girl." She refused to weep; she was upright and dignified even in her grief. "My younger sons are dead," she said. "But there is still Cassell. He must rebuild the tribe, and when we have buried our dead we will look to the future and not the past."

"You will not seek revenge?" Mon asked quietly and Kusha shook her head, her shoulders straight and proud.

"We have no time for revenge," she said. "Now we must care for the wounded. Will you help? I see you have brought your bag of medicines."

"Yes, I will help." Mon knew she had no choice but to stay. Much as she wanted to return to Dervil and tell him what had happened, she was needed here and these people were her friends. As though reading her thoughts, Kusha touched her arm lightly.

"You would be welcome to travel with us when we leave," she said quietly. "We could always use your skills and our way of life is a good one."

Mon nodded. "Thank you, Tribe Mother, I will think about what you say."

She left Kusha and went to where the wounded were gathered under the shade of the trees. Fortunately, many of the injuries were slight. It seemed that the main object of the soldiers was simply to take the English girl because, had they wished, they could have wiped out the entire tribe.

It was almost nightfall when Mon at last made her way back along the dusty route to the hut. Her body ached from bending for hours over the wounded men and she would have spent the night in the camp if it had not been for Dervil. She longed to lie in his arms and smell the masculine scent of him.

She heard a rustle to one side of her and froze for a moment, wondering who was lurking in the darkness of the trees. She edged forward and smiled in relief as she heard the soft neighing of a horse.

"Come on then, my fine lad." She took the bridle in her hand and patted the animal's head. If she could calm the creature, she would be able to ride home in comfort.

After a few minutes, she gained the animal's confidence and swung herself lightly into the saddle. She sent up a small prayer of thanks, happy to be making her way more rapidly toward home. She guessed that the horse must have belonged to one of the soldiers. It was a fine, well-groomed animal, elegantly accoutred. She would release the creature once she arrived at the little hut; she would not like to be accused of horse-thieving.

The hut came into sight and Mon's heart began to beat rapidly. She pictured Dervil waiting inside for her, the candlelight flickering over his handsome face. Perhaps he would make love to her tonight, hold her in his arms and fill her with passion by his touch.

She saw the door open as she approached and Dervil came outside, his strong arms reaching up to lift her to the ground. He looked at the horse, studying the saddle and the scarlet blanket beneath it. She watched him in bewilderment.

"If I'm not mistaken, this is one of Tsar Alexander's horses. Where on earth did you get it?"

"I found the stallion in the woods," she said. "I was very happy not to have to walk all the way home." She looked up at him, impatient with his interest in the animal. "Don't you want to know what I have learned?" she said, slipping her hands into his.

He gave her a quick look. "Well?" he said sharply. "Are you saying that you have found Seranne?"

He looked tense and strained and Mon felt her spirits drop. He was not going to forget the girl as easily as she'd hoped.

"She's gone," she said quickly. "She was at the camp but last night she disappeared." Mon felt his bruising hold on her arms.

"She didn't just disappear. Did the soldiers of the Tsar take her?"

"Yes, they took her," she said. "She was quite happy to go with them, they didn't take her by force." She leaned against him. "The girl is all right, Dervil. She does not need you—not the way I need you. Can't you forget her and stay with me?"

He appeared not to hear her. "That means she will be taken to St. Petersburg. The Tsar is a civilized man; he will look after her. I trust those ruffians at the camp treated my wife with respect."

"They are not ruffians," Mon said in defense of the people who had become her friends. "She was given the highest honor the tribe could bestow, she was to have been Cassell's bride."

"Cassell?" His voice was low.

"He is the tribe leader, the woman was to marry with him," Mon said.

She knew there was more to the story than that. Somehow the golden-haired one had disgraced herself, but exactly what had happened was a mystery.

"What are you hiding from me?" Dervil said.

She shook her head. "Nothing. All I know is that this morning when I went to the camp there had been a battle and I saw the girl go away with a soldier who had gold on his coat."

"On horseback I should take only a few hours to reach St. Petersburg." It was almost as if he were talking to himself and Mon felt the thrust of pain. He was going to ride away out of her life without a qualm. She could have hated him if she had not loved him so much.

"No!" She clung to him, pressing her face against his shoulder and he became conscious of her despair.

"I'm sorry, Mon," he said, his arms around her gently. "She's my wife. You knew I couldn't stay here forever." He tipped her chin up so that he could look into her face. "Now, listen to me. I didn't ever lead you to believe that I was in love with you."

He spoke the truth. He had lain with her and given her great joy but he had never said he loved her, and she'd been content to take whatever he offered. Now, with the thought of his leaving, she felt her life stretch before her unendingly. Perhaps one of her potions that brought on the long sleep would be the solution.

"Stay at least for tonight," she begged. "It isn't asking much and you won't catch up with the soldiers before morning anyway. She will be safe with the great Tsar Alexander, you said so yourself. Please, give me this last gift and I will never ask anything of you ever again.''

He looked up at the darkness of the sky and then uncertainly at her pleading face. At last he relaxed and drew her close to him.

"You are right Mon," he said softly. "It's doubtful I would cover the ground to St. Petersburg tonight. I'll leave at daybreak." He carefully tethered the horse to the post at the side of the hut, and taking Mon's hand led her inside to where the single candle flickered down to a stump and then went out.

It was like an omen, Mon thought, the snuffing out of her life, but first she would live a lifetime's loving in the few hours that were left.

He was so ardent yet, even as Mon felt him pierce her body, mingled with her joy and ecstasy there was a feeling of loss. This would be the last time she would hold him in her arms, then they would be empty. Suddenly she decided there would be no tomorrow.

When he slept, she rose from the bed and lit a fresh candle. She brought out her potions and studied them before drinking from one of the small flasks. She looked up to see that Dervil had stirred. He was staring at her, his silver eyes full of questions. She smiled at him regretfully.

"Yes, I want to die but you bear no blame. You have given me happiness beyond imagining. I can't live without you, so I have made my choice."

The room was becoming darker already and Dervil seemed to move toward her at a slow, ponderous pace. He took her arm and shook her, a cloud over his eyes.

"You mustn't die, Mon." He brought her a cup of

water, forcing the liquid between her lips. She tasted salt like brine and then she was retching violently. She felt faint and so ill. Why didn't he just let her die?

But he was determined to save her life. Mon was aware of his presence throughout the haze of the days that followed. Within her was the warm feeling that he had not left her alone, in spite of his wish to find his woman. That proved he must love her, if only a little.

She lay on her bed not knowing if it was night or day. She was laughing one minute and crying the next. All through the long hours and days he was beside her, caring for her, repaying his debt.

As the days stretched into a week and then two, Mon became aware of something else. She had sensed changes in her life rhythms but she had hardly taken any notice. Now, however, she could not fail to realize that growing inside her was Dervil's child. As she lay in bed, allowing him to feed her thin warm gruel, she felt movement and she knew that her own life had been spared for this end, that she should bear the Englishman's son and bring him up to manhood.

No longer did she cry that her arms would be empty. She accepted that Dervil would leave her once she was well. She would not tell him of the baby he had planted within her, for he might come later and take the child away. That was a secret she would keep. Once she was recovered and had said good-bye to Dervil, she would pack up her few belongings and join with the tribe of Cassell.

She no longer wished to live alone; she wanted people around her who would care for her and her baby when he came. A warm glow came into her heart and she sat up and smiled at Dervil who was sitting anxiously at her bedside.

"All will be well now," she said, and the truth felt good within her heart.

15

Fenn Cornwallis coughed a little as he walked along the elegant corridors of the Tsar's palace in St. Petersburg. He had arrived in Russia in the spring, just in time to experience the sudden cold snap that fell like a blight over the country. The icy wetness had affected his health and the long hot summer, remarkably lengthy by Russian standards, had improved the dry cough only a little.

Tsar Alexander the First, Emperor of Russia, had been concerned about the Englishman and had sent for someone to nurse him back to health. It was strange, Fenn reflected, that only now when autumn was in full flood had he discovered that his brother and Seranne had made the journey from England to be at his bedside.

He had been astounded to hear the story of the shipwreck and of the death of his brother Dervil. The subsequent abduction of his sister-in-law by the gypsy leader they called Cassell was now the talk of the palace. Seranne had come a long way from the little innocent she had been when they met in her native Devonshire.

He congratulated himself now on the fact that he had convinced Alexander of Seranne's willingness to become his mistress. The Tsar had taken an immediate interest in the girl when she had been brought to his palace. Half-naked, suffering from shock and fatigue, she had nonetheless looked beautiful. Her skin was tanned a pale gold by the sun and her hair fell in shining masses over her naked breasts. Fenn himself might have been inclined to renew the old relationship that had existed between them had he not felt he would be better rewarded by bartering with Alexander for the use of her charming body.

It had been very discreetly done, of course, as befitted a gentleman's agreement, but Fenn had come out of the bargain considerably richer, well content with the gift of gold and the priceless amethyst brooch Alexander had given him for his trouble.

He had yet to speak with Seranne, convince her that the Tsar would brook no refusal, but he anticipated little trouble in that quarter. His dear sister-in-law would surely find the handsome Alexander a more civilized bedmate than the ruffian of a gypsy had been.

He tapped the door of the room lightly and went inside without waiting to be bidden. Seranne was in the huge canopied bed, looking small and frail against the silk of the sheets.

"Are you better?" He smiled, knowing that his charm still served him well in spite of the decline in his health. At any rate he had suffered no lack of Russian beauties with whom to amuse himself during his stay at St. Petersburg.

Seranne looked at him coolly, her eyes wide and still incredibly innocent. It was difficult to believe she had been at the mercy of the gypsy menfolk for the best part of the summer.

He crossed the room and sat beside her, taking her small hand in his. Her skin was creamy and he could see the gentle swell of her breasts under the night-gown she was wearing. Something stirred in him for a moment and then impatiently he brushed the feeling aside. There was no room for remembering or for conscience. The Tsar was not a man to be thwarted.

"Alexander has done you the honor of inviting you to dine and drink with him." He smiled warmly, unaware of her rising panic. "He is a handsome man as well as being rich and powerful. You should consider yourself honored by his interest in you." He leaned forward, speaking confidentially. "Come now, dress in your finest gown and make yourself agreeable. You'll be well rewarded."

"No!" The word exploded from her rosy lips and Fenn stared at her as though she had suddenly grown two heads.

"What?" he said sharply. "You can't refuse the Tsar of Russia! Don't be absurd."

Tears came into her eyes. If Fenn had not known better, he might have mistaken them for a girl's natural fear of losing her chastity.

"I will not be the plaything of the Tsar," she replied. "I'm not a harlot, whatever you might think."

"Of course not." Fenn decided it would be best for the moment to humor her, but somehow he would have to make her understand that she had no choice in the matter. He had given Alexander his word that Seranne would go to his apartment that night and he was not going to allow the girl's sudden scruples to ruin the arrangement.

"Look, Seranne," he began persuasively. "This man has the power of life and death here, don't you realize that? He's determined to have you, and if you refuse him, I'll be blamed."

Seranne fell silent, biting her lip and Fenn pressed home his advantage.

"In any case, my dear Seranne, does it really matter if you sleep with Alexander after all that has happened to you? Remember this, he is a kindly, civilized man; he will treat you far better than any gypsy could."

"I did not sleep with Cassell," Seranne said quickly. "He intended to marry me, you must believe me." She leaned toward him and, breathing in the rich scent of her, Fenn regretted for a moment that he himself was not going to enjoy her.

"You might be speaking the truth," he said. "But who is going to believe you? No, my dear, you are a very different prospect from the young innocent who left England's shores, you might as well realize that, here and now."

"Fenn, please, don't make me do this." Seranne was clinging to his hand, begging him in such an earnest, endearing way that Fenn kissed her soft mouth impulsively, almost inclined to renege on his deal with Alexander and keep her for himself. Her response was startling.

"Don't!" She recoiled from him as though he was poison, rubbing her lips with the back of her small hand, staring up at him with large reproachful eyes. Who did she think she was anyway? Anger filled him and he moved away from the bed.

"Be ready when I come for you tonight," he said sharply, "otherwise it will be the guards who will take you to Alexander and, before they do, they

might decide on a little amusement with you themselves."

He walked quickly from the room, his anger making him cough. The bitch, pretending to be the little
innocent! As if anyone would believe that. Who did
she think she was deluding? Not him, certainly; he
knew her too well, much too well. He returned along
the corridor to his room. He would rest a little during
the heat of the afternoon. He felt quite out of sorts
and it was all the fault of that little whore back there.
Well, she would do as he said or it would be the
worse for her. He went into his room and closed the
door silently behind him.

Seranne was in tears. She sat up in her bed, trying
to think clearly. It seemed to her that though Fenn
called Cassell a ruffian, he was worse than the gypsy
leader had ever been. He was acting as little more
than a procurer for the Tsar. The trouble was
Seranne believed he spoke the truth when he said that
Alexander had the power of life and death over them
both.

She had survived the months in the encampment
without once having been forced to betray her own
inclinations or her love for Dervil, and it seemed
ironic that when she'd apparently reached safety she
was at her most vulnerable.

She rose from the bed and went to the window.
The air in the room was hot and sultry; it was as
though this summer had no end. Seranne longed for
the cool green fields of England. If only she could
put back the clock and start afresh from the time her
aunt introduced her to the Cornwallis brothers. She
would have seen through Fenn's facile charm at once
and she would have recognized the qualities pos-

sessed by Dervil. But it was no good worrying about
what was past, she could not change it in any way. It
was the present she must think about: what was she
to do when the Tsar summoned her to his presence?

The question was still unanswered an hour or two
later when there was a tap on her door and a woman
she had never seen before entered the room. She was
tall and slim, her hair severely styled and to Seranne's
surprise she spoke in French.

"You are feeling rested, *ma chere*?" she asked
solicitously. "I see there is some color in your pale
cheeks now. When they brought you here from the
clutches of that horrible man, I thought you were
standing at death's door."

She took a seat beside the bed and stared in open
curiosity at Seranne.

"I hear those people have very strange rites. Did
you take part in any ceremonies?"

She leaned forward eagerly, her eyes half closed as
she waited for Seranne's reply. She seemed excited
and Seranne felt a strange stirring of resentment that
she could not explain.

"I can't talk about it, I'm sorry." She stared at the
woman, her chin lifted. "May I ask you who you are
and what is your business with me?"

"Oh, how silly! I am no one of importance, I
simply came to help you dress. Your dear brother-in-
law Fenn asked me to find some suitable gowns as
you had nothing of your own."

"Thank you for the kind thought," Seranne said
slowly. She wanted the woman to go and leave her
alone. She felt uncomfortable under the scrutiny of
those heavy-lidded eyes, and she had the strong
suspicion that this woman's role was to attend to the
wishes of the Tsar's mistresses.

"Oh, goodness me!" The woman rose to her feet. "I'm not doing this out of kindness, *chèrie*. Now, we have a variety of clothes including undergarments as well as shoes at our disposal. Let me see." She put her head on one side, studying Seranne. "You are small but well made . . . I think I know the sort of gown that would suit you very well."

She swept to the doorway and, without a backward glance, went as quickly as she had come.

Seranne felt bemused; it seemed that all the high-born Russian ladies were taught to speak French from birth, though with Napoleon invading the country it was a practice that must surely be discontinued.

The creak of her door drew her attention and then Fenn was leading the way across the carpet followed by a young girl carrying an armful of clothes. The servant laid them carefully on the bed and bobbed a curtsy before hurriedly leaving.

"It's time, Seranne," Fenn said slowly, his eyes alight with amusement. He stood, hands folded across his chest, watching her as she turned over the silk gowns without any interest. She was startlingly beautiful, her body more mature than he remembered, her breasts full and high, her hips well curved. She was desirable and mysterious and it was no wonder Alexander wanted her.

Seranne retreated behind the screen at the end of the room and began to dress, fear burning within her as she struggled with the high-waisted gown. She had grown used to the simple skirts and bodices favored by the gypsy women and her hands faltered as she slowly fastened the row of buttons down the back of the dress. She slipped her feet into the softly colored pumps and at last she was ready.

Fenn was tapping his foot impatiently on the floor when she emerged from behind the screen and he grasped her arm, propelling her along the corridor without even bothering to speak to her. She was aware of high ceilings and dazzling chandeliers and then she was being pushed unceremoniously into a vast bedroom. She shrank against the door, looking around her with fast-beating heart and dry lips.

There was a gorgeously draped bed dominating the room and, standing guard alongside it, two soldiers in the uniform of cuirassiers. Both men were tall, their height accentuated by the leather helmets topped with horsehair crests and bearing the motif of the imperial eagle. Gilt epaulettes gleamed in the candlelight and both men wore silver waist sashes with orange strands.

One of the soldiers rested his hand on the saber hanging at his side and Seranne hastily averted her eyes. She feared these harsh-faced soldiers more than she had ever feared the gypsy leader.

She stared around her, seeking an escape from the room. Her eyes were drawn upward to the highly decorated ceiling with white patterns in grisaille, which at first appeared to be raised plasterwork but was merely an illusion created with paint.

To her left, on a low table, stood an exquisite gold basin inlaid with lapis lazuli and amber. It contained scented water that was heady and sweet. Seranne moved toward it very slowly, watching the soldiers carefully, fearing they might attack her at any moment. In sheer desperation, she had decided to overturn the basin, cause confusion during which she might make her escape from the room. She didn't allow herself to consider what she would do then. As she touched the cold rim of the vessel, the door suddenly opened and she froze in dread.

He was taller even than his soldiers. The Tsar Alexander stood smiling at her and as he advanced across the room she saw that he limped slightly. He was handsome, with fair curling hair, broad in the shoulders, lithe and slender at the hips. He came directly to where she was standing and put both hands on her arms, holding her away from him, studying her with a scrutiny that was almost cold.

He spoke in Russian but so quickly that she couldn't even guess what he was saying. He clicked his fingers and one of the guards leaped to attention, bringing the Tsar a tray containing crystal glasses sparkling with wine.

Alexander held a glass to Seranne's lips, almost forcing her to drink. The wine was sharp and clear and Seranne coughed a little as it touched her throat.

Then the Tsar suddenly drew her to him, holding her close, and his lips came down on hers, crushing and bruising. Too surprised to draw away, she leaned against him, struggling for breath.

He scooped her up and placed her none too gently on the bed and then he was laughing at one of the guards, gesturing to the man to undo the many buttons at the back of Seranne's gown.

"No! Don't touch me, please!" Seranne said quickly but Alexander either did not understand or did not care about her protests. He held her flat against him and she felt the big clumsy hands of the guard break open the buttons; then, between them, he and Alexander pulled the gown away from Seranne's shoulders and down over her hips.

The guard resumed his position at the head of the bed, staring straight ahead of him, as though nothing untoward was happening. He fingered the saber at his side and the gilt fitting gleamed. It was a silent threat and Seranne knew there was no escape.

Alexander quickly removed her underclothing, tearing at the fine fabric in his haste. His eyes were alight and she felt as though he were a bird of prey and she his victim. She couldn't believe this was really happening to her as her last garment was removed and she fell back against the pillows.

The eyes of the guards flickered over her as she huddled, completely naked, down into the softness of the bed. She watched in horrified fascination as Alexander stripped off his dressing gown and then knelt between her legs, his big hands forcing her knees apart.

"No," she said but the word was like a sigh. It was obvious that he was completely dominated by passion now and nothing she could say would make any difference. He meant to have her and she was too terrified to fight him.

He remained upright between her thighs as he penetrated her body. He thrust forward pitilessly and Seranne felt she was being torn apart. He held her legs wide with his hands, savagely moving against her unyielding flesh. There was no gentleness in him; she was not a woman to be loved and caressed and wooed, she was merely a chattel, a means of bringing him bodily release.

His movements went on and on, and now the guards were openly watching the spectacle, smiling a little as she grimaced with pain. One spoke to the other in Russian in quick, soft sentences and made a gesture toward his own body. Seranne closed her eyes, pressing back the tears that rose to burn beneath her lids. She had escaped from Cassell and the gypsy laws only to be brought to this. She felt she couldn't stand the pain and humiliation a moment longer.

Alexander's large hands gripped her breasts, the fingers biting into her flesh until she could have screamed. His thrusting became increasingly frenzied and then he uttered a low, guttural noise before falling heavily onto her, covering her body with his so that she could hardly breathe.

He lay there panting for a moment and then raised himself up on his elbows, smiling down at her in satisfaction. He spoke in halting English. "You see how it is, my dear; we Russians know how to make love. We have stamina and vigor and I'll wager that your gypsy leader did not make it last so long as I."

Seranne tried to reach out and cover herself with the counterpane but one of the guards pulled the cover back again. The Tsar laughed.

"You are surely not shy, little one, not after the many men you have had at the camp?" Still laughing, he ran his finger along the outline of her breast, tweaking her nipple. He climbed from the bed and walked across the room, pouring himself another drink, gulping it down without a pause. He was like a stallion as he stood there quite unconcerned about his nakedness, and Seranne realized that he had no idea he had raped her. He simply thought he was yet another man to add to the long list he imagined she'd been with at the gypsy camp.

Fenn must have put the idea into the Tsar's head, and for a moment anger flared in her. Then she sank back onto the pillows with a feeling of hopelessness, tears coursing down her cheeks.

Alexander came back to her and stretched out at her side, his hand caressing her cheek.

"What is it, why do you cry? Have I failed you?" There was real concern in his voice and Seranne found herself blurting out the story of her stay at the camp.

"I was never taken by Cassell or any of his men," she sobbed, trying to speak slowly so that the Tsar would understand. "I was going to be his bride—mother of his children—I was held in respect right up until the last moment. . . . And then somehow everything went wrong and I was accused of many things that weren't true."

"Don't be sad," he said gently, not understanding a word of what she'd said. "I didn't give you enough time and that I regret." He smiled at her. "But I will make it up to you, I will give you jewels and many gowns of the finest velvet. I will take care of you."

He raised himself over her and Seranne saw that he was aroused once more. Before she could speak, he was upon her again and was thrusting against her, forcing her reluctant body to yield to his.

He was so fierce that Seranne felt she could not endure it. It took all her strength of will not to scream out loud. It was a relief when at last he relaxed against her, holding her close to him, trying in his own way to convey his gratitude to her.

He was not an evil man, she realized; he had simply been misled about her. He imagined she welcomed his advances; it was inconceivable to him that she might be revolted by his touch.

He drew on his gown, went to a chest in the corner of the room and from it he took out a thick gold bracelet set with rich rubies. He slipped it onto her wrist with a smile and leaned over and kissed her.

"Tonight, you will have the honor of sleeping with

me in my bed," he said gently. "I will prove to you that I am a man capable of great things with a woman of my choice."

Seranne sank back against the pillows, closing her eyes, feeling utterly defeated. She almost wished she had died back there at Cassell's camp because then her torture would be ended. As it was, she felt used and cheap and she did not know how she was going to live with herself in the clean light of day.

16

Seranne woke with Dervil's name on her lips. Her cheeks were wet with tears, and as she moved she touched warm flesh and remembered with a sense of despair what had happened the previous night. She edged over to the side of the bed as far away from Alexander as she could, but her movement disturbed him. He opened his eyes and looked at her without recognition for a moment, then his eyes warmed to laughter.

"Seranne, my sweet, pale English beauty, why have you drawn away from me? Come." He reached out a long arm and slipped it around her shoulders, drawing her close to him, his touch more gentle than it had been the night before.

"I didn't do you justice last night." He leaned over her, looking down into her face. "I was too full of good wine and my own selfishness." Under the bedclothes, his hand fondled her breasts and inwardly Seranne was tense, her hands clenched to her sides, hating him. He treated her body as though he had every right to explore its secret places.

"I will enjoy you, Seranne. . . . You are a jewel to be worn with pride."

She heard his words with dismay; she hated him and what he was doing against her will. Yet her anger ebbed, for Alexander spoke with kindness, treating her as though he cared for her. She was totally vulnerable. All she could do was lie passively as his hands began to explore her body with ready familiarity.

He cupped her breast in his hands and his mouth was warm against her skin. She longed to recoil but she forced herself to stay still and quiet, allowing him to do as he pleased.

"You are beautiful, little Seranne," he murmured in his thick, accented voice, "but there is no life, no spirit in you. I cannot touch your heart."

She wanted to scream at him that her heart and soul belonged to Dervil, and always would, even though she had lost him. She would have kept her body pure too if the choice had been hers to make. It wasn't, but though Alexander could command her submission he would not force her to respond to him.

He pressed his hands down the flat of her stomach, sliding his fingers over her slender hips, touching her legs, her thighs, his breathing harsher as his passion grew.

Her eyes flickered to where the guards still stood at attention and she knew they were covertly watching what was happening in the great bed.

"Do your men have to stay?" she said in a small voice as Alexander bent to kiss her mouth. He stared at her in surprise for a moment and then gave a careless shrug.

"Pay them no heed. They must stand guard at all times. Do not concern yourself with their presence, it is of little consequence."

He threw back the bedclothes, exposing the length of her body, and she shuddered, trying to hide herself with her hands.

Her small protest ignored, Seranne resigned herself to the humiliation of being taken again by the Tsar in the presence of his soldiers. She winced as he possessed her with renewed swiftness and vigor, piercing her tender body with hard thrusts, knowing nothing but his passion as he rode her with less sensitivity than he might show a spirited filly that needed breaking in. She tried to remain expressionless, aware of the curious looks from the two guards, but as her ordeal went on and on she felt the tears flow down her cheeks. She brushed them away with the back of her hand, afraid of Alexander's anger should he see her distress.

Later, he had hot water brought up to the bedroom and he insisted on washing Seranne himself, much to her embarrassment. She stood in his porcelain bath as immovable as a statue, while Alexander tenderly smoothed soap over her breasts and down between her buttocks, his hands caressing, his mouth kissing hers from time to time.

"You have bewitched me," he said. "I am entirely fascinated by your beautiful body, I can think of nothing but making love to you." He paused. "Only one thing upsets me, Seranne. You are lacking in passion and I feel I do not please you."

How could she tell him the truth—that she endured, not enjoyed, his attentions, that she would like nothing better than for him to leave her alone? She hung her head, unable to speak. Alexander knelt before her, pressing his mouth into the hollow between her thighs. She closed her eyes, wondering how she could go on accepting his familiarities without protest. He looked up at her.

"You are tired? I prove too much for you, is that it?"

She nodded slightly, allowing him to draw any conclusions he wished. Her spirit seemed to have vanished; she was apathetic, unable to fight the despair that had fallen like a cloud over her since the moment the Tsar had first violated her body. Until then, she had been able to think of Dervil with some sort of peace but now she had betrayed his memory and there seemed no point in anything anymore.

Alexander wrapped her in a towel and, laughing, carried her to the fireplace, sitting her on his knee and patting her dry as though she were a child.

"We shall have our food served up here in my chamber," he told her. "I will have a rest from the state affairs and we shall be alone together for a little while." He kissed her lips and the damp tendrils of hair around her face. She closed her eyes with a feeling of revulsion as he slipped the towel away from her shoulders, his eyes greedy as they rested on the fullness of her breasts. "You are so white and so beautiful, Seranne," he said, his fingers on the pinkness of her nipple, squeezing a little before placing his lips on her breasts.

She tried not to shiver but her body was numb. Would he never be sated? Was she to suffer his lovemaking at all times of the day and night? She didn't know if she could bear to live under such strain.

"You are chilled," he said. "We will have some refreshments before I take you back to bed. I mean to warm you to life, my pale English girl.''

A procession of servants brought food on silver trays, small delicacies to tempt any but the most jaded palate, but Seranne could not eat, not even to be polite. The moment she put a piece of game pie cooked in fluffy pastry into her mouth she felt as though she would be ill.

She was very conscious of the fact that she was wearing nothing under the silk robe given to her by Alexander after her bath. It was as though she were to be ready at all times should he call upon her to make love. *Love!* The very word was a bad joke, she thought bitterly. Love didn't enter into the arrangement. It was simply that he had the use of her body whenever he chose even though he did make some attempt to show her a little consideration.

The woman with the severe hairstyle whom Seranne had met the previous day came into the bedchamber, smiling at Alexander, kissing his cheek lingeringly, her hands on his shoulders.

"Are you enjoying the girl?" she said in French.

Alexander frowned, moving away from her as he picked up a succulent piece of chicken between his fingers. "I have told you not to speak French," he said. "It is the language of our enemy, can you not remember that, Madelaine?"

She pouted a little and touched his cheek with a white, beringed hand. She leaned over him with easy familiarity and helped herself to some food from his plate.

"I am half-French myself, Alex, dear—or had you forgotten that?" She smiled at him, her large eyes sweeping over him and then over Seranne, as though trying to gauge the atmosphere between them. "You have not answered my question, Alex. Are you enjoying her or is she as cold as she looks?"

She spoke in Russian now and Seranne understood a little of what she was saying. She kept her eyes downward, however, waiting with a sense of tension, hoping the Tsar would agree that she was indeed cold.

"She will warm, given time," he said. "At least she is young and fresh, not an old experienced hand like yourself, Madelaine. Just because you were my first woman, you presume too much. I will not have you prying into my life. Now go." He spoke with an amiable impatience and the woman grimaced at him. She leaned forward and whispered something in his ear. His eyes darted quickly to Seranne and then he nodded.

Madelaine went out, swinging her body in the slim-fitting gown of heavy red satin that shimmered sensuously over her hips. Alexander's gaze followed her and Seranne harbored the sudden hope that he might return to his old love, especially when he found that Seranne would never warm to his caresses as he hoped.

Madelaine returned after a few minutes with a crystal glass containing a glowing amber liquid, which she held out to Seranne.

"Come along, drink it quickly. It is a remedy for poor spirits; it will do you good." Her English was faultless and Seranne wondered how such an obviously well brought up lady could so lower herself as to wait upon the Tsar's women.

Madelaine spoke quickly to the Tsar in Russian and Seranne managed to make out some of what she said. She stared at her empty glass in horror. It appeared that Madelaine had administered some kind of love potion to her.

The drink seemed to burn her throat and her blood began to race. Her skin was tingling as though suddenly alive to sensations and when Alexander touched her shoulder, heat coursed through her entire body. She suddenly longed to fling herself into his arms.

He reached out, with tantalizing slowness, and pushed her gown from her shoulders, his fingers leaving brushstrokes of fire as they touched her skin.

"Beg me," he said, smiling at her. "Down on your knees and beg."

His face seemed to waver before her eyes as, obeying him, she dropped to her knees. She pressed her face against the hardness of his body, aching for him to take her. One part of her yearned for him, but another part of her cried out at what she was doing. Her sense was eserting her and she tried desperately to shake away the effects of the drink. With an effort, she rose to her feet, but the Tsar drew her gown from her and she stood before him naked. Then it was his turn to kneel.

She was torn in two. Her body was singing under Alexander's strong fingers and as he knelt before her, his mouth on her stomach, she flung her head back, arching herself like a wanton, waiting for him to bring her delight. The other side of her stood watching the spectacle in disgust and disbelief. Her head was beginning to reel and the two parts were quickly merging into one, a being crying out for bodily satisfaction.

The Tsar set her down on the carpet and straddled her body with his. He seemed to be quenching a fire between her thighs and she wanted his thrusting to go on and on and never stop. She could hear a woman laughing in the background but she didn't care. All she wanted and needed was relief from the desire that was almost a pain.

She pulled Alexander's face down to her own, kissing his lips, his neck, his strong shoulders, and when he fell panting on top of her she cried out for him to start all over again.

He laughed and caught her up in his arms, carrying her to the bed and she clung to him, holding him close, her eyes closed, her head flung back in ecstasy as he lay beside her, his fingers probing, moving, his mouth on her breast.

She was possessed. In her mind, he had become Dervil and they were tossed by the stormy seas and she was happier than she had ever been in the whole of her life.

Fenn, walking in the heat of the afternoon, stood for a moment under the high arched windows of the Tsar's room. He heard unmistakable sounds of passion and he grimaced to himself, recognizing Seranne's voice, even though he couldn't make out what she was saying. That she was enjoying herself was quite obvious, however; he felt a deep regret and a slight surprise at the thought. By all accounts the Tsar was a vigorous and strong lover and it was becoming doubtful that Seranne would ever want to leave him.

Fenn stared ahead of him as he continued on his way through the grounds. Ahead of him he saw a figure coming toward him on horseback. He recognized the rider at once and his mouth was suddenly dry. His brother! Dervil was alive! Fenn was frightened of the consequences of his hasty action in giving Seranne to Alexander and felt a moment of utter panic.

He took the few minutes in which Dervil was dismounting from his horse to pull himself together and then he went forward, hands outstretched, as though delighted to see his brother safe and well.

"We thought you were at the bottom of the sea," he said quickly. "It's wonderful to see you! What happened? Where have you been all this time?"

"That will keep," Dervil said, slowly eyeing his brother's face with suspicion. "Is Seranne here at St. Petersburg?"

"Yes, she's safe," Fenn said and caught at Dervil's sleeve as he made for the steps of the palace. "Wait. There is something you should know."

"All I need to know is that my wife is alive," Dervil said, and then he became aware of the embarrassed look on his brother's face. "What is it? Come on, Fenn, don't keep me waiting." His voice was dangerously quiet and Fenn shuddered.

"Seranne has become the Tsar's mistress," he said in a rush, deciding that the truth was the best policy, or at least half of the truth. There was no need to mention his bargain with the Tsar.

"I don't believe you," Dervil said, the words jerked from him as he gripped Fenn's collar. "If he has raped her, Tsar or not, I'll kill him!"

Fenn thought quickly. A scene would not help him at all. He had a good life here and he didn't want it spoiled because of his brother's hotheadedness. He remembered the noises he had heard under Alexander's window and drew his brother toward the spot, hoping the little love scene was not yet over.

It was not. The sounds of passion came clearly on

the quiet air and Dervil's face changed, becoming almost as gray as his eyes.

"The vixen," he said, and before Fenn could stop him, he had turned and run toward the entrance of the palace, his dark hair flying behind him.

Fenn followed at a more sedate pace; he did not even try to run these days because of the weakness in his chest. He hoped that his brother would have the good sense not to offend the Tsar but then Dervil had always been hasty and lacking discrimination. Some people thought of Fenn as calculating but at least *he* did not rush into a situation without looking very carefully at the consequences.

He followed Dervil up the wide staircase and saw him cautiously open a door. Fenn walked silently up behind his brother. Peering over Dervil's shoulder, he saw Seranne lying naked across the bed, laughing hysterically, with Alexander beside her, his hand cupping her breast.

The couple were unaware of intruders. Even as Fenn watched, Seranne put her arms around the Tsar's shoulders, drawing him down toward her. He heard his brother utter a soft exclamation and then Dervil strode along the corridor, his face beaded with sweat.

"The whore!" he said in a low fierce voice. "I will never forget or forgive her for this as long as I live."

He made his way toward the spacious, carpeted landing and bounded down the stairs as if all the demons in hell were at his heels. Fenn leaned over the elegant gallery and called to his brother, careful not to raise his voice too loud.

"Where are you going, Dervil?" He saw his brother pause and look back at him; if he hadn't known Dervil better he could have sworn there was regret in his silver-gray eyes—but of course it was just a trick of the hot Russian sunlight.

"I'm returning to England," Dervil said in a flat voice. "There is nothing to keep me in Russia any longer." He looked up at Fenn with something of his old sarcasm. "If you become ill again, you will have your sister-in-law to look after you. I don't doubt she does that very well too." He turned and left the palace, and shortly afterward, Fenn heard the sound of a galloping horse. He sighed with relief; that had been just a little difficult. A smile twisted his lips. Seranne could not have rid them of Dervil more effectively if she'd set out to try.

He went to his room and sat on the bed. He felt very tired. This Russian weather was no good to him at all; it was either too hot or too cold. He shivered, determined to forget about his brother's sudden unwelcome appearance. Dervil had depressed him with his sarcasm and anger and Fenn was only too glad that he had not thought to place the blame on anyone except Seranne herself. It could quite easily have been a nasty situation, very nasty indeed, except that the quiet, subdued Seranne had suddenly turned into a wanton.

He lay back on his pillows and was almost asleep when the door opened and Madelaine came into the room, her bright eyes full of an invitation he could not resist.

He took her in his arms and she gave a low laugh. "It has quite inspired me," she said.

Fenn suppressed the irritation he felt at her cryptic statement. She was always doing that, making a mystery out of everything and waiting to be coaxed into telling him.

"What has inspired you?" he said and she laughed

again, her arms creeping round his neck.

"Why, giving that prim little miss an aphrodisiac of course." She kissed him and then leaned back in his arms. "It was quite amusing to see how badly she wanted dear Alex once that elixir began to work. I think she will exhaust him before nightfall."

Fenn laughed delightedly, smoothing back Madelaine's dark hair, his hands cupping her face.

"Have I ever told you how clever you are?" he said, and, ignoring her puzzled look, he drew her down into the bed and began to unfasten her gown.

17

Seranne had been living a dreamlike existence ever since she had drunk the elixir given her by Madelaine. She had difficulty in telling if it was night or day, her eyes were unusually heavy and her brain sluggish. But she did remember the frenzied lovemaking between herself and Alexander, and she remembered too imagining that she had seen Dervil standing in the doorway.

He had seemed so real. His hair swung back darkly from the strong set of his face and his eyes were the silver-gray she remembered so well.

As she slowly shrugged off the effects of the drink, she began to feel shame and disgust. She had coupled with Alexander in the manner of a whore, discretion thrown to the winds as she craved physical satisfaction. She was quite ready to believe that she would have lain with anyone so long as the heat of her body was quenched.

She realized it was not her own fault; she had been influenced by the drug and she had been powerless to avert the events that followed. Nevertheless, she despised herself. She became so low in spirits that she began to feel nothing really mattered anymore.

The winter came down quite suddenly and she looked out of her window one morning to see a heavy blanket of snow covering the ground. She heard the servants saying it would be a short winter, coming late as it did, and she heard too that the cold and ice were defeating the French army, driving them back the way they had come, depleting Napoleon's troops so badly that it seemed only a handful would ever return to France.

But all that was unimportant to Seranne, immersed in her own private misery, and even though she could see that Alexander was becoming impatient with her continued apathy, she could do nothing to rouse herself from it.

When the Tsar came to her bed, she accepted him with total lack of response. Now he was merely using her body, without trying any longer to please her. She knew the day must come soon when he would find fresh amusements and it could not come quickly enough for her.

She had barely spoken to Fenn, though she saw him of course at the brilliant balls given by Alexander. It was on these occasions that the Tsar was most demanding. He read the interest in other men's eyes and knew that Seranne's pale beauty was something of a novelty. On such nights, he would weary her with his repeated attacks on her body.

He did not treat her gently any longer; indeed, it seemed he was incapable of anything but the vicious assaults on her which brought him the satisfaction he craved.

The wintry weather was keeping the entire population of St. Petersburg close to their homes, so the palace became the focal point for glittering meetings. Seranne was shown off like a doll in a glass case: all could look but none must touch.

Alexander came to her room one evening in fine spirits and told her that there was to be a ball in celebration of the French retreat.

"They have been driven back by the Russian winter," he said joyfully. "The snow has them on the run and I shall follow the army of Napoleon into Europe as soon as I have organized my own troops." He kissed her shoulder. "In the meantime, Seranne, we shall continue to enjoy our alliance."

She attempted a smile. She could think of nothing to say to him. She could not bring herself to lie, yet to tell him the truth—that his touch merely aroused revulsion in her—was out of the question.

"Be cheerful," he said, tipping her chin up so that he could look into her eyes. "I have a surprise for you, a fine burgundy velvet gown so that you will look even more beautiful and desirable at the ball."

He drew her onto his knee, his hand slipping inside the bodice of her gown, freeing one of her breasts. His touch was heavy, far from gentle, and Seranne had to force herself to be calm and not to scream out loud. How she hated his persistence.

"Your lovely breasts will be shown to advantage," he said with satisfaction. "The gown has been fashioned so that it plunges deep in front, your skin will look so creamy in comparison to the rich velvet.''

She tried to move away but he held her fast. ''Take off your clothes, little Seranne,'' he said breathlessly. ''I want to make love to you right here and now.''

''But I'm expecting one of the servants to bring refreshments at any moment,'' Seranne said quickly. ''Perhaps it would be better if we waited until later.''

''I cannot wait.'' He pushed her up against the wall and lifted her skirts. Seranne held him away, her heart beating swiftly, her mouth dry.

''Please, Alexander, not like this—let's at least go to bed.'' She spoke almost desperately.

He took no notice of her and she felt his hand touch her stomach, smoothing her skin, pushing her clothes aside impatiently.

''No, Alexander.'' She tried to twist away but he slipped his hands round her buttocks, holding her so tightly that she winced in pain.

He was panting like some great beast and then he lunged at her awkwardly, hurting her in his effort to achieve penetration. She moaned aloud. His lips were on her neck and he was murmuring to her, unaware of her pain and humiliation.

''You see how you like it? It feels good, does it not? I am a big, strong man and I can satisfy even you. Say it, Seranne, say you like it.''

Seranne had suffered agonies in her efforts not to offend the greatest man in the whole of Russia, but to endure being held against the wall like a country wench was too much for her to bear. She pushed at his shoulders, her puny strength making no impression as he lunged again and again.

''Say you like it,'' he repeated breathlessly and something in her mind seemed to burst like a thousand stars.

"No!" The word was wrung from her and she felt her fists tighten into small hard weapons with which she hit out at the man subjecting her to such degradation.

He stopped moving for a moment in sheer surprise, then he uttered a curse and twisted her hand up against the wall above her head. She was pinned in such an awkward position that she screamed in pain.

He continued the assault on her body with ruthless strength until at last, sated, he let her fall to the ground. She lay there sobbing, her hair covering her face. Alexander pulled her to her feet.

"You hate me so much?" he said, his voice clipped and hard. Seranne tried to draw away from his imprisoning hands.

"No, I don't hate you," she said truthfully. "But I cannot love you either, or desire you."

She was afraid to look at him and there was a long silence which grew more tense as the minutes passed. She expected him to flare up in anger, to hit her even, but he simply sat looking at her as though he couldn't believe his eyes.

At last he spoke. "Then I shall not trouble you again," he said with dignity. "I do not have to force my attentions on any woman."

She hung her head. "Forgive me, your Excellency. The lack is not in you but in myself. I can feel nothing for any man because the only one I ever loved is dead."

"Very well." The Tsar spoke levelly, as though discussing a business proposition. "You will continue to come to my room for the time being but I will not touch you." He gave her a long look. "I cannot have it said that any woman has tired of me. You understand?"

Relief was sweet and it made her generous as she smiled at him. "No one will learn anything from me," she said. "In any event, it must have been noticed at court that you are less ardent toward me of late. It may be you've found someone more worthy of your attentions."

He shrugged. "You are very sensible and I will be sorry to lose you." He looked at her carefully. "Are you sure there is no man in the court who takes your fancy? Once I have formed a new relationship there is no reason why you shouldn't find a lover." He smiled thinly. "Remember you could have any man you chose now, because you have been my mistress."

"There is no one," Seranne said quickly.

"That is all then." The Tsar rose to his feet. "But at the celebration ball, we shall dance the polka together and everyone will believe that you are still madly in love with me."

He left her then, and Seranne fell onto the bed exhausted. She slept for almost an hour, at peace now that the ordeal of being Alexander's mistress was over.

The ball was magnificent. Candles gleamed in huge chandeliers and the paneled hall rang with the sound of laughter and music. It seemed that the French retreat had eased the atmosphere of strain which had hung over everyone during the heat of the summer, bringing a lightheartedness that was infectious.

Seranne was almost happy in the knowledge that once the dancing and festivities were over she could go to her own bed and be left entirely alone. She smiled as she saw Alexander dancing with a tall, silky-haired young girl. She wore a pale pink gown that billowed as she swung into the Tsar's arms. It looked as though he was wasting no time in showing the world that he had a new conquest.

He danced with Seranne several times, laughing down at her with such friendliness that Seranne wondered why she'd ever been afraid of him. Why had she taken so long in telling him how she felt? she wondered. But then, perhaps she had chosen just the right moment, when his desire for her was on the wane and there was a new paramour eager for his attentions.

Fenn came toward her, threading his way between the dancers, his eyes hard. She felt her heart flutter with nervousness, knowing instinctively that the Tsar had made the situation known to him.

"So it's over then," he said without any preliminary greeting. "He's tired of you much sooner than I thought. You couldn't have been trying very hard, could you?"

"It's nothing whatsoever to do with you," she heard herself saying bitterly. "I think you have lined your pockets well at my expense."

"If it had gone on a little longer, I should have done much better—and you too, dear sister-in-law—but then I suppose you've been too stupid to ask for gifts."

"Please, Fenn, just leave me alone," Seranne said quietly. "I have no wish to quarrel with you. I just want a little peace, that's all."

A tall young man with heavy eyebrows and a thick moustache came over to where they were standing and bowed over Seranne's hand. She caught a glimpse of the sudden, speculative light in Fenn's eyes and knew at once what he was thinking.

The young man asked her in a low, guttural voice if she would care to dance. Seranne shook her head.

She could see that Fenn was wondering if he could make something out of the situation and she intended to dispose of that idea at once.

"Thank you, no," she said firmly to the young man. "I'm waiting for the Tsar Alexander to ask me to dance and in the meantime I think I shall just sit and rest."

The young man bowed and left her and Fenn gave her a look of utter exasperation. He came closer to her and spoke quietly.

"What are you saving yourself for, Seranne? You have the reputation of being one of the most exciting courtesans perhaps in the whole country, so why not use it? You could make yourself a great deal of money and some fine friends too." He looked around the glittering ballroom. "Don't you realize that there are people here from all parts of the world? Rich, influential people. You could if you wished become one of the most sought-after women in the land."

"Why do I need riches?" Seranne asked him in a low voice. "I was born rich, remember, and it brought me no happiness. I was kept so isolated from the everyday way of living that when *you* came I actually mistook you for a fine man." She turned a little way from him, tears brimming in her eyes. "As for friends, I have none, not here, except for perhaps the Tsar himself. All the rest want to do is make use of me—you most of all, Fenn."

He touched her arm. "Look, Seranne, this is not the time to start weeping," he said impatiently. "The Tsar is approaching. Try to appear pleased to see him. He might yet find you attractive enough to want you occasionally in his bed."

Alexander swept her into his arms and as the music

began Seranne was whirled around into the fast moving dance, her hair flying away from her face, the soft material of her gown clinging to the curves of her body.

"You look most beautiful tonight," Alexander said as he drew her closer to him. "I almost regret giving you up. You do not feel inclined to change your mind about me, do you, Seranne?"

She smiled. "What has happened to the young girl in the pink dress? Is she not waiting impatiently for you to return to her?"

"Perhaps," Alexander said. "But it is my way to keep such women waiting, they are too eager and that cools my ardor." He leaned closer to her. "It is the reluctant ones like you who have the power to arouse passion."

They danced in silence for a moment and then Alexander spoke again.

"I see that you are already the center of attention. It is being rumored that our affair is waning and the young men are all anxious to be first with you. Is there one you like?"

"No," Seranne said shortly. "I have told you that there is no one I want, no one at all."

"Very well," Alexander said. "But if I thought there was a lover I should be very angry. It would not be good for you to take another man while still officially my mistress."

"I will have no difficulty remembering that," Seranne said quickly. "I assure you once more, there is no one."

He swept her to the side of the ballroom and released her, smiling down at her from his great height. Yet, in spite of his apparent warmth, she sensed something different in him, almost as though he didn't believe that she had formed no other attachments.

It was an evening that Seranne would be happy to see come to an end. She danced again several times with Alexander, but though she tried to speak to him, he was inclined to be offhand, almost hostile, and at last she simply gave up the struggle and remained silent.

She was relieved when the guests began to drift away and she was able to retire. She felt hot, in spite of the coldness of the weather outside, and she was happy to take off her gown and to rinse her face from the bowl of scented water that stood on the table beside her bed.

Seranne was almost asleep when she heard the handle of her door begin to turn. She sat up quickly, holding the bedclothes around her. She felt her heart begin to beat fast as a large figure loomed out of the dimness.

"Alexander?" she said, wondering if he was going to break his word and impose himself upon her once more, but when there was no reply from the man coming toward her, she began to feel afraid.

She opened her mouth to scream but then a hand clamped over her face and a warning hiss forced her into silence. She tried to struggle as she felt the man slip into bed beside her. Her hand came in contact with his cheek and the heavy eyebrows and she knew at once it was the young man who had approached her at the ball.

"How dare you!" she said in a fierce whisper. "Get out of my room or I'll scream so loud I'll arouse the entire palace."

"Come along, you do not fool me for one minute," the man said heavily. "The Tsar has finished

with you. Everyone knows the dark-haired woman
shares his bed tonight. Come, let us enjoy ourselves
—you will not regret it, I assure you.''

"Get out of my room!'' She slipped from his grasp
and made for the door but he caught her before she
could open it and flung her roughly to the floor.

"Why are you resisting me?'' he asked in bewilderment. "Is it that you like to fight?'' He lay across
her, pressing his mouth against hers, and she twisted
away from him, crying out her disgust and anger.

She scrambled to her feet and this time she managed to open the door, running out into the long corridor and standing for a moment in uncertainty before making her way to Alexander's room.

She flung the door of the royal bedchamber wide
and stopped in her tracks. Alexander was kneeling
between the legs of the dark-haired girl who was
writhing in ecstasy under his touch.

"Leave us!'' His voice held anger and outrage and
it was a moment or two before Seranne had the
presence of mind to close the door on the scene of intimacy.

Of the young man who attacked her there was no
sign. She felt it doubtful if he would return now that
she had made such an uproar, but once inside her
bedroom she pushed home the heavy bolt, just in
case there were any other intruders.

She realized that Alexander must be terribly angry
with her. He was not the sort of man who would easily forgive her rashness in rushing uninvited to his
room. All the same, she felt that once she'd explained
the reason for her haste, he was bound to understand.

She slept only fitfully and in the morning was not
surprised to find Madelaine knocking at her door,

telling her in a peremptory manner that the Tsar would see her before breakfast.

She dressed quickly, wondering what Alexander would say. Surely, once he fully understood the circumstances, he would be forgiving.

Alexander was sitting up in bed wearing his burgundy dressing gown and he was obviously in a very bad mood. As Seranne was ushered toward the bed by Madelaine she realized that Fenn was present too. He was standing near the window, looking pained and indignant.

"We wish you and your brother-in-law to leave the palace at your earliest convenience." The Tsar spoke as though she were a complete stranger. His eyes were cold and his features set in hard lines. In the early light of morning, he looked more than his thirty-five years.

"If I could explain about last night—" Seranne began but he held up his hand for silence.

"I do not wish for explanations. It was unpardonable for you to come to my room the way you did, and what the reason was I do not care."

"But I was attacked in my own room," Seranne burst out. "And I turned to you for protection, is that so strange?"

"You are no longer entitled to my protection," the Tsar said icily. He leaned back against his pillows and stared at her, his eyes hard and angry. "As to this attack, I find that difficult to believe."

Seranne fell silent. She could not talk to the Tsar. Even in the height of his passion they had not communicated. For a brief time he had appeared to offer his friendship, but that was gone now; all he felt for her was disdain.

"As soon as the snow melts, you will return to

England," he said positively. "Now leave us and please remain out of sight until you go. I have no wish to see you again."

Seranne inclined her head and moved out of the room to be followed at once by Fenn.

"You fool," he said angrily. "You little fool." He gripped her arm tightly. "Well, you shall pay for your stubbornness when we get back home! You'll pay—and in full."

18

It was with mixed feelings that Seranne stepped ashore onto English soil once more and she was acutely aware of the deep differences in her own personality. It had been a young eager girl in love with life who had left these same shores less than a year ago and now that girl was gone forever.

Fenn dealt with everything as he'd done from the moment the Tsar of Russia had cast Seranne aside. She had the deep-rooted suspicion that Fenn had bargained with Alexander, talking him into making a parting gift of sizable value intended to console Seranne for the loss of her position in the palace.

She did not know if it had been money or jewels the Tsar had given to Fenn, and what's more she did not really care. She found she cared about very little these days. She had sunk into an apathy that was increasingly difficult to shake off.

The arrangements were that she should accompany Fenn to London; once there, she assumed he would see to it that she had her own establishment. To be left alone was all she asked.

She badly needed time to find herself again and now, as they rode through the rainy London streets, she found it difficult to associate herself with any of the events that had taken place in Russia.

Hearing the swish of wheels on the wet road and seeing the ordinary English faces of people around her, it seemed inconceivable that she had lived with a band of gypsies, taken part in their rites and later became the mistress of the Tsar of Russia. But it was all in the past now and she badly wanted to forget it.

The house where Fenn took her was on the outskirts of the city. It was a tall, elegant building with a look of tranquility about it that appealed to Seranne immediately. Inside, there was an air of worn leather and the smell of beeswax which brought memories of her old home in Devon rushing back into her mind.

"I think I'd like to rest," she said to Fenn. "May I choose my own room?"

"I suppose so." Fenn said ungraciously. "But I have merely borrowed the house for a few months. There has been no time to make any permanent arrangements."

Seranne went up the wide curving staircase and wandered along the corridors opening doors. She looked into the rooms, breathing in the atmosphere of the place that seemed dear and familiar even though she had never seen the old house before. It was just that she was home again in England, she told herself; everything here was so entirely different from Russia that she needed to reassure herself it was all real.

She settled at last on a moderate-sized room that already had a cheerful fire burning in the grate. The crackling of the logs and the drum of the rain on the windows was so homey that Seranne sat on the bed and cried.

There was a tap on the door and a young girl in a neat cap and apron brought in the tea tray. She set it down on a small table near the bed and bobbed a curtsy.

"Afternoon, madam," she said. "I'm Betsy. The master told me to ask if there's anything you need."

By the way the girl spoke, it was obvious that she had fallen under Fenn's spell already. Now Seranne wondered how anyone could be taken in by his facile charm.

"Thank you, Betsy." Seranne made an effort to control her tears, wiping them away surreptitiously with her fingers. "This looks fine, I don't think there's anything else just now."

The girl went to the door. "I'll help you to unpack later, shall I, madam? That is if you haven't brought a maid of your own."

"That's very kind of you, Betsy." Seranne was regaining her composure. "I would very much appreciate your help."

When she was alone, Seranne took off her coat and bonnet and laid them across the bed. She put the tray near the fire and sat on the floor, drinking the fragrant tea, relishing the warmth of her surroundings. She was feeling something like contentment creeping over her, although she doubted whether she would ever find true happiness again.

After tea she curled up on the bed and slept. There were no wild dreams to disturb her, so when she woke she felt refreshed and rested.

She was surprised to see that it was dark in the gardens behind the house. A pale watery moon was sliding from behind the clouds, and for a moment she shivered, recalling her initiation into Cassell's tribe under the huge, brilliant silver moon of Russia. It was so unreal now, almost as if she had only dreamed the experience, and yet she could remember in clear detail how she had almost been executed before the Tsar's men had rescued her.

"Seranne! I'm speaking to you." Fenn was coming into the room toward her and she stared at him absently for a moment, unable to bring herself back to the present.

"Look alert for heaven's sake," he said impatiently. "We have a visitor—Lord Prayton—so come downstairs at once. And be sure to look your best."

"I'd prefer to stay in my room," Seranne protested, but Fenn brushed her words aside.

"Nonsense!" he said. "This is Lord Prayton's house, we are here by his generosity, so you must at least be civil to him. How do you think it would look if you didn't even put in an appearance?"

"All right," she said wearily. "I'll be down in a little while, just give me a chance to find something to wear."

"That is all arranged," Fenn said quickly. "While you slept, I had your clothes hung in your wardrobe. And mind you take care over your appearance. I'm tired of seeing you in those dowdy clothes you insisted on wearing aboard ship." He smiled cruelly at her. "Clothes won't alter what's under them, you know. Dull colors won't bring you respectability."

"Leave me alone," Seranne whispered, but the truth of what Fenn said cut her to the heart. He was right; she was little better than a whore and nothing was ever going to change that.

When she looked among the gowns hanging in her cupboard, she realized that Fenn was determined she would look the part of a courtesan. All her modestly cut gowns were missing, leaving only those with low-cut bodices fashioned from thin, clinging material that revealed more than concealed.

It was clear she would have to wear one of them; the only alternative was the outfit she had traveled in and that was mud-stained and creased, not fit to wear before guests.

She did find a shawl, however, and with this draped around her almost naked shoulders, she felt a little more comfortable. She left the peace of her room reluctantly and went down the stairs, surprised to hear the ring of laughter from the dining room. It was feminine laughter and there seemed to be quite a lot of people present from the sound of the voices.

Fenn came to her side at once and deftly removed the shawl before she could make any protest. She felt all eyes turn toward her and was aware of her breasts protruding from the low-cut gown.

"This is our famous, or should I say infamous, Seranne," Fenn said out loud. "Now don't all you gentlemen clamor at once, there will be ample time to get to know more about her colorful past."

Seranne felt so humiliated that she longed to rush from the room, away from the curious, amused eyes that stared as though she was a caged animal. But Fenn was propelling her forward, leading her to a vacant seat beside an elderly, white-haired man whose lined face and crinkled eyes looked out of place amongst the crowd of younger, more boisterous guests.

"Good evening, my dear," he said as she sat

beside him. He sounded kindly and almost sympathetic and she forced herself to smile at him.

"Good evening," she replied and then fell silent, unable to think of anything to say. She had lost the art of small conversation and so she sat and listened to the rest of the party as they laughed uproariously at remarks she found not in the least funny.

"You don't appear to have a very large appetite." The man beside her spoke close to her ear and she glanced up at him quickly.

"No, I'm not very hungry. I expect the traveling has left me a little tired."

"I'm sorry, my dear, perhaps we should have delayed our little gathering, allowed you time to recover." He smiled. "From what I hear, you had an exceedingly eventful visit to Russia."

As he spoke, there was a sudden silence. Everyone was waiting for her to speak and Seranne looked round wildly for a way of escape. It was Fenn who broke the silence.

"Seranne is too modest," he said with a thin smile. "Tell them how much the Tsar depended on you, Seranne." He looked round the room. "She was more in his bedchamber than out of it."

One of the women leaned forward, eyes avid as she stared at Seranne.

"I've heard the Tsar is a veritable stallion—is it true?" She did not wait for a reply. "We shall have to have a little meeting at my house—just us ladies— and then, dear, you can tell us all the fascinating details."

Seranne felt sick but she could think of no way of getting out of the room without making a spectacle of herself. She looked down at her hands and then she heard Fenn speak again.

"That's not all," he went on mercilessly. "Seranne was the captive of a gypsy leader for some time, and the tribe indulged in all sorts of interesting rites, did they not, Seranne?"

"I'm sure no one wants to hear about that." Her voice sounded weak even to herself and there was a bubbling laugh from the woman who'd spoken to her.

"Oh, how lovely! What I would give to be in your shoes, dear! You must know all there is to know about men."

Seranne could bear it no longer. She rose to her feet and threw down her table napkin, trying to control her tears.

"I'm sorry, I'm not very good company tonight. I have been so long traveling that I'm exhausted. Please excuse me."

She left the room. But Fenn came after her. He gripped her arms, holding her cruelly.

"What do you think you are doing?" he said fiercely. "These people are very influential and that gentleman at your side was Lord Prayton himself. What must they be thinking of you?"

"They no doubt think I'm the whore you painted me," she said bitterly. "Let me go, Fenn, please, I just want to rest. I'm so tired of it all."

To her relief, he released her and strode away. She hurried up the stairs, making for the silence of her bedroom with its warm crackling fire.

She had no idea why Fenn was being so cruel. He seemed to delight in humiliating her, making her out to be something she was not. She had slept with Alexander—that she could not deny—but none of it had been from choice. Deep inside, she was surely not a wicked person?

She quickly took off the clinging, revealing gown and lay down on the bed. She was so utterly weary that she ached in every bone. Her eyes grew heavy and she slept.

In the morning, Betsy arrived with a breakfast tray, a smile on her face. She placed the tray on the table and bobbed a small curtsy.

"There's a lady downstairs," she said. "She says she's your Aunt Mildred, and as Master Fenn is out, I didn't know what to do."

Seranne felt joy flooding through her. "Oh, send her up at once," she said quickly. "And please bring another cup."

Mildred had not changed one iota. She still dressed in the height of fashion, her coat edged with fur and fitting snugly on her hips. Her bonnet sported a bright feather that drooped over her smooth brow.

"My dear girl!" She embraced her niece and they clung together for a long moment while Seranne tried to swallow the threatening tears.

"Let me look at you." Mildred held her at arms' length, head on one side. "Hmm, you're a little thinner and you have shadows under those eyes of yours, but you don't really look as I'd expected."

Seranne sank back into the warmth of the bed. "What did you expect then, Aunt?" she asked, puzzled.

Mildred took her time answering. She removed her gloves and hat and sat in the chair near the fire.

"The rumors about your return have been going around London for more than a week." She paused, maddeningly, to unbutton her coat. "We have heard of your adventures in Russia, my dear, and I fully expected a hardened courtesan.'' She smiled. ''Instead, you are still my dear niece, and you have not lost any of your innocence from what I can see.''

Seranne lowered her eyes. ''There is some truth in what you must have heard,'' she said quietly. ''I did live with a gypsy tribe but I was never violated by any of the tribesmen.''

''And the rest—the story about the Tsar Alexander? What of that, my dear?'' Mildred probed gently.

Seranne sighed. ''I had no choice but to become his mistress. Fenn saw to that.''

''I understand,'' Mildred said. ''The Tsar is a great and powerful man. It would be difficult for an inexperienced English girl to resist a man like that.'' She paused, pursing her lips thoughtfully. ''And what did Fenn Cornwallis have to do with it? I suppose he gained in some way from your alliance with the Tsar Alexander.''

''He did,'' Seranne said wearily. ''But whatever he gained, it makes no difference now. I became Alexander's mistress and nothing can change that.''

''Was he good to you, my dear?'' Mildred said briskly. ''What I mean is did the Tsar leave you well provided for? He must have given you something. He's a wealthy man and I can't imagine him being penny-pinching.''

Seranne shook her head. ''I don't know. I was too sick at heart to think or care about gifts or rewards for my services.''

''But surely you must have liked Alexander a little, my dear. You don't go to bed with someone you despise, do you?''

''I didn't despise him,'' Seranne said. ''But Aunt,

I didn't consent to what took place, either. Alexander had two guards posted at his bedside; I didn't dare protest at what he did to me."

Mildred's eyebrows shot up. "You do surprise me, my dear. I thought that even if you didn't love the Tsar, you might at least have enjoyed him."

"It wasn't like that. Whenever Alexander took me, it was always under protest."

"*Always?* Are you sure about that?" Mildred's eyes were penetrating and Seranne found herself coloring.

"There was one time . . . I was given an elixir, it did strange things to me. I thought Alexander was . . . Well, I didn't really know what was happening. Everything was mixed up."

"You were drugged, my dear, is that it?" her aunt asked.

Seranne nodded. "Yes, I suppose so. It all sounds so unlikely now, but that was the only time I ever gave myself willingly, and afterward I felt so ashamed."

Mildred rose to her feet. "I think you'd better dress now, my dear, and in the meantime, I'll go and have a talk with Fenn. There are one or two matters I'd like to discuss with him."

Mildred left the room quietly, her thoughts in a turmoil. This sad, defeated Seranne was not what she'd expected at all. After what Dervil Cornwallis had told her on his return from Russia, she'd had the distinct impression that her niece was the Tsar's mistress from choice. Dervil had said that he had seen his wife in the arms of Alexander, apparently savoring every minute of his attentions.

Mildred was inclined to believe that her niece had spoken the truth, however, and if that was the case, Dervil must have seen his wife with Alexander on the one and only occasion she had displayed any passion.

Fenn stared at Mildred in surprise when she walked into the drawing room. He had just returned to the house and had been unaware of her presence.

"What did you tell my niece about Dervil's arrival at the palace in St. Petersburg?" she demanded.

"I told her nothing," Fenn answered, taken off guard. He shrugged. "What was the point? Dervil had found out she was Alexander's new plaything and he wanted nothing more to do with her."

"All this is your fault," Mildred said sharply. "I can imagine you allowing Dervil to see Seranne and the Tsar together, then telling him he was better off without her."

"It's the truth isn't it?" Fenn said. "She's no good for my brother."

"Huh!" Mildred snorted. "You don't care about your brother. All you have ever cared about is yourself. What if I should go to Dervil and tell him all this?"

Fenn laughed. "I doubt if he would believe you. He saw her in the Tsar's bed and she was enjoying herself, make no mistake about that."

"Under the influence of a drug, of course. That's a point you omitted to mention," Mildred said flatly. "And you say she knows nothing of Dervil's visit, nothing at all?"

"No," Fenn said impatiently. "I didn't see any reason to tell her—why should I?"

"Oh, my dear lord," Mildred said quietly. "You know what this means, don't you? She still thinks he's dead, drowned at sea. How could you be so cruel?''

Fenn laughed. ''And do you think it would be kind to let her know he's alive and believes her to be a whore?''

''She has to be told,'' Mildred said softly. ''For better or worse she has to know that Dervil is here, living in London, not three streets away. What if he should take it into his head to come and visit you?''

''That's most unlikely,'' Fenn said. ''He's a very unforgiving man.'' He smiled and leaned back in his chair. ''There's nothing you can do for Seranne but leave her in my hands. I don't want you interfering.''

Mildred spun on her heel. ''To the devil with you! I mean to tell her that Dervil's alive and there's nothing you can do to stop me.''

19

Seranne knew that Mildred was still talking, still trying to explain everything to her, because she could see her mouth opening and closing, but she understood nothing except that Dervil was alive. He had not died in the tempestuous seas off the Russian coast as she'd believed all these months. He had survived, cared for apparently by a strange Russian girl.

He had followed her to St. Petersburg, searching for her, only to find her in the arms of the Tsar of

Russia. He had been led to believe that she was Alexander's mistress from choice.

"How can I live with the knowledge that my husband is alive and thinks the very worst of me?" she said in a low voice. Mildred took her hand.

"Don't look like that, Seranne. We shall try to see Dervil, explain exactly what happened. Everything will be all right, you'll see."

"No." Seranne shook her head. "He is further from me in spirit now than if I had really lost him to the sea. He must hate me—and who could blame him?"

"Perhaps we could force Fenn into telling him the truth," Mildred suggested desperately. "Dervil would have to believe his brother, you know that."

Seranne gave a short laugh. "Can you see Fenn risking his neck to clear my name? He would be afraid of what Dervil might do to him. No, Fenn won't tell the truth."

"I suppose not." Mildred rubbed her niece's cold fingers, trying to bring some warmth into them. "You know, Seranne," she said with an element of surprise in her voice, "you've changed, become more self-reliant. I suppose you've grown up."

"Why should that seem strange?" Seranne's voice was hard. "I've experienced a great deal in the last few months. I've had a husband, remember, and I have lived in the palace of St. Petersburg as mistress to one of the most powerful men in the whole world. Do you wonder that I've grown up?"

"My dear, don't be bitter," Mildred said. "I understand how you must have suffered, but you are still young, you have a lifetime in which to find happiness."

"The only happiness for me would be in my husband's arms," Seranne said quietly. "I love Dervil so much that it's like a constant pain inside me." She drew away from her aunt in sudden impatience. "Oh, don't let's sit here making useless conversation. We could walk a little, get some fresh air. It might do me some good."

"Very well, dear." Mildred smiled brightly. "If that's what you want, then we'll go out and I can show off my new hat."

Seranne wondered afresh at her aunt's ability to remain so cheerful. Perhaps it was the way she could put any worries out of her mind as though they did not exist.

Fenn gave them both a sour look as they passed the drawing room, but Mildred ignored him, her head held high, the bright feather dancing over the brim of her hat. Seranne took her arm as they left the house together, thankful for Mildred's strength.

"You must tell me all about yourself," Seranne said as they stepped outside into the street. "It will make a pleasant change from talking about my problems."

It was a strange feeling to be walking along the hard, wet pavements of London with a gray sky overhead and the trees slowly budding into new life. Seranne drank it all in, vowing never to leave English shores again.

"There's very little to tell about myself, dear," Mildred said, but there was a coy smile on her lips and Seranne, with a new sensitivity, realized her aunt was happy and in love.

"Well, what's his name?" she asked smilingly. "Come along, you must tell me all about it—you know I want to be happy."

"It's Phillip." Mildred's voice came out in a rush, as breathless as that of a young girl. "Phillip Carey. I thought I'd lost him forever when he went away but he missed me so much that he came back for me." She paused. "I know it must be hurtful that I'm happy while you're so miserable, Seranne, but I might as well tell you. We're planning to be married, and then I will travel abroad with him." She put her hand on Seranne's arm. "But I'll stay for a while if you need me, dear, you know that."

Seranne felt tears prick her eyes; it must have cost Mildred sorely to make such an offer.

"Don't be foolish, Aunt Mildred," she said. "Take him while you have the chance. I want you to be happy with the man you love. Even if you did stay here, it wouldn't help me solve my problems, would it?"

They walked in silence for a moment and then Mildred took Seranne's arm, pointing to a large house set well back from the road under the shelter of the dripping trees.

"That's where Dervil lives. Shall we go in and see him, dear—try at least to speak to him and make him see sense?"

"No!" Seranne said at once, panic rising within her. "I couldn't face him, not now." She stood for a moment, looking at the empty windows, finding it difficult to believe that somewhere in the mellow old house was the husband she'd believed was lost to her forever.

She longed for him with a sudden intense pain. She remembered his passion, his almost saturnine looks and his dry, warm humor. She wondered how Fate could have been so cruel as to take away the one man she could ever love and then to place her right on his doorstep, so that his nearness was a torment.

"I can't stay here," she said to Mildred. "I suddenly feel chilly, and it's starting to rain." But she knew that her coldness had nothing to do with the weather. Mildred smiled at her, understanding.

"Very well, my dear. I'll return to my own little house and to Phillip. Would you like to come with me? You don't have to stay with Fenn, you know."

"I'll be all right." Seranne spoke quickly, knowing she could not intrude into her aunt's life. "But thank you for everything, Aunt Mildred."

"Oh, don't talk as though you'll never see me again." Her aunt's briskness hid the very real affection that had grown for her niece. "I'll be here for some time yet. We'll meet often before I leave London, you can wager on it."

When Seranne entered the house, there was an air of excitement in the way the servants were busy polishing the woodwork in the hall and arranging fresh spring flowers around the various rooms.

From the kitchen came the smell of roast lamb and Seranne stared around her, wondering what had prompted all the preparations.

Betsy darted past on her way to the drawing room and Seranne caught her arm.

"What's happening?" she asked, frowning. "Why is everyone so busy?"

"It's Lord Prayton, madam," Betsy said eagerly. "He's going to take up residence here again tonight, didn't you know?"

"No, I didn't," she replied, puzzled. "But I thought he'd loaned the house to Mr. Cornwallis and myself indefinitely."

Betsy shrugged. "I don't know about that but his

lordship has quarreled with his . . ." She looked around to make sure no one was listening. "He's had words, like, with his ladyfriend." She winked. "You know what I mean, don't you, madam?"

"Oh, I see." But Seranne was nonplussed. Lord Prayton, from what she remembered of him, was a white-haired old man; she would have thought him well past the age for ladyfriends. "Thank you, Betsy."

She walked toward the drawing room and looked inside but there was no sign of Fenn. She hurried upstairs and along the corridor, her skirts billowing behind her. Fenn looked up when he saw Seranne framed in the doorway of his room.

"This is a surprise visit," he said. "But come into my bedroom by all means, though I didn't expect to see you in such intimate surroundings ever again."

"I just wanted to ask you what is happening," she said coldly. "I understand Lord Prayton is returning home tonight. Won't our presence here be an intrusion?"

"On the contrary," Fenn said. "His Lordship particularly asked for us to stay on a while. He's a very rich and very generous man—you could grow to like him."

"I don't intend to stay and find out," Seranne said crisply. "I think it's about time I found somewhere of my own to live. What you do, of course, is entirely up to you."

"I see." Fenn smoothed his chin. "Well, houses are not that easy to find. I should give the matter a great deal of thought if I were you."

Somehow Seranne had the impression that Fenn was merely humoring her and that he had some trick or other up his sleeve.

*　*　*

It was much later in the day when Seranne heard the wheels of a coach stopping outside in the street. She looked down to see Lord Prayton entering the house while servants ran around him, carrying a whole variety of luggage. Whoever his ladyfriend had been, he must have spent some considerable time with her, Seranne thought with a glimmer of humor. Who would have thought it of a man his age?

She decided not to go downstairs to dinner, and sent her apologies through Betsy, pleading a headache. To her surprise, Fenn came marching into her room without so much as a by-your-leave and stood in front of her, tapping his foot impatiently.

"You must come downstairs," he said angrily. "Lord Prayton is our host, have you forgotten that? Make some effort to be friendly, for heaven's sake. Don't you ever think of anyone except yourself?"

"And who should I be thinking about? You?" Seranne turned on him suddenly. "I owe you nothing. You let me believe Dervil was dead when you knew he'd come looking for me, and that is the one thing I will never forgive."

He caught her arm. "I don't give a damn what you think of me. But you will *not* offend Lord Prayton. You'll come down to dinner even if I have to carry you."

She saw the ruthless determination in his face and her flash of spirit evaporated. What did it matter after all if she made an old man happy by her company? Perhaps Fenn was right and she was being selfish.

"Very well," she said. "I'll come down presently, but don't expect any sparkling conversation from me."

He released her. "Sparkling conversation is not what a man wants from a woman like you," he said harshly and she was aware of the rich color running into her cheeks.

"Leave my room," she said in a low voice. "And don't come over the doorway again, do you understand?"

Without answering, he turned on his heel and walked away. Seranne had to fight to control the anger that made her tremble. She would go down to dinner, but only for the sake of courtesy to Lord Prayton. Tomorrow she would start to look for her own establishment. She would be better living away from Fenn Cornwallis and all the terrible memories his presence evoked.

She made a real effort to be polite to the elderly man who sat at her side, his eyes crinkling with good humor, his hands shaky as they rested on hers.

"My dear," he said softly, "you do not know the pleasure your company gives me. You are such a charming and beautiful young lady, it's an honor to have you under my roof."

She smiled up at him. After all, it had been kind of him to lend his house, kinder still to continue to offer his hospitality, even though now it might be quite inconvenient for him to have visitors.

"The honor is mine," she said, knowing the words were trite and meaningless. Yet she was unable to feel any interest in the conversation. She felt quite dull and weary and when she announced she would retire early she was surprised at the ready way Fenn jumped up from the table and held the door open for her.

Once she was in bed, she felt herself begin to relax. Since standing outside Dervil's house, her nerves had been strained to the limit. She didn't know how she had managed to get through the evening. But it was over now and tomorrow she would begin the search for a home of her own.

She was almost asleep when there was a light tap on the door. Reluctantly, she lit the candles, pulling on her robe.

"Your lordship," she said in surprise. "What's wrong? Are you ill?"

He was a ludicrous sight, standing there in a nightshirt that revealed the thinness of his legs while on his head was perched a nightcap that did nothing to improve his looks.

"Ah, Seranne, you'd play games with me would you?" He entered the room and closed the door quietly, smiling at her as if they were conspirators. "Well, my sweet little girl, are you not going to welcome me?" he said, holding out his arms to her.

"You're insane." Seranne drew away from him, clutching her robe around her. He laughed a little and came nearer, his eyes glittering. She could smell wine on his breath and turned away from him in revulsion.

"But what's wrong?" he said. "The Cornwallis lad told me you'd be eager for me. I have a great deal to offer a girl like you. I'm a very wealthy man, and when the time comes for us to say good-bye—why, I could make sure you had another protector."

He made a sudden grab for her, and with surprising strength pulled her against him.

Seranne had a sudden vision of her life as it could be, going from one man to the next, a plaything to be discarded when her usefulness was ended. This was what Fenn had planned: to make her available for

Lord Prayton so that she could become his new mistress.

She burst into tears so suddenly that she startled herself as well as the old man. He released her, staring at her with surprise written all over his lined face.

"Why are you crying, child?" he said, his graying eyebrows coming together in a frown.

Seranne tried to answer but tears choked her throat and blinded her eyes. She turned, and in a frenzy of anger and misery ran down the stairs and out into the street. She heard a voice calling her but she ran even faster, her bare feet making little noise on the wet pavement.

She ran until she was exhausted. When she stopped for a moment to regain her breath, she became aware of the rain soaking through her thin nightclothes.

A carriage drew up beside her and she cowered against a doorway, terrified that Lord Prayton might have come after her. A light swung over her head, dazzling her, and then she heard a muttered oath.

"Good God!" The voice was Dervil's and everything was forgotten as Seranne rushed into his arms, almost knocking the lamp out of his hand in her haste.

"Help me—please help me . . ." she whispered, clinging to his arm as he tried to hold her away from him. He opened the door of the house and she followed him inside. The warmth and comfort of the house swept over Seranne as she stood in the hallway. What instincts had led her to Dervil's door, she didn't know. But as she looked up at her husband, her love for him was still strong and pure in spite of all that had come between them.

"What's all this?" he said briskly. "Have you suddenly tired of your way of life?''

He walked up the stairs and she ran behind him, clutching at his sleeve.

''For God's sake stop sniveling,'' he said, and at the harshness of his voice, tears started afresh. He took her into a bedroom and pulled a blanket from the bed, wrapping it around her, and she realized she was shivering.

''Please,'' she said. ''Just let me stay here until morning. I'll find somewhere of my own then, but don't make me go back. I ask this one thing of you—then I'll leave you alone forever, if that's what you want.''

''That is exactly what I want.'' His silver-gray eyes were hostile as he stared down at her, and Seranne felt as though she were dying inside. ''You can sleep here,'' he said shortly. ''As you are still legally my wife I suppose I have some responsibilities, but don't count on too much or you'll be disappointed.'' He turned away from her and she almost reached out her hand to stop him leaving.

''Dervil, don't you want me even to explain the reason I'm here like this?'' she said, her voice choked.

''What's to explain?'' he said. ''I can guess that one or other of your lovers has upset you and you had nowhere else to go. You'll no doubt patch everything up in the morning.''

''It's not like that!'' The words were a cry for mercy, but he simply shrugged, as though tired of the conversation.

''Try to get some sleep,'' he said in a hard voice. ''Otherwise you'll have trouble living up to your reputation as London's most beautiful whore.''

''It's not true,'' she said in a whisper.

He raised his eyebrows as though amused by her. "The little innocent act is lost on me, Seranne," he said. "I know you too well. I actually saw you with my own eyes enjoying the attentions of the Tsar. What could you say now that would change that?"

Her shoulders drooped and she sank down onto the bed, her head bowed.

"It's a strange thing to have your wife talked about all over London as the town's most beautiful whore. I'd say you were the lowest little slut it was ever my misfortune to meet."

The door closed behind him and Seranne lay back wearily on the bed, too deeply hurt to even cry. She wanted nothing more than to fall asleep, never to wake again.

20

"Damn your hide, Cornwallis!" Lord Prayton was wrapping himself in an embroidered Chinese silk robe, his face red as he stared belligerently at Fenn standing in the doorway. "Did you or did you not tell me the girl was willing? I've never forced myself on any woman in my life and at my age I don't intend to start."

"I'm sorry." Fenn was exasperated by Seranne's stupidity. What on earth did the girl want from life? She had just turned down one of the most powerful men in London.

"I've made an utter fool of myself," Lord Prayton continued, "and I swear you'll pay for it. Well, don't just stand there looking stupid—go after the girl! She's out in the rain wearing nothing but her night-clothes. Bring her back. I won't be made a laughing-stock of all over town, do you understand?"

Fenn heard the beating of the rain against the windows and the last thing he wanted to do was to venture out on such a night. Since returning to London, his cough had worsened, the damp air having an adverse affect on his health.

"She'll come back," he said, unaware of how callous he sounded. "I don't see where else she can go."

"That's not good enough." Lord Prayton was fastening his buttons. "It's up to you to find her if you ever want to be accepted in London society again."

Fenn drew on his top hat, cursing the old man under his breath. Lord Prayton was an old fool, but it wouldn't do to make an enemy of him, for his influence was far-reaching.

As he went out into the blustery darkness, he thought bitterly of what he'd like to do to Seranne. Who in God's name did she think she was, refusing a man like his lordship? In a couple of years' time, when her looks started to fade, she would be sorry she had not taken advantage of such a good opportunity to set herself up in style.

He walked briskly through the rain, searching the streets in the vicinity of the house. It stood to reason she couldn't have gone very far, not dressed as she was. She must be hiding in a doorway or perhaps down some basement steps. The girl must be completely mad.

He was soaked through in a very short time and he cursed again, his anger against Seranne mounting. He would teach her a thing or two when he got his hands on her. She would have to learn that if she wanted him to look out for her interests she needed to be a little more accommodating. Lord Prayton was old, he was quite aware that the man wouldn't be the most vigorous lover in the world, but surely Seranne was experienced enough to handle such a lover with discretion.

He suddenly brightened. It could be that Seranne had gone to Mildred's house. It was so obvious a solution that he wondered why he hadn't thought of it before. He changed direction and hurried along the wet streets with more purpose in his stride. Just wait until he caught up with the little whore—he'd give her something to think about.

Mildred received him wearing a diaphanous robe over a rose-colored nightgown. She stared at Fenn in amazement and ushered him into the small drawing room with obvious lack of enthusiasm.

"What on earth are you doing here at this time of the night?" she said in her forthright way. Staring at her smooth face, Fenn wondered if she were cleverly concealing the fact of her niece's presence.

"It's Seranne," he said, coming straight to the point. "She's disappeared. Isn't she here?"

He could tell by the blank look on Mildred's face that he had guessed wrongly.

"Disappeared?" she repeated, her eyes wide. "What do you mean she's disappeared? What have you done to her?"

"I've done nothing," he said impatiently. "She's just lost her senses, if you ask me. She rushed out into the rain wearing only her nightclothes."

"Something must be very wrong," Mildred said fiercely, her face coloring with anger.

"Don't get hysterical." Fenn was feeling distinctly wet and uncomfortable. His clothes were clinging to him and already his chest was beginning to tighten. He began to cough and even Mildred could see that he was not well.

"Oh for heaven's sake come nearer the fire," she said. "Get out of those wet clothes. I'll call Phillip."

"Phillip?" Fenn asked in surprise. "Who's Phillip?" He undid his coat and handed it to Mildred and she took it with a shudder, shaking the raindrops from it.

"Phillip Carey," she said flatly. "We are shortly to be married, so have a care what you say. He's a man of fierce temper."

While Mildred was gone, Fenn sat shivering before the fire that was dying low in the grate. He felt a headache coming on and he rubbed his eyes, unable to see the room clearly. All he longed to do was lay his head down somewhere soft and sleep. He leaned back and closed his eyes.

Later he wasn't quite sure what had happened. He vaguely remembered being put to bed and then he was raging with thirst. He thought he saw the sun shining once when he opened his eyes, but then all was darkness again. The only thing clear to him was that he had come down with the fever he had contracted in Russia and it was all the fault of that whore Seranne.

The object of Fenn's jumbled thoughts was at that moment eating a solitary luncheon, picking at tender chicken breasts cooked in wine. But she had little appetite.

Seranne at last left the long table and walked away from the emptiness of the dining room into the hall. She stood looking around her for a moment. The silence was heavy and oppressive. She knew she could not take much more. The agony of being under the same roof as her husband and yet being treated by him as little more than a stranger was tearing her apart.

He had provided for her well enough in the last two days. He had purchased the necessary articles of clothing she needed, going out of his way to see that she lacked for nothing. Nothing, that was, except for what she most craved: a small sign of softening in his attitude toward her.

She spun around, startled, as the door to the street opened and a gust of rainy wind swept into the hall. Dervil took off his hat, shaking the rain from it and his silver-gray eyes stared at her without expression.

She wondered what he would do if she ran into his arms and begged him to listen to her. She longed for the right words to tell him that she loved him and had always loved him.

"Why on earth are you standing about in the hall?" he said abruptly. "This isn't the warmest part of the house, and you already have a chill. You're causing me enough trouble without falling ill."

"I was just on my way into the drawing room," she said quickly. "Have you eaten? If not, there's some cold meat in the dining room or I could ring for some tea, if you like."

He stared at her for so long that she felt uncomfortable. His expression told her that he did not want her to run his affairs. He was master in his own house and her concern was unwelcome.

She left him and went into the drawing room,

hardly able to hold back the tears. She sat before the fire, her fists clenched as she made a supreme effort to control herself. If she should cry now he would simply think it was another attempt to gain his sympathy.

A few minutes later, he joined her and stood at the hearth looking down at her. He was so handsome it was unbearable. She wanted his lips on hers with a hunger that was almost driving her mad. She needed him; he was the only man in the world she could ever love.

"When are you leaving?" His harsh words were like cold water dashed in her face. "I don't want to hurry you but I think it's about time you made some other arrangements."

She was flustered. "I don't know. I suppose I could see Aunt Mildred. She might take me in until I found somewhere of my own."

She felt empty. Mildred would not want her; she was going to be married to the man she loved. There was no place she could go to find sanctuary, at least not in London. It might be just as well if she traveled home to Devonshire. Perhaps in Hussey Hall she might find some peace.

"That sounds like an excellent idea," Dervil was saying. "I shall take a ride over to Mildred's this evening. Don't wait up for me, I will most probably be late. I can let you know what has been decided in the morning."

Her heart sank. He couldn't wait to be rid of her. Did he really hate her so much? She watched as without another word, Dervil strode from the room, closing the door, leaving her alone with her emptiness.

*   *   *

Fenn's condition was worse. His temperature had risen and the room had become blurred, the furniture had taken on grotesque unreal shapes. He saw Mildred coming toward him as though from a great distance and then she was leaning over him.

"Your brother is here." Her voice was totally lacking in sympathy and when Fenn shook his head, muttering that the last person he wanted to see was Dervil, Mildred smiled.

"Well, like it or not you're seeing him," she said. "And you must tell him the truth about what happened in St. Petersburg."

"No." Fenn shook his head weakly. "I won't do it. Dervil would kill me." He turned away from her in outrage. Here he was lying sick and Mildred was blabbering on about telling the truth to Dervil. As though it mattered now.

"If you don't do as I say, then I won't be responsible for what happens," she said evenly.

With a sigh, he struggled to raise his head. "What do you mean?" His voice was thin and weak and he fell back against the pillows, cursing all women and Mildred in particular.

"I mean that however ill you are, I shan't get you a physician until you do as I ask."

"But that's blackmail," he said in dismay.

"Call it what you like." Mildred folded her arms across her ample bosom, a look of determination on her face.

"All right," he whispered at last. He was quite sure Mildred was capable of keeping her word and closing the door on him, leaving him to rot. Why on earth did his brother have to turn up now?

Dervil came into the room and stood at the bedside, staring down at him with those strange eyes of his. Fenn took a deep breath, trying to think of words that would explain the situation and yet leave himself in some way exonerated from any blame.

"Mildred said you wish to talk to me." Dervil spoke flatly, as though he could barely tolerate being in the same room as Fenn.

"Yes, well, it's a small matter really," Fenn said weakly. "But you know what women are."

"I have a fair idea," Dervil answered him dryly. "But I haven't got all night. What do you have to tell me?"

"It's about Seranne," Fenn said, and immediately his brother's face took on a closed look.

"Yes, what about her?" he said harshly. "She came to me wearing nothing other than her night-clothes. What happened to drive her out into the night like that?"

Fenn gasped for breath. "I don't know how to begin."

"Get on with it, man." Dervil spoke with growing impatience. "I didn't come here to see you, I simply wanted Mildred to give her niece a home. I don't see why I should be troubled with her."

"It all started in Russia," Fenn said quickly before his courage failed. "Seranne believed you were dead, lost at sea. She was taken captive by a band of gypsies. She swears none of them harmed her, though of course it's in her own interest to lie."

Dervil walked over to the window and stood looking out into the street. Fenn had no way of knowing if his brother believed him or not.

"When the Tsar's men rescued her, she was just about to be executed," Fenn continued. "She was in a state of shock and, as I wasn't well enough to look after her, Alexander took care of her."

"I know," Dervil said in a hard voice. "I saw them together, remember?"

Fenn sighed. "Yes, well, that wasn't exactly what you thought. Seranne had been given an elixir, a love potion bought from some witch woman. It apparently worked well." He shrugged. "She could not help herself."

"A love potion bought from a witch woman?" Dervil repeated and it was as though he was immersed in some secret thoughts of his own.

"It sounds farfetched, but that's what happened," Fenn went on. "Then the Tsar grew tired of her—she was too spiritless for him, I suppose. She never really wanted him as a lover in the first place."

Dervil looked at him in dawning anger. "It was *you*, God help me! *You* stood to benefit from it all—and what's more I believe it's you who has been spreading the talk about my wife. What was the final outrage that made her run from you? Tell me!"

"I was only trying to help her." Fenn cowered back against the pillows, shaken by the naked fury in his brother's silver eyes. "She needed a protector, you must see that," he continued pleadingly. "And who better than Lord Prayton?"

"I could tear you apart with my bare hands," Dervil said in a low, taut voice. He moved menacingly forward but Mildred caught his arm.

"No, Dervil, violence is not the answer." She smiled. "I think that Fenn will find himself unwelcome in London society hereafter. He might even be forced to leave the country." She drew Dervil toward the door. "He'll be punished, have no doubts on that score. Go home to her, Dervil," she said softly. "You love each other, that much is quite clear, so don't give up this chance of happiness."

To Fenn's intense relief, Dervil left the room without a backward glance. Mildred would have followed him but Fenn called to her.

"When are you going to bring me a physician?" he said plaintively.

To his surprise a smile spread across her face. "You don't need a physician any more than I do," she said flatly. "All that remains of your sickness is a slight chill. Good night, Fenn."

He fell back on the pillows, his eyes closed.

Seranne was in bed, unaware of what had happened. She stared wide-eyed at the flickering candlelight on the ceiling, listlessly trying to put her thoughts in some sort of order. The only clear issue to emerge from her mind was that she was nothing more than a nuisance to the man she loved.

She heard the door downstairs open and close and wondered why Dervil had returned early. She shivered in sudden apprehension. Perhaps Mildred had refused to have her stay and he was angry.

Footsteps came running up the stairs and her heart began to pound. Her door was flung open and Dervil, his hair hanging untidily over his forehead, stood staring at her. There was something different about him, something she couldn't quite explain, and there was a strange light in his silver eyes.

He began to take her clothes out of the wardrobe. There wasn't much, just the few things he had bought her. She stared at him, wondering if he was going to put her out on the street there and then.

When he had removed everything from the cupboard, he took her belongings away and she heard a great deal of slamming of doors. She shrank down in the bed, her heart beating fast.

He returned and stood staring down at her for a moment. Then suddenly he bent over and scooped her up into his arms.

"What are you doing?" she asked in a small voice, almost faint at the nearness of him, breathing in the masculine scent of his skin and feeling the softness of his hair as it swung against her face.

Without answering, he carried her along the corridor and into his own bedroom, pushing the door shut with his heel. She had a swift impression of somber-colored drapes and plain, manly furnishings before he set her down on the bed.

"I don't understand," she whispered, staring up at him. "Why have you brought me here?"

He knelt down beside her and suddenly his hands were gentle on her cheeks, cupping her face, forcing her to meet his eyes.

"You are my wife—where else should you be but in my bed?" he said softly.

"But, Dervil . . ." Her voice trailed away as he kissed her lips, stopping her from speaking.

"Don't say anything," he murmured. "We have all the time in the world to talk, later." He pressed her backward against the pillows and his hands slid down to her breasts, caressing, teasing in the old way that never failed to rouse her.

"Oh, God," he said thickly. "I've never ceased to love you and want you." He pushed the soft material of her gown away from her shoulders so that her breasts were revealed in all their glowing beauty.

She looked into his face, hardly daring to believe that what was happening was real and not simply a dream. But what she read in the silver-gray eyes brought a surge of joy like a flame searing through her blood.

Whatever had happened in the time he had been absent, it had greatly changed his attitude to her. Instinctively, she knew she had his full forgiveness and understanding.

"Oh, my love." She melted against him as his hands traveled over her body, touching the intimate secret places in a way he knew would bring her delight. He kissed her breasts, her stomach, her thighs, so lightly it was almost a butterfly touch.

When his flesh joined hers, she drew a deep, shuddering breath, knowing that if she died at this moment she would die fulfilled. He cradled her and together they rose to the heights of a joy that transcended anything Seranne had ever experienced before.

Their union was complete, the coming together of spirit as well as flesh and love flowed like a golden river around their entwined bodies. The past was wiped away and the future spread out before them, rich with promise.